D0011411

*RIDING
THE
RAP*

Also by Elmore Leonard

Fiction

Nonfiction

Praise for **ELMORE LEONARD**
and *RIDING THE RAP*

"Vintage Leonard. . . . He keeps you guessing, turning pages, gnawing your way to the end."
—*San Francisco Chronicle*

"His books defy classification. . . . What Leonard does is write fully realized novels using elements of the classic American crime novel and populating them with characters so true and believable you want to read their lines aloud to someone you really like." —*Dallas Morning News*

"*Riding the Rap* shows Elmore Leonard at the top of his form. Whatever you call his novels, they always read like Elmore Leonard, distinctive in style and vision, brilliantly inventive in plot and characters."
—*Los Angeles Times*

"Another masterpiece from the master. . . . Leonard has never been better." —James Crumley

"The finest thriller writer alive." —*Village Voice*

"Nobody but nobody on the current scene can match his ability to serve up violence so light-handedly, with so supremely deadpan a flourish."
—*Detroit News*

"*Riding the Rap* made me feel like a kid again. Kept me up until four in the morning. When Elmore Leonard's people start talking, I can't help myself, I have to listen." —Lawrence Block

"No one can beat Elmore Leonard when it comes to mordant humor and shockingly bizarre situations."
—*Orlando Sentinel*

"Vintage Leonard. Don't miss it. . . . Following Raylan Givens through the sea grape and palmetto, the lonely freeways and the shopping centers of South Florida, watching the crazies through his eyes, is worth the price of this book."
—*Cleveland Plain Dealer*

"A plot as syncopated and smooth as Leonard's legendary dialogue. . . . Comedy and brutality converge in this loopy thriller—which may be the only American crime novel in which Jell-O provides a crucial clue." —*Newsday*

"No one creates more realistic sleazebags than Leonard. This time, Arno and Givens are up against three of the slimiest—and most hilarious—characters Leonard ever created." —*Denver Post*

"The hottest thriller writer in the U.S." —*Time*

"No one writes better dialogue. No one conveys society's seedier or marginal characters more convincingly. . . . Leonard's sardonic view of the world proves immensely entertaining, and not a little thought-provoking." —*Detroit Free Press*

"Elmore Leonard is a distinctive American artist, the way our great jazz musicians are. He proves once again with *Riding the Rap* that there is still his sound, and then everybody else's."
—Mike Lupica

"*Riding the Rap* is the work of an old master—it's taut, fierce, and mesmerizing." —Stephen Hunter

"Tart, hip, and funny. . . . As well as inimitable nutball characters and that unmistakable dialogue, *Riding the Rap* is shot through with sly, mordant street wisdom." —*Chicago Sun-Times*

"As always, Leonard's cinematic grasp of scene and setting, his ability to arouse within us a helpless sympathy for even the lowest of his characters, his quirky pacing and plot twists, and his sly humor and artfully oddball prose sear our eyeballs and keep the pages turning." —*Miami Herald*

"Nobody but nobody in the business does it better. . . . Leonard has a great feel for misfit alliances, and in novel after novel, he nails them in all their menacing, gut-busting funny glory." —*New York Daily News*

"Elmore Leonard is at the top of his game." —*Seattle Times*

"The contemporary master of American crime fiction. . . . Suffice it to say that while *Riding the Rap* demonstrates again that Elmore Leonard is no slouch when it comes to pulling together a dandy plot, it is for his dead-on characterizations and pitch-perfect dialogue that we read his books." —*Atlanta Journal-Constitution*

"Leonard advances his plots in spare, cinematic fashion, saving the terse conversational give-and-take by which his characters make themselves known. Raylan Givens . . . is the prototype Leonard hero: alert, knowing, and unillusioned." —*People*

"The coolest, hottest writer in America."
                        —*Chicago Tribune*

"Elmore Leonard has the best ear for dialogue in the crime-writing biz. Under Leonard's control, *Riding the Rap* glides to a conclusion both violent and funny."   —*Playboy*

"As well as a master storyteller, Leonard is one of our funniest writers, and for decades has richly dramatized elements of our culture. *Riding the Rap* is wonderful."   —Andre Dubus

ELMORE LEONARD

RIDING THE RAP

wm

WILLIAM MORROW
An Imprint of HarperCollins*Publishers*

For Christine

This book is a work of fiction. The characters, incidents, and dialogue are drawn from the author's imagination and are not to be construed as real. Any resemblance to actual events or persons, living or dead, is entirely coincidental.

RIDING THE RAP. Copyright © 1995 by Elmore Leonard, Inc. Excerpt from *Raylan* copyright © 2012 by Elmore Leonard, Inc. All rights reserved. Printed in the United States of America. No part of this book may be used or reproduced in any manner whatsoever without written permission except in the case of brief quotations embodied in critical articles and reviews. For information, address HarperCollins Publishers, 195 Broadway, New York, NY 10007.

HarperCollins books may be purchased for educational, business, or sales promotional use. For information, please e-mail the Special Markets Department at SPsales@harpercollins.com.

FIRST HARPERTORCH PAPERBACK PUBLISHED 2002.
FIRST HARPER PAPERBACK SPECIAL PRINTING PUBLISHED 2010.
FIRST WILLIAM MORROW PAPERBACK EDITION PUBLISHED 2012.

Library of Congress Cataloging-in-Publication Data is available upon request.

ISBN 978-0-06-212247-6

15 16 RRD 10 9 8

one

Ocala Police picked up Dale Crowe Junior for weaving, two o'clock in the morning, crossing the center line and having a busted taillight. Then while Dale was blowing a point-one-nine they put his name and date of birth into the national crime computer and learned he was a fugitive felon, wanted on a three-year-old charge of Unlawful Flight to Avoid Incarceration. A few days later Raylan Givens, with the Marshals Service, came up from Palm Beach County to take Dale back and the Ocala Police wondered about Raylan.

How come if he was a federal officer and Dale Crowe Junior was wanted on a state charge . . . He told them he was with FAST, the Fugitive Apprehension Strike Team, assigned to the Sheriff's Office in West Palm. And that was pretty much all this marshal said. They wondered too, since he was alone, how he'd be able to drive and keep an eye on his prisoner. Dale Crowe Junior had been convicted of a third-degree five-year felony, Battery of a Police Officer, and was looking at additional time on the fugitive warrant. Dale Junior might feel he had nothing to lose on this trip south. He was a rangy kid with the build of a college athlete, bigger than this marshal in his blue suit and cowboy boots—the marshal calm though, not appearing to be the least apprehensive. He said the West Palm strike team was shorthanded at the moment, the reason he was alone, but believed he would manage.

And when he put his hat on and drove off with Dale Junior in the confiscated two-year-old Cadillac he was using, a dark blue one, an Ocala officer said, "He believes he'll manage . . ."

Another officer said, "Don't you know who that is? He's the one the Mafia guy drew on last winter in Miami Beach, the two of them sitting at the same table, and this marshal shot him dead. Yeah, Raylan Givens. It was in the paper."

"That why he didn't give us the time of day? I doubt he said five words. Shows us his star. . . ."

The one who had read about Raylan Givens said,

"I didn't get that impression. I saw him as all business, the kind goes by the book."

He said to Dale Crowe Junior, "I know you think you can drive when you've had a few. How good are you when you're sober?"

This marshal not sounding like the usual hard-ass lawman; Dale Junior was glad of that. He said, "I had a Caddy myself one time, till I sold it for parts and went to work at Disney's. You know what I tried out for? Play Goofy. Mickey Mouse's friend? Only you had to water-ski and I couldn't get the hang of it. Sir, I like to mention that these three years since I took off? I been clean. I never even left the state of Florida all that time, not wanting to be too far away from my folks, my old mom and dad, except I never did get to see them."

The marshal, Raylan Givens, said, "If you're gonna talk I'll put you in the trunk and I'll drive."

So neither of them said another word until they were south of Orlando on the Turnpike, 160 miles to West Palm, Dale Junior staring straight ahead at the highway, flat and straight through Florida scrub, boring, holding it right around sixty so as to make the trip last, give him time to think of a move he might try on the marshal. The man didn't appear to be much to handle, had a slim build and looked like a farmer—sounded like one, too—forty years old or so; he sat against his door, seat belt fastened, turned somewhat this way. He had on one of those business cowboy hats, but broken in; it looked good on him, the way he wore it cocked low on his eyes.

3

Dale Junior would feel him staring, though when he glanced over the marshal was usually looking out at the road or the countryside, patient, taking the ride as it came. Dale Junior decided to start feeling him out.

"Can I say something?"

The marshal was looking at him now.

"What's that?"

"There's a service plaza coming up. I wouldn't mind stopping, get something to eat?"

The man shook his head and Dale Junior made a face, giving the marshal an expression of pain.

"I couldn't eat that jail food they give you. Some kind of potatoes and imitation eggs cold as ice." He waited as long as he could, almost a minute, and said, "I don't see why we can't talk some. Pass the time."

The marshal said, "I don't care to hear any sad stories, all the bad luck and bum deals life's handed you."

Dale Junior showed him a frown. "Don't it mean anything I got nothing on my sheet the past three years, that I've been clean all that time?"

The marshal said, "Not to me it doesn't. Son, you're none of my business."

Dale Junior shook his head, giving himself a beat look now, without hope. He said, "I'll tell you, I thought more'n once of giving myself up. You know why?"

The marshal waited, not helping any.

"So I could see my folks. So I'd know they was okay. I didn't dare write, knowing the mails would be watched." When the marshal didn't comment Dale Junior said, "They do that, don't they?"

"What?"

"Watch the mails?"

"I doubt it."

Dale Junior said, "Oh, well," paused and said, "My old dad lost one of his legs, had it bit off by a alligator this time he's fishing the rim canal, by Lake Okeechobee? I sure wish I could see him before we get to Gun Club. That's where we're going, huh, the Gun Club jail?"

"You're going to the county lockup," the marshal said, "to await a sentence hearing."

"Yeah, well, that's what they call it, account of it's off Gun Club Road. So you're not from around there, huh, West Palm?"

The marshal didn't answer, seeming more interested in the sky, clouds coming in from way out over the ocean.

"Where you from anyway?"

"I live down in Miami."

"I been there once or twice. Man, all the spics, huh? My dad's never been to Palm Beach or seen the ocean. Never got any closer'n Twenty Mile Bend. You believe it? Spent his whole life over there around Belle Glade, Canal Point, Pahokee . . ." He waited, eyes on the road before saying, "You know, if we was to get off near Stuart we could take Seventy-six over to the lake, run on down to Belle Glade—it wouldn't be more'n a few miles out of the way and I'd get to see my folks. I mean just stop and say hi, kiss my old mom . . ." Dale Junior turned to look at the marshal. "What would you say to that?" He waited and said, "Not much, huh?"

"Your old dad's never been to Palm Beach or seen the ocean," the marshal said, "but he's been up to Starke, hasn't he? He's seen the Florida state prison. You have an uncle came out of there, Elvin Crowe, and another one did his time at Lake Butler. I think we'll skip visiting any of your kin this trip."

Dale Junior said, "My uncles're both dead."

And the marshal said, "By gunshot, huh? You understand how I see your people?"

Now he said, "You can speed it up some."

Dale Junior looked over at him. "You want me to break the law?"

Raylan didn't answer, staring at the open vista of flat land to the east, what he imagined the plains of Africa might be like.

"We could use some gas."

"We'll make it," Raylan said.

"Fort Drum service plaza's coming up."

Raylan didn't say anything to that.

"Aren't you hungry?"

This time Raylan said, "I'll see you get something at the jail."

"I ain't had a regular meal," Dale Junior said, "since the day I was arrested, and you know what it was? A hamburger and fries, some onion rings. That night for supper I had potato chips. See, all day I was out looking for work. I *had* a job, working for a paint contractor? Scraped down and sanded this entire goddamn two-story house and the guy lets me go.

That's what they do, they use you. My trade, I drove a big goddamn cane truck from the fields to the sugarhouse—back before I had that trouble and had to take off. Now, the way the system works, what's known as the free-enterprise system? They're free to use you on some dirt job nobody wants and when you get done they fire you. Four dollars an hour, man, that's the system, as good as it gets."

Raylan watched him as he spoke, Dale Junior staring straight ahead, rigid, arms extended, hands gripping the top arc of the steering wheel. Big hands with bony white knuckles. Raylan turned a little more in the seat harness to face him and raised his left leg a few inches to rest it against the edge of the seat. He could feel his service pistol, a Beretta nine, holstered to his right hip, wedged in there against the door. Handcuffs were hooked to his belt. A shotgun, an MP5 machine gun, his vest, a sledgehammer and several more pairs of cuffs were in the trunk. He had left the Palm Beach County Sheriff's Office about nine this morning. Almost five hours up to Ocala, then had to wait around an hour for the paperwork before getting his prisoner. By then it was after three. Now, more than halfway back, it was starting to get dark.

"The night I got stopped," Dale Junior said, "I had like four beers and the potato chips while I shot some pool—that's *all*. Okay, driving home, this place where I been staying with a friend, I'm minding my own fucking business, not doing anything wrong, I get pulled over. Listen to this: On account of one of my taillights ain't working. The cops get me out of the car, tell me to walk the line, touch my fucking nose, they give me all this shit and take me in for a Breathalyzer. Okay, I want to know who says it's fair. I'm clean three years, been working on and off when I could find a job, and now I'm gonna get sent up to FSP?" Dale Junior said. "Do five years, maybe even more'n that on account of a busted *tail* light?"

Raylan got ready.

Dale Junior said, "Bull*shit!*" Turned his head and strained against his seat belt as he swung at Raylan backhand to club him with his fist and Raylan brought his leg up under the arm coming at him and punched the heel of his cowboy boot hard into Dale Junior's face. The car swerved left, hit the grassy median and swerved back into the double lanes, Dale Junior hunched over the wheel holding on. By this time Raylan was out of his seat belt, had his Beretta in his right hand and was holding it in Dale Junior's face, waiting for him to look over.

When he did, Raylan said, "Pull off the road." He waited until they were parked on the shoulder before reaching around to get his handcuffs. He said to Dale Junior, "Here, put one on your left wrist and snap the other one to the wheel."

Dale Junior, blood leaking from his nose, stunned but still irate in Raylan's judgment, said, "I can't drive handcuffed to the steering wheel."

Raylan held up his free hand for Dale Junior to look at and began rubbing the tips of his thumb and index finger together. He said, "You know what this is? It's the world's smallest violin. A fella did that in a movie where these six scudders wearing black suits go and rob a jewelry store and they all get killed. You see it? It was a good one."

They drove on toward West Palm with darkness spreading over the land, Dale Junior getting used to the handcuffs, looking over as the marshal said, "Put your lights on." Saying then, "Everybody's got problems, huh? Different kinds for different people. Account of you think you're tough you're going up to State Prison where you'll have to prove it."

Dale Junior said, "You gonna report what I did, get me another couple of years up there?" and had to wait.

The marshal taking a few moments before he said, "Last month I went to Brunswick, Georgia, to visit my sons. One's ten, the other's four and a half, living up there with their mom and a real estate man she married name of Gary, has a little cookie-duster mustache. Winona calls the boys punkins, always has. But this Gary calls them punks. I told him not to do it, my sons aren't punks. He says it's short for punkin, that's all. I told him, 'I don't care for it, okay? So don't call them that.' If I'd known about you then I could've told Gary your story and said, 'That's what a punk is, a person refuses to grow up.' "

"I asked you," Dale Junior said, "if you're gonna bring me up on a charge."

"You hear your tone of voice?" the marshal said, sitting over there in the dark. "I'm not your problem."

It was quiet in the car following the headlights along the Turnpike, neither of them saying another word until they came to the tollbooth and the marshal paid the man and they got off on Okeechobee Boulevard in West Palm. The marshal told him to go east to Military Trail and turn right and Dale Junior told him he knew the way to Gun Club. Okay?

Now there were streetlights and signs and stores lit up, back in civilization.

"Your problem," the marshal said, "you can't accept anyone telling you what to do."

Dale Junior only grunted, feeling another sermon coming.

The marshal saying now, "If you can't live with it, don't ever get into law enforcement."

"If I can't live with what?"

"Being told what to do, having superiors."

Dale Junior said, "Oh," slowing down and braking for a yellow light turning red, thinking, *Jesus, what I always wanted to do, get into law enforcement.*

It was as they coasted to the intersection and stopped they got rammed from behind.

Raylan felt himself pressed against the seat harness, his head snapping back and forward again. He heard Dale Junior say "God *damn!*" and saw him gripping the wheel, looking up at the rearview mirror now. Raylan got his seat belt undone before looking around to see the headlights of a pickup truck close behind the Cadillac's rear deck. Now it was backing up a few feet, the driver making sure the bumpers weren't locked together.

"Goddamn jig," Dale Junior said.

Two of them, young black guys coming from the

pickup now as Raylan got out and walked back toward them: the one on the driver's side wearing a crocheted skullcap, the other one, his hair done in cornrows, holding something in his right hand Raylan took to be a pistol, holding it against his leg, away from a few cars going past just then, all the traffic Raylan could see coming for the next few blocks. They were by a vacant lot; stores across the street appeared closed except for a McDonald's.

The pickup truck's bumper, higher than the Cadillac's, had plowed into the sheet metal, smashing the taillights on the left side and popping the trunk, the lid creased and raised a few inches.

Raylan recognized the revolver the guy held, a .357 Mag with a six-inch barrel; he had one at home just like it, Smith & Wesson. Raylan kept his mouth shut, not wanting to say something that might get these guys upset. This was a car-jacking, the guys were no doubt wired and that .357 could go off for no reason. Raylan looked at the damaged trunk again, studying it to be occupied.

The one with cornrows and the gun against his leg said, "You see what I got here?"

Raylan looked him in the eye for the first time and nodded.

The one in the crocheted skullcap walked up to the driver's side of the Cadillac. The one with cornrows said to Raylan, "We gonna trade, let you have a pickup truck for this here. You see a problem with that?"

Raylan shook his head.

The one in the crocheted skullcap glanced back this way as he said, "Come here look at this."

The moment the one with the cornrows turned and moved away Raylan raised the trunk lid. He brought out his Remington 12-gauge, then had to wait for a car to pass before stepping away from the trunk. Raylan put the shotgun on the two guys looking at Dale Junior handcuffed to the steering wheel and did something every lawman knew guaranteed attention and respect. He racked the pump on the shotgun, back and forward, and that hard metallic sound, better than blowing a whistle, brought the two guys around to see they were out of business.

"Let go of the pistol," Raylan said. "Being dumb don't mean you want to get shot."

He used two pairs of cuffs from the trunk to link the car-jackers together—had them do it left wrist to left wrist and right wrist to right wrist side by side— and had them slide into the front seat next to Dale Junior.

Would he have shot them? Dale Junior kept quiet wondering about it. One of the cops back in Ocala had told him he'd better behave while in this marshal's care, but he hadn't thought about it until now. He could feel the shoulder of the car-jacker sitting next to him, the one with cornrows, pressing against his arm. Now the marshal, back there in the dark with his shotgun, was saying, "Fellas, this is Dale Crowe Junior, another one believes it's the system's fault he's ill-tempered and feels it's okay to assault people."

Saying then, after a minute, "I know a fella sixty-seven years old, got rich off our economic system running a sports book, has more money'n he can ever spend. But this man, with all his advantages, doesn't know what to do with himself. Mopes around, drinks too much, gets everybody upset and worried so they'll feel sorry for him."

The car-jacker next to Dale Junior said, "You was to lemme go, I'll see the man don't bother you no more."

Dale Junior thought the marshal would tell him to keep his mouth shut, maybe poke him with the shotgun. But nothing happened like that and there was a silence, no sound from back there in the dark until the marshal said, "You miss the point. This friend of mine—his name's Harry—he isn't bothering me any, he's his own problem. Same as you fellas. I don't take what you did personally. You understand? Want to lean on you. Or wish you any more state time'n you deserve. What you'll have to do now is ride the rap, as they say. It's all anybody has to do."

t w o

Harry hired a Puerto Rican bounty hunter to go after the sixteen five this guy Warren "Chip" Ganz owed him. Warren Ganz III, living up in Manalapan, Palm Beach County.

"Those homes up there on the ocean," Harry said to the collector, "with the boat docks across the road, on the Intracoastal? They have to go for a few mil, so you know he's got it. The guy phoned in his bets, NFL the entire season, some college basketball, NCdouble-A and NBA play-offs . . . You know I'm out of business. So my sheet writers are closing the books, checking the slow pays, I find out this Warren Ganz was using three different names. He'd call up to place a bet and say, 'This is Warren.' Once in a while he'd say, 'This is Cal.' Most of the time, though, he used Chip. Call up and say, 'This is Chip.' One of my rules, forty years in the business—going back to the syndicate days—twenty years running my own book, you have to always know who you're doing business with. Lately, though, I've had things on my mind you might've heard about—those people trying to whack me out, for Christ sake. It can shake you up, take my word, somebody after you like that. I'm trying to retire and I got these loose ends to take care of." Harry said, "So how about fifteen hundred?" Which represented the vig, the profit Harry would have made if Chip Ganz paid off on his bets like everybody else. Harry said, "A bounty hunter, Christ, you shouldn't have any trouble."

The Puerto Rican, a slim, good-looking guy with dreamy eyes and a ponytail he twisted into a knot, said he was no longer a bounty hunter, but still knew how to find people. His name was Roberto Deo-gracias and was known as Bobby Deo and Bobby the Gardener.

Bobby said, "This guy's name is Cheep?"

"You got it," Harry said. "Chip Ganz."

He loved guys like Bobby Deo; they'd do anything for a price, whatever you had to have done.

* * *

A couple of days later Bobby phoned Harry at his apartment in the Della Robbia Hotel on Ocean Drive, Miami Beach.

"The mother of this guy Chip Ganz owns the house where he's living. The father, Warren Ganz, Junior, paid two hundred thousand for it in sixty-five, died and left the estate to his wife. Two point three-five acres on the ocean worth four to five million now. That's an estimate, comparing it to places along there sold in the last few years."

"How do you find that out?"

"You call the office of the Property Appraiser."

"They tell you all that?"

"They have to, Harry. Is no secret."

"So he lives there with his mother?"

"The mother is in a nursing home in West Palm, but I don't know if there's something wrong with her or she just getting old or what. I have to check, maybe go see her. So Mr. Chip Ganz, I'm pretty sure, lives there alone. Nine thousand square feet, man; swimming pool, tile patio, the house white with a red tile roof they call Mediterranean, Harry. It could be a beautiful place, but it's in bad shape." Bobby the Gardener speaking now. "I mean the property is overgrown, needs to be landscaped. You can barely drive into the place."

"Maybe," Harry said, "it's for sale."

"Maybe, but it's not listed. When I went up there he wasn't home, so I walk around the place, look in some of the windows at the living room, the dining room. There almost no furniture in the downstairs. Like he's selling it, maybe a piece at a time and his mommy don't know about it. Big three-car garage has a Mercedes-Benz in it, ten years old, needs some bump and paint work."

Harry's voice on the phone said, "Shit. Well, it doesn't look like he's gonna have my sixteen five, does it?"

Bobby Deo said, "Let me see what I can do." And drove back to the Ganz estate: along Ocean Boulevard past walls of flowering oleander and wind-blown Australian pines to the spray-painted sign in the vegetation that said PRIVATE DRIVE and below it KEEP OUT. Bobby backed into the drive, eased his Cadillac through the vegetation growing wild and stopped when he heard it scraping the car. He got out and walked along the drive through sea grape, palmettos, sabal palms, past an old gumbo-limbo spreading all over the place, through this jungle to the house with no furniture in it. He looked again in windows to see the rooms still empty before walking around to the ocean side of the property and was pretty sure he'd found Mr. Chip Ganz.

In a lounge on the red-tiled patio, reading the paper and smoking a joint, ten-thirty in the morning.

Bobby's first impression of Chip Ganz, he saw a skinny guy in his fifties trying to look hip: the joint, a full head of hair with gray streaks in it brushed back uncombed, and tan. Bobby had never seen an Anglo this tan and thought at first Chip Ganz was lying there with nothing on but his sunglasses. No, the guy was wearing a little swimsuit, a black one. Or it was his underwear. Bobby had some like it with the name Bill Blass on them; he had them in red, blue, green, different colors. This Chip Ganz was the kind wanted you to think he was cool: the way he lowered the paper now and looked this way, but not acting surprised to see a person he didn't know watching him.

Bobby said, "How you doing, Chip?" and took time to look around, notice the sea grape taking over the frontage along the ocean. "Your property needs a lot of work. You know it?"

The guy seemed to be interested, putting the paper down and pushing up to lean on his arm, the joint pinched between his thumb and his finger. He said, "Is that right?"

"I use to work as a gardener," Bobby said.

"Yeah? What do you do now?"

"Harry Arno ask me to come by. You know what I'm talking about?"

"I have a pretty good idea," Chip said to the guy coming toward him now in a white guayabera shirt hanging starched over his waist—but the real thing if he was doing collection work. The guy standing at the lounge now looking down at him.

"You want to check me out, call Harry. Ask him is Bobby Deo here to pick up what you owe him."

An accent to go with the Latin-lover look. Chip took his time. He said, "NBA championship, I've forgotten the line, but I seem to recall I took the Knicks, put down five against the Rockets."

"You put down five three times under different names," Bobby said. "You owe fifteen plus the fifteen hundred juice and another fifteen hundred for expenses, driving here from Miami."

"That's eighteen big ones," Chip said, giving the collector a thoughtful look. "Which I don't happen to have at this point in time. Or even the sixteen five I actually owe, if you want to look at it, you know, realistically."

"Look at it any way you want," Bobby said, "I know you can get it."

Chip opened his eyes to look innocent and a little surprised.

"I can? Where?"

"From your mommy."

Bobby watched Chip Ganz draw in on the joint and then swing his legs off the lounge to sit up; but when he tried to rise, Bobby stepped in close. Now Chip had to lean back with his hand supporting him from behind to look up. He offered Bobby the joint and Bobby took it, inhaled, blew out a cloud of smoke and said, "Jamaica," handing the joint back to him.

Chip shook his head, saying, "Ocala Gold, home-grown," in that strained voice, holding the reefer smoke in his lungs. He tried to get up again, but Bobby stood there, not moving.

"I want to show you something."

"I saw it," Bobby said. "You don't have no furniture. So what happen, you lose all your money and your mommy won't give you none, uh?"

Chip's head was almost waist high, his face raised. "She lets me live here and that's about it."

"She don't love you no more?"

"She wigged out on me. Has hardening of the arteries, Alzheimer's, I don't know. She's in a home."

"I know, I went to see her," Bobby said, "find out if she want some landscaping done. She don't say too much that makes sense, does she?"

Bobby had to wait while Chip toked on his reefer again, acting hip with his tan and his long hair, the guy creased and weathered up close, showing his age, in his fifties. He blew the smoke out and shrugged before he spoke this time.

"So you see my problem. Lack of funds and a mommy who won't give me any. Christ, who barely communicates. But Harry knows I'm good for it. I'll pay him as soon as I can."

"You got it wrong," Bobby said. "I'm your problem." He took a fistful of Chip's hair and pulled up, the guy straining his neck and hunching his shoulders, eyes coming wide open. "You get the money and pay me by the day after tomorrow, forty-eight hours. How does that sound to you?"

It wasn't a question Bobby expected the man to answer, so he was surprised when Chip said, "Or what?" For a few moments then Bobby stared at the face looking up at him, waiting for him to answer.

"You think I'm kidding?"

It was a question the man could say yes or no to if he wanted, but this time he kept quiet, didn't change his expression.

"What I do," Bobby said, "I told you I use to be a gardener? I'm an expert at trimming all kind of shrubs so they look nice. Like what you need done around here—is so overgrown." Bobby reached behind him, beneath his shirt hanging loose, and brought out a pair of pruners from a leather sheath on his hip, held the curved cutting blades in Chip's face and squeezed closed the red handles that fit his grip and felt good in his hand. "So I use this for pruning. You don't pay me the day after tomorrow I prune something from you. Like what do you think, this part of your ear? You don't need it—you don't wear no earring, do you? Okay, you still don't pay in two more days, I prune the other ear. You don't look so good then. Okay, you still don't pay then I have to prune something else like, let me see, what's a part of you you never want me to prune? What could that be?"

Chip surprised him saying, "I get the idea." Pretty calm about it.

Maybe it was the weed let him talk like that. Bobby said, "It's not just an idea, man, it's a promise, every time you don't pay."

"That's what I mean, Bobby, I believe you."

Using his name now, like they knew each other.

Bobby let go of his hair and Chip sank back down to rest on his arms. He moved his head in a circle, like he was working a stiffness from his neck before he looked up again. This time he said, "You stand to make three large, right? Fifteen hundred representing Harry's vig and another fifteen you added on yourself, that Harry doesn't know about. For coming up here, you said. What's it take you, an hour and a half?"

Bobby waited, not saying anything, because the guy had it right about what he was making.

"Let me ask you something," Chip said. "When you're not doing Harry Arno a favor, what do you do, strictly collection work?"

"What do you want to know for?"

"I'm wondering if I might be able to use you."

The guy kept surprising him, sounding now like he was in charge. Bobby said, "Yeah, how do you pay? Sell some more furniture?"

"Indulge me, okay? I'd like to know how you make your living, how you deal with people. I've got something going that might interest you."

Bobby hesitated. But he was curious and said, "I do collection for Harry once in a while. Harry, or different shylocks call, they want me to lean on some guy. I was a repo man also and a bounty hunter. I did work for bail bondsmen, went after people who took off, didn't appear in court when they suppose to."

"Defendants that jump bond," Chip said.

"Yeah, I bring them back so the bail bondsman don't lose the money he put up. The bail bondsman goes after most of the ones himself, but there some others—a guy leaves the country, say he goes back to Haiti or Jamaica? Those the ones I went after."

"What if you couldn't find the guy? Or for some reason you weren't able to bring him back?"

"I went after a guy," Bobby said, "he was mine. There was no way he didn't come back with me."

Chip said, "You mind if I get up?" Raising his hand he said, "Here," and Bobby took the hand and pulled him up from the lounge. It was okay, not like the guy was telling him what to do. Bobby saw they were about the same height, though Chip Ganz seemed taller because he was so thin, flat in front from his chest down past ribs you could count to the bump in his swimsuit, skinny with round, bony shoulders. The guy looked at the joint, what was left of it, dropped it on the tiles but didn't step on it, Bobby watching him. Now he started across the patio toward open French doors and what looked like a room in there with white furniture, Bobby following him. When he was almost to the doors, Chip stopped and looked back over his shoulder.

"How come, if you were this star at bringing back fugitives, you don't do it anymore?"

"They have a law now on the books, nine oh three point oh five, a convicted felon isn't allow to do that kind of work."

"You've done serious time," Chip said, nodding then, telling Bobby, "That's what I thought," before he turned and went in the house.

Bobby reached the French doors before Chip paused again, glancing around to say he'd be right out, and continued through this sunroom, all bamboo and wicker furniture with white cushions. Bobby watched him open a door to what looked like a study, all dark wood paneling in there. He caught a glimpse of a big TV screen and a guy he believed was Phil Donahue before Chip went in and the door closed.

Bobby stood looking at the door in there across the sunroom. It was okay. The guy said he'd be right out and Bobby believed him.

What was he going to do, leave? Sneak out the front? Skinny middle-aged guy living off his mommy? What could he do?

three

A video surveillance system was hooked to the TV set in the study. Push a button on the remote control and a black-and-white shot of the patio area, the driveway, the front entrance, or a room upstairs would appear in the lower right-hand corner of the screen. Push another button, the TV picture would go off and the surveillance video would come on the whole screen.

That's what Louis Lewis, watching TV in the study,

finally did: put the video of the patio on big so he could watch Chip and the Latino he recognized, Bobby Deo, just talking at first, Chip smoking his weed and now Bobby Deo taking a hit.

Louis Lewis was originally from the Bahamas. He had come here as a little boy with his pretty American mama and a daddy who played steel drums; Louis could sound Bahamian if he wanted to, but preferred being African-American and worked at it. A popular variation, he tried an Islamic name, Ibrahim Abu Aziz, till Chip started calling him Honest Ib and then Boo for Abu and Louis decided that was enough of that shit. He went back to being Louis Lewis, a name his daddy said would make people smile and he'd be a happy fella. He'd never gotten into Islam anyway, just played with the Arab name for a time, looking for respect more than smiles.

Louis used the remote to check the front drive and saw Bobby's Cadillac among the vegetation. Now he pushed a button and was watching Phil Donahue on the big screen again, Phil talking to three women who weighed over five hundred pounds and their normal-size husbands. It was getting good, the ladies mentioning how they made out in bed, hinting around at how they did it, fat ladies acting cute. But now in the little square, down in the corner of the screen, Bobby Deo had his pruners out, holding the snippers in Chip's face and Louis pressed the button to turn the fat ladies off and put the patio show on the big screen. Still watching, he raised the lid of the chest that was like a cocktail table in front of the red leather sofa he was sitting on, the oak chest matching the paneled walls, and brought out a sawed-off pump-action shotgun.

Louis believed the business out there was about money Chip owed somebody, the man not knowing shit how to bet and always into bookies down in Miami. Louis knew Bobby Deo from a time before as the kind of man you'd rather have on your side than against you. He saw Bobby now as a man was set straight, had on expensive clothes—even if they were Latino—had a fine car he left out front. Yeah, he knew Bobby.

Now they were talking again like they'd come to some kind of agreement, Chip no doubt bullshitting the man—yeah, Bobby helping him up now, talking some more, Chip coming in the house now. So Louis worked the remote to put the fat ladies back on big and the patio in the corner of the TV screen, Bobby appearing again, looking around. Chip would come in to see him with the shotgun watching the fat ladies and their little hubbies. . . . Telling Phil yeah, they had a normal sex life, but not saying what was normal to them or exactly how they did it, the fat ladies acting like they knew something nobody else did, like a special thing they could do with those big bodies that would pleasure a man some special way. Or crush him, Louis thought, they roll over on the little hubby sound asleep.

Just then Chip came in—didn't say anything right away—came over and took the remote from Louis and punched the patio back onto the screen big.

"You see him threaten me?"

Not sounding scared especially; keyed-up some.

Louis held up the cut-down shotgun in one hand, said, "Look here, I was ready to back you up. I know the man, Bobby Deo? I know if you try to trip on him, mess with his head, you best shoot the mother-fucker, put him down quick. But then I see you work-ing it out between you, talking like everything's cool."

"You know him," Chip said. "Does that mean per-sonally, or you've heard things about him?"

"I didn't say I know *of* him," Louis said, not caring for Chip's attitude at the moment, "I said I know him. That means what it says."

Chip was all into himself, not catching Louis's tone. He said, "You see what he did? Grabbed me by the hair?"

"Took out his pruners, yeah?"

"Threatened to cut my ears off. . . ."

"Must be you owe somebody money, huh?"

"Harry Arno, sixteen five. Only this guy wants eighteen with expenses. He calls me Cheep."

The man sounding just a speck shaky now. Usually he could put on being superior even with nothing to back it.

"Give you a couple days to pay, huh, or he start to snip. Bobby Deo was a bounty hunter. Now he does collection work when there's enough in it for him. What else you want to know? Being light-skin Puerto Rican he thinks all the ladies are crazy about him. What the man is basically, he's an enforcer. You un-derstand? You want somebody taken out and you can pay high dollar, he'll do it for you."

Chip said, "Is that right?" raising his eyebrows. Interested but not, in Louis's judgment, wanting to show it.

"He got sent to Starke on a homicide, shot some dude he was suppose to be bringing in. Doing his rap he was the man up there among the Latinos."

"Same time you were there."

"Was where we first bumped into each other." Louis said, "You understand if you're thinking to hire Bobby to take out Harry Arno it cost you more than what you owe Harry."

Chip surprised him, looking pleased at the idea and saying, "Actually what I was wondering, if you and Bobby got along okay."

"You mean like if me and him was to work together? Have a mutual interest in common?"

Louis watched Mr. Chip Ganz standing there in his underwear almost naked, hands on his bony hipbones, looking at Bobby on the TV screen before looking this way again.

He said, "What do you think?"

Making it sound like he was throwing it up in the air and it didn't matter to him one way or the other.

Louis said, "Bring Bobby in on the deal so he leave you alone, huh? Won't be snipping off any your valuable parts."

"We could use another guy," Chip said. "We've talked about it enough."

Louis said, "You want to hire him?" trying to make the man come out and say it.

"It's an idea."

"Get somebody knows how to do the job," Louis

said, " 'stead of sitting around discussing it to death?"

Chip didn't care for that kind of talk. He said, "My friend, the idea is foolproof. What we've been discussing is who we start with."

He was watching the TV screen again. Louis looked over to see Bobby Deo in that P.R. shirt like he was going to a fiesta, Bobby now inspecting the swimming pool: the pool scummy and ugly with the filter system shut down to save money, algae growing in it like seaweed and turning the water brown.

"Say you put the deal to him and he likes it," Louis said, "you still owe Harry. He sent Bobby; he can send somebody else."

Chip said, "Not if Harry isn't around," and like *that* the man's confidence and superior attitude were back in place. Like the whole conversation had been leading up to the Chipper delivering his punch line. *Not if Harry isn't around.*

Louis said, "Hey now," seeing the sly grin on the man's face, knowing exactly what the man was thinking.

"Hire Bobby," Louis said, "to get Harry Arno."

The man nodded. "What do you think?"

"Depends if Harry's the kind we looking for."

"He's loaded," Chip said. "All the time he's running his sports book he's supposed to be cutting the wiseguys in? He's skimming on them. A sheet writer that used to work for Harry told a friend of mine it's a fact. Twenty years he skimmed something like two grand a week over what he made for himself. Finally the wiseguys got suspicious . . . You must've heard about it."

"I was upstate at the time," Louis said, "but I heard, yeah, they send a guy to whack Harry out and he shoots the guy dead and takes off?"

"Went to Italy for a while," Chip said, "comes back —I don't know the whole story, but it's like it never happened, all the trouble he had with the wiseguys. But now the feds've shut him down, he's out of business."

Louis noticed Bobby Deo on the diving board now, hands in his pockets, looking down at the scummy pool. Louis said, "So Harry's closing his books, collecting what's still owed him, huh?" watching Bobby on the TV and realizing the man's hands weren't in his pockets, he had his business out and was right then taking a leak in the swimming pool. Louis said, "You see what he's doing?"

After a moment Chip said, "He spotted the camera and thinks I'm watching him," the man not sounding too surprised. "Letting me know he doesn't care to be kept waiting. Anyway," Chip said, "I even thought of Harry as a possibility, when we were making out the list. I was gonna mention him to you, see what you thought?"

"Say he's got all this skim money," Louis said. "Where you think he keeps it?"

"That's the first thing we find out." Chip was looking at the TV screen again, at Bobby Deo coming away from the pool toward the house. "How much Harry's got liquid he can get his hands on." Chip moved across the room, glanced at Louis to say, "Here we go," and opened the door.

He stood waiting as Bobby came through the sunroom into the study, Bobby looking at the TV screen, the empty patio showing, then at Louis standing with his hands on his hips, then at the shotgun lying on the sofa.

"You understand," Chip said, "you were covered all the time you were out there. If you hadn't put those snippers away when you did, you could've taken a load of buckshot in the ass. I just want you to know that."

The man talking now with backup, confident as can be. Louis watched Bobby turn his way.

"You work for this guy?"

Louis shrugged. "We got something on."

Chip said, "I believe you know my partner, Louis Lewis?"

Presenting one ex-con to another, the man watching to see the effect on Bobby Deo, a different situation than when they were outside. Louis and Bobby looked at each other with no expression to speak of.

Bobby saying, "Use to be Abu, the Bahamian Arabian," with a mild expression now, pleasant enough.

And now Louis showed a slight smile telling him, "I gave up that shit once I got my release. What we'd like to know, Señor Deogracias, the bill collector, if you think you ready for the big time."

See what he thought of that.

But then Chip stepped in saying, "What Louis means—something we've been talking about here— we wonder if you'd be interested in a proposition."

Bobby looked at Louis and Louis said, "A score, a big one."

Bobby seemed to consider it for a moment. He said, "How much we talking about?"

Louis had to smile, the man showing his greed, wanting to know the take before asking what it was about.

"We'll be dealing in millions," Chip said, "with a way to keep it coming in as long as we want."

Bobby said, "What's the split?"

"Three ways, we all get the same."

"You say millions—nothing to it."

"At least a couple mil each time we score. This is no one-shot deal."

"Yeah, what is it? What do we do?"

"We take hostages," Chip said and waited while Bobby Deo stared at him.

No doubt running out of patience, so Louis gave him a hint. "Like the Shia took those hostages over in Beirut? You know what I'm saying? Over in Lebanon—blindfolded them, kept them chained up? Like that."

Chip said, "Only we'll be doing it for profit."

"You talking about kidnapping," Bobby said.

"In a way," Chip said, "only different. A lot different."

four

By the time Raylan got to Joyce's apartment in Miami Beach it was too late to go out to dinner. He mentioned he'd tried to call her three or four times. Joyce said she forgot to turn her machine on—nothing about where she was all afternoon. She fixed him scrambled eggs and toast and made herself a drink. Finally, sitting at the kitchen table while Raylan ate his supper, Joyce said, "Harry got picked up for drunk driving."

"Today?"

"A few weeks ago. They took his license away for six months."

"I told you it would happen."

"I know. That's why I haven't said anything."

"He still drinking?"

"He's trying to quit." She paused and said, "I've been sort of driving him around. Harry's looking for customers who still owe him money."

"You realize you're aiding in illegal transactions?"

Joyce said, "Oh, for Christ sake," and there was a silence.

Raylan got up to get a beer from the refrigerator. Joyce asked him, as she always did, if he wanted a glass. Raylan said no thanks. After another pause, aware of himself and aware of Joyce sitting with her drink, he said, "Why don't you put that new Roy Orbison on?"

She said, "All right," but didn't move, lighting a cigarette now, a new habit she'd picked up being around Harry. The first time she played the new Roy Orbison for him the CD came to "The Only One" and Joyce said if she were still dancing she'd use it in her routine. Joyce had moved her hips to the slow, draggy beat and showed Raylan where she'd throw in the bumps. " 'Every one you know's been through it.' Bam. 'You bit the bullet, then you chew it.' Bam." Raylan liked it.

When they were first getting to know one another, almost a year ago, he'd told her how he'd worked for different coal operators in Harlan County, Kentucky, where he grew up, and before joining the Marshals

Service. He told her, "I've worked deep mines, wild-cat mines, the ones you go into and scratch for what's left, and I've stripped."

Joyce said that time, "So have I."

He said, "Pardon me?"

She hadn't wanted to tell him too soon about working as a go-go dancer when she was younger—one of the few topless performers, she said, without a drug habit. Like it was okay to dance half-naked in a barroom full of men as long as you weren't strung out. He told her no, it didn't bother him—not mentioning it might've been different if he'd known her when she was up there showing her breasts to everybody. No, the only thing that bothered him now was her devoting her life to poor Harry.

She'd say she wasn't devoting her life, she was trying to help him.

Sitting at the kitchen table again Raylan thought of something and began telling about the bust he'd taken part in that morning. Telling it in his quiet way but with a purpose:

How they went to an address out in Canal Point to arrest a fugitive known to be armed and dangerous. Banged on the door and when no one came a strike team officer yelled at the house, "Open up or it's coming down!" So when still no one came they used a sledgehammer—what the strike team called their master key—busted in and here was a woman standing in the living room no doubt the whole time, not saying a word. One of the strike team, a sheriff's deputy, told her they had a warrant for the arrest of Russell Robert Lyles and asked was he in the house.

The woman said no, he wasn't, and had no idea where he might be. The deputy said to her, "If Russell's upstairs, you're going to jail." And the woman said, "He's upstairs."

Raylan waited for Joyce, saw her nod, but that's all; she didn't say anything. She didn't see the point he was trying to make.

So Raylan said, "You understand it wasn't like the woman was giving the guy up, telling on him. There was nothing she could do, so she said yeah, he's upstairs."

Joyce nodded again, uh-huh. "So did you get him?"

She still didn't see the point.

"We got him. Even with all the commotion, busting the door down? The guy was still in bed."

"Did you shoot him?"

Looking right at Raylan as she said it and it stopped him, because he could see she was serious, waiting for him to answer.

"We had to wake him up."

Nudged the guy with a shotgun—the way it actually happened—the sheriff's deputy saying, "Rise and shine, sleepyhead."

But that wasn't the point either. What he wanted Joyce to see, she had as much chance of helping Harry Arno as this woman had of hiding a fugitive. There was a silence. "I didn't like to bust into somebody's house," Raylan said. "I asked the woman why she didn't open the door. She said, 'Invite you in for iced tea?'"

There was another silence until Raylan said, "You

know Harry's an alcoholic," and saw Joyce look at him as if she might've missed something, one minute talking about apprehending a fugitive . . . "You know that, don't you?"

"He's trying to stop."

"How? Is he in a program? He won't admit he's got a problem, so he makes excuses. It's what alcoholics do. You left him, he's depressed and that's why he's drinking again."

Joyce said, "As far as he's concerned . . ."

"You dumped him. After how many years you've been going with him on and off? How serious were you?"

She didn't answer that.

"Honey, alcoholics never blame themselves when they mess up. It's your fault he was drinking and lost his license, so he gets you to feel sorry for him and drive him around, drop whatever you're doing."

She said, "Well, I'm not working." Meaning she hadn't gotten any calls to do catalog modeling.

"Come on. The man's sixty-seven years old acting like a spoiled kid."

"He's sixty-nine," Joyce said, "the same age as Paul Newman. Ask him."

They picked at each other using Harry as the reason, not nearly as lovey-dovey as they used to be, that time right before he shot Tommy Bucks and was temporarily assigned out of the Miami marshals office.

A situation Raylan blamed on the assistant U.S. attorney who reviewed the shooting:

This very serious young guy all buttoned-up in his seersucker suit, but acting bored to indicate his self-confidence. He wanted to know why Raylan was sitting in a crowded restaurant with a man known to be a member of organized crime when he shot him. Raylan told him the Cardozo Hotel lunch crowd was out on the porch and Tommy Bucks had his back to a wall, a precaution the man had no doubt been taking since his childhood in Sicily.

The assistant U.S. attorney asked if they'd had some kind of disagreement. Raylan said he believed it was his job as a marshal to disagree with that type of person, a known gangster. The assistant U.S. attorney said he couldn't help but wonder if the shooting might not have been triggered, so to speak, over a busted deal, an argument over some aspect of an arrangement Raylan had with this individual. Not flat accusing Raylan of being on the take, but coming close.

He said then he'd heard a rumor that, sometime earlier, Raylan had given Tommy Bucks twenty-four hours to get out of town or he would shoot him on sight. That wasn't exactly true was it? The assistant U.S. attorney sounding as though he saw humor in this without believing a word of it.

"I gave him twenty-four hours to get out of Dade County," Raylan said. "Tommy Bucks was sitting at that table when his time ran out. Armed. A witness saw it and called out, 'He's got a gun!' It was confirmed and put in the police report. What happened then, Tommy Bucks drew on me and I shot him."

The assistant U.S. attorney said if this was true, it sounded as though Raylan had forced Tommy Bucks to draw his gun so he would have an excuse to shoot him.

Raylan said, "No, he had a choice. He could've left. He had, he might still be alive; though I doubt it."

Raylan's boss, the Miami marshal, thought it best to get him out of that U.S. attorney's sight for a while, pulled him off warrants and assigned Raylan to the Fugitive Apprehension Strike Team in Palm Beach County, working out of the Sheriff's Office. It was the type of duty Raylan liked best, enforcement, way better than standing around in a courtroom or shuffling papers in Assets and Forfeitures. Except that in a way it was like being exiled: have to drive two hours up to West Palm in the morning, two hours back at night to Joyce's place or the house he'd rented in North Miami, that freeway traffic wearing him out. It was another reason things weren't as lovey-dovey with Joyce—they didn't see each other as much.

Or maybe the distance, the drive, arguing about Harry, maybe none of that had anything to do with the way things were between them.

He wondered about it, sitting at the kitchen table with Joyce, thinking of something she'd said a minute ago. He'd told her about apprehending the fugitive and she asked if he'd shot him. Serious, wanting to know.

She asked now if he wanted another beer.

Raylan said, "Did you think I had shot that guy today?"

"I wondered, that's all."

"Really? A guy lying in bed asleep?"

"I saw you shoot and kill a man," Joyce said.

Not twenty feet from the table when he shot Tommy Bucks three times, Joyce watching it happen.

She said, "But we've never talked about it, have we? How you felt?"

He wasn't sure how he felt. Relieved? It was hard to explain. He said, "It scares you, after, thinking about it. I don't feel sorry for him or wish I hadn't done it. I didn't see any other way to stop him."

"It was a personal matter?"

"In a way."

"Man to man. You have an image of yourself, the lawman."

"It's what I am."

She said, "You want to know what I wonder about? What if he wasn't armed?"

"But he was."

"You know that?"

"He wouldn't have been there without a gun."

She said, "Let me put it another way. If you knew he didn't have a gun, would you have shot him anyway?"

"But he *did*. I don't know what else to tell you."

She said, "Well, then think about it."

"I'd like to know what *you* think," Raylan said. "Would I have shot him knowing he was unarmed?"

Joyce said, "I don't know." She waited a few moments and said, "You want another beer or not?"

f i v e

Harry got to the restaurant in Delray Beach at ten to one, a little early. He wasn't going to have a drink, had made up his mind driving here; but as soon as he was seated he ordered a vodka and tonic and paid the waiter. He'd have one, that's all. It was nice here on the terrace, watching people going by, like a sidewalk café. One-fifteen Harry ordered another drink and told the waiter to run a tab. He got the drink and took it inside with him to the pay phone, where he dialed Bobby Deo's number in Miami Beach and got no answer, no recorded message. He walked out to the terrace among the Friday afternoon lunch crowd and sat down at the table in the shade where he'd left his cigarettes and change. He talked to the waiter for a couple of minutes about this and that, ordered a double Absolut on the rocks with a twist, and watched a girl holding a deck of cards pausing at tables to say a few words, but not having any luck until she came to a woman seated near Harry. The woman, wearing quite a lot of makeup, gold-framed sunglasses and earrings, asked the girl to sit down. Harry heard the woman say she was sick and tired of customers acting bitchy, throwing their credit cards, treating her like a servant. He didn't hear the girl's voice until she said, "The Eight of Swords. Yes, there's a lot going on you feel you have to put up with, more than you think you can handle." The girl speaking slowly, with kind of a southern accent. "So, let's see. The Ace of Wands. You don't feel you're getting anywhere, but you've learned a lot about yourself. Isn't that true?" The woman said something Harry couldn't hear. Then the girl's voice again. "The Prince of Swords reversed. Hmmmm." She said, "Well, you're not afraid to take on challenges," and something about a painful situation that hadn't been resolved. "The Three of Wands. Hmmmm, now I see a past-life connection. . . ." Harry ordered another drink.

At two he tried Bobby Deo again. No answer.

He phoned Joyce. Her message voice came on. He waited and then said to her machine, "I've been here over an hour, corner of Atlantic and A1A—or Ocean Boulevard, Ocean Drive, I don't know, they're all the same thing—Delray Beach, right? You were there when he phoned, isn't that what I told you? Said he'd have sixteen five for me. Well, he isn't here." Harry was aware he sounded as if he was blaming Joyce. The thing that irritated him, she wasn't home. But then realized that if she was, she'd ask him how he got to Delray Beach. He'd tell her and she'd jump on him for driving without a license, suspended on account of the DUI, and he'd have to listen to her nag him about it. So it was just as well she wasn't home and he had to talk to the machine. Jesus. He said, "There's a girl here with tarot cards going around to the tables. Maybe I should have her tell my fortune. The way things're going . . . I don't know, I'll call you later." He returned to his table to find the little girl with the tarot cards waiting for him.

She said, "If you don't mind my making an observation, I see a lot of confusion and struggle going on inside you."

A nice-looking girl, dark hair down past her bare shoulders, wearing one of those tube tops, a white one. Harry pulled a chair out for her. As they were both sitting down he said, "Honey, when a guy says he's gonna meet you to hand over fifteen grand, in cash, and he doesn't show, there's a good chance your emotions will be right out there for all to see. You don't need those cards to tell I'm fairly pissed off —if you'll pardon my French—though you might take a peek and tell me if I'm ever going to see the son of a bitch again. Roberto Deogracias—I should've known better."

The little girl waited, hands folded on top of her tarot cards. Harry was looking for the waiter as she said, "I saw the confusion in you when you first came in and sat down."

"Nervous anticipation," Harry said. "Let's have a drink."

"What I perceived," the girl said, waiting then for Harry to look at her, "was not anticipation, but deep feelings about a choice you have to make. Something to do with unfinished business."

Harry looked off again saying, "Is that right?" caught the waiter's eye and raised his hand.

"You're trying to decide whether or not in the next few weeks you should leave here."

Harry turned in his seat to face her.

"If you ought to quit your business and go someplace else to live."

He was staring at her now, this kid calmly looking back at him, her hands folded. He said, "How do you know that?"

"I see you sitting at a sidewalk café. Not like this one or this kind of view." She gestured to take in the terrace, the street, cars parked at meters, the beach and the Atlantic Ocean out there. "I see an older, more tropical setting. I want to say like on the Mediterranean, the Riviera."

Harry kept staring at her. "That's amazing."

"Am I right?"

"Close enough. The Italian Riviera, I have a villa

over there near Rapallo, up in the hills above the town."

The girl said, "But you don't know if you should go back."

Harry laid his arms on the edge of the table and hunched over to get closer to her. "Maybe you can tell me what I should do."

"Well, if you'd like a reading . . ."

"With the cards?"

"It's up to you. I'll be honest, though, I don't think the cards have any power in themselves. It's because you touch them—when I ask you to shuffle the cards? Then I get a read off your vibrations. Another way is if I hold something of yours that you own, something personal. Or I touch your hands."

Harry straightened and pushed his hands toward the center of the table. He saw her smile, her hands moving toward his now, and felt her fingertips.

"How do you know how to do this?"

"I have psychic powers."

"I mean is it something you learned?"

"You can get better at it," the girl said, "but you have to be born with some degree of paranormal abilities. When I was just a little girl I'd get pretty intense psychic impressions. It was funny because I thought everyone knew the things about people that I did. Things just come to me, like I see a picture or hear a voice?" She closed her eyes. "I see you at that sidewalk café. Yeah, it's in Italy, 'cause I see a sign . . . You look, well, at peace, like you have everything you want." Her eyes opened. "And yet you don't know if you should go back there."

Harry kept quiet; he watched her close her eyes again. She had nice eyelashes, dark and long, a nice soft mouth.

"The reason you think you ought to go back involves some kind of unfinished business. You own property over there?"

"I leased a villa."

"What about investments?"

"Over there? I don't have any."

"There're funds involved . . ."

Harry waited.

She paused again, then opened her eyes. "Maybe we should start with why you wanted to live in Italy. The unfinished business doesn't have to have anything to do with, you know, *business*. I'm pretty sure, though, it relates to something that happened in the past."

Harry said, "Well, I was there during the war. . . . You know, you might be right. And I kept going back, thinking about living there someday. But then when I did make the move it was, well, different than I thought it would be."

"How was it different?"

"For one thing it was winter, a lot colder'n I ever imagined. There were other things, too. The villa's drafty, hard to heat . . . The language can be a problem, trying to order in a restaurant . . ."

The girl said, "So even though there're good reasons why you don't want to go back, you still feel the urge."

"If that makes sense," Harry said.

"Well, I think this *urge*," the girl said, "is caused by

the unfinished business you're not aware of. And the unfinished business, whatever it is, has to do with something that happened in the past."

Harry thought about it. He shook his head saying, "I don't know what it could be. Outside of I signed a lease for the villa, paid in advance . . ."

"When I say 'in the past,'" the girl said in her quiet tone, looking directly at him, "I don't mean that time during the war, or on one of the trips you took since then. I'm talking about a soul connection, something you feel strongly about, that took place during one of your past lives."

Harry said, "Wait," straightening up a little more, "are we getting into reincarnation here?"

He felt the tips of her fingers move on his hands, touching his knuckles.

She said, "It's the feeling I get. You don't have to, you know, believe in it yourself."

Harry said, "No, go on," and had to smile. "You see me living in some other time, like maybe hundreds of years ago?"

"It's not something I actually *see*. You're going to have to tell me about it."

"But I might've been a real Italian at one time? Or going way back, like maybe even a Roman?"

She gave him a nice smile with a shrug. "Would you like to find out?"

"If it's true," Harry said, "then I might even've been somebody, huh? I mean like a well-known figure."

"It's possible." She said, "All we have to do is regress you, take you back to some time in the past and you can tell me about it, who you were, what it was like. . . ."

"How do you do that?"

"I use hypnosis, take you back gradually and you tell me where you are, what's going on. Have you ever been put under hypnosis before?"

"Not that I can remember."

She said, "I can't promise results, but I think you'd be a good subject. Would you like to try it?"

"I'd love to," Harry said. "But you don't do it here, do you?"

"No, you'd have to come to my house. I'm just up the road." She waited.

And Harry said, "Right now?"

"It's okay with me."

He watched her get up from the table, this slender girl in her tube top, not much up there, and tight jeans hugging her hips and thighs. She sure didn't look like a fortune-teller. Now she got a wallet out of her hip pocket, fingered through it and brought out a business card she handed him.

"Here's the address, it's on Ramona in Briny Breezes? Three miles up A1A on the right-hand side. If you come to a trailer park you've passed it."

Harry glanced at the business card. He looked up to see the girl waiting.

She said, "It's a hundred dollars. Is that okay?"

Harry shrugged. "No problem. You take cash? I'm the kind of guy, I like to pay cash for everything, keep it simple. I bought that Caddy out there across the street, the white one? Cadillac Seville, I paid cash for it."

Now the girl gave him a cute shrug with her shoulders and a smile saying, "Whatever way you like to do it," and started to walk off.

Harry wondered in that moment if fortune-telling was her only game: if there might be more than getting hypnotized in store for him. He called after her, "Hey, I'm Harry Arno."

She paused to look back and nod.

Harry watched her walk into the restaurant before he looked at the business card again. Above the address on Ramona in Briny Breezes it said:

Rev. Dawn Navarro
Certified Medium & Spiritualist
Psychic Readings

From inside the restaurant's dim light she watched the waiter arrive with Harry Arno's drink. She watched him take it from the waiter's hand and drink it down and then stand up to pay his bill, taking cash from his pants pocket, leaving what he owed on the table and picking up her business card, taking time to look at it again.

She came out to the doorway now to watch Harry leave the terrace and cross the street to the white Cadillac he'd paid cash for. When finally he drove off and was through the light at Atlantic Avenue heading north, she turned to the phone on the wall next to her, dropped in a quarter and dialed. After a few moments a voice came on. She said, "Hi, we're on our way," and hung up.

s i x

Louis and Bobby Deo sat parked in Bobby's black
Cadillac on a street they had to find called Ramona.
Louis saw it as a low-rent neighborhood of little Florida houses in need of fixing up, the home hidden
among old trees and shrubs. Nothing better to do, he
asked Bobby how come people that named streets
couldn't get it straight? Come up Ocean Boulevard it
was the same as A1A till along here it became Banyan Boulevard; go up the line a half mile it was

Ocean Boulevard again. How come, if it was the same road? Bobby took time to look over at Louis, then turned back to look straight ahead again. Bobby somewhere in his head, Louis decided, not wanting to talk. Not much of a talker anyway. No doubt his mind fooling with the hostage proposition, Chip's part still a question in Bobby's mind, Bobby asking on the way here if Chip knew what he was doing.

The way Louis explained it, he said, "The man wants to be bad. Understand? Get into a hustle that pays on account of he don't have a trade, only a rich mama forgot who he is. The man thinks he's a sport, loves to gamble, bet on games. Only he don't know shit how to pick any winners. What the man does have is ideas, ones that might pay or not, like this taking hostages. The thing about his ideas, they different. Understand? Kind of gigs haven't been tried that I know of. The man watches the news on TV and reads the paper to get his ideas. The idea of the hostages, the idea of snatching one of these millionaires cheating on their savings-and-loan business you read about. What the man don't have is experience."

Bobby said, "Can he keep his mouth shut?"

Louis said, "We'll watch he does."

Louis was letting it become "we" to get next to Bobby and know what he was thinking, and because they were both in the life and had done state time. Bobby for shooting a man Bobby said pulled a gun on him instead of paying what he owed and went up on a manslaughter plea deal. Louis convicted on felony firearms charges when he took part in the drive-by of a dwelling with MAC10's converted to full auto.

Louis went up without copping—naming any names to have his time cut—and was respected among the population, all the homeboys up at Starke, where he met Bobby Deo. After they'd got to know one another some Bobby said to him, "How come you homes call each other nigga?"

Louis said, "Mostly when you trippin' on some motherfucker, giving him a bad time, you say it. Understand? Or you say it, you not trippin' but vampin' on him some and you say it like you calling him 'my brother.' Either way is fine."

So what happened, Bobby Deo tried him that time in the yard at Starke. Looked Louis in the face with kind of a smile and said, "Yeah, nigga. Like that?" To see how Louis would take it, the man standing there waiting.

Louis said to him, "Yeah, like that. Only it ain't fine for somebody to say it ain't a brother. Understand? Unless you being P.R. has nigga in you?" Louis looking Bobby Deo in the face the same way Bobby was looking at him, eye to eye.

Bobby said, "You asking me, uh? You not accusing me of having mixed blood or what some call tainted? No, I'm not one of you."

Louis saying then, "So I know you and you know me, who we are. You know you fuck with me you got the whole population of homes on your untainted ass." It was a question of respect was all.

The only time Bobby said more than a few words it was about his working as a repo man. Sitting here waiting for Harry's car to show up reminded him.

Bobby saying yeah, he did that work for loan companies, repossess cars when the owners got behind in their payments. Now, he said, repo men were called recovery agents and drove a van they called an illusion unit. All it looked like was an old beat-up van, no company name on it, but had a winch with a motor in the back end. Go in a ghetto neighborhood to pick up a car with a wrecker? Man, everybody knew why you were there, they stand around the car you want and make it difficult. With the illusion unit you took your time. Wait for a chance to park in front of the car. When nobody was around, open the back, winch the front end of the car up, hook on the support bar and drive away. He said, "We could do Harry's car that way."

"We get the key off him and drive it," Louis said. "What we need to go to all that trouble for, borrow somebody's il*lu*sion van?"

"I'm saying it's a way to do it," Bobby said, sounding like a hard-on, like a man who thought he was always right.

While they sat waiting, Chip was already in the house; his car, his mama's tan Mercedes, up by the trailer park next door, in some trees.

"You have the idea of using the fortune-teller," Bobby said, "you see Chip? He was angry he didn't think of it."

"I noticed that," Louis said.

"She know what we're doing?"

"She don't want to know. She delivers Harry for a price and that's it."

"How much?"

"Fifteen hundred."

"That's low," Bobby said, "to take a risk. You have the money to pay her?"

"When we sell Harry's car."

"You mean when I sell it," Bobby said. "If this guy I know, he gives me a thousand or two until he moves the car, I keep it for making the deal. Then when he pays me the rest, you and Chip get some of it."

Louis was thinking he could sell the car himself, ship it to Nassau—he'd done that plenty of times in his youth—but didn't say anything about Bobby's arrangement. Keeping the peace, for the time being.

He said, "So we don't pay Dawn right away. It ain't like she can take us to court."

What Bobby was thinking now, watching the fortune-teller's house, there could be a problem with her. He knew it without knowing the woman. Felt it looking at the house, the vegetation almost hiding it: an old melaleuca rotting inside itself, palmettos that had never been cut back growing wild across the front windows. A woman who lived alone in a house like that had problems. And a woman with problems, man, could make you have some of your own.

When the white Cadillac rolled past, crept up the street to stop in front of the house, Louis said, "Here we go," sitting up now, alert. "Your friend Mr. Arno. Man, it worked, huh? I wasn't sure it would."

Bobby watched Harry get out of the car and stand looking at the house, his hand resting on the mailbox mounted on a crooked post.

Louis said, "Man's older than I thought."

Bobby didn't say anything. He had no feeling about Harry, one way or the other.

Now a compact Toyota came past them, faded red, trailing a wisp of smoke from the tailpipe. The car braked and turned into the drive that looked like gravel and weeds. Bobby watched Harry Arno walk over to greet the woman getting out of the car, saying something to her, Bobby seeing the fortune-teller for the first time. He said, "She isn't bad," sounding a little surprised.

"She's something else," Louis said. "Can tell you things about yourself you never even knew."

The house reminded Harry of Florida forty years ago, a little stucco crackerbox with jalousie windows where a garage door used to be. He said to the girl, "Nice place you have," trying to sound like he meant it.

She didn't say anything. Took him past a sign next to the front door that said:

PSYCHIC READINGS

DREAM INTERPRETATIONS

PAST-LIFE REGRESSIONS

and into a room full of dark furniture from some
other time and a gray leatherette recliner that
seemed out of place. She touched the backrest saying, "I'd like you to sit here, if you would, please, and
try to relax. Close your eyes if you want."

He got in the chair and looked around at all the
clutter, knickknacks, dolls, little china and ceramic
figures and a few stuffed animals, an old teddy bear,
all of it here and there on bookshelves and side tables. On the walls, an Indian rug with a design that
looked something like the zodiac, and a framed print
of Jesus—that one where he's surrounded by little
kids.

Reverend Dawn Navarro said, "I was thinking on
the way here, I asked if you had any investments over
in Italy and you said no, just the villa you leased."

"That's right," Harry said, still looking around.
The recliner faced the doorway into the room with
the jalousie windows that used to be a garage. He saw
more clutter in there—old aluminum lawn chairs, a
plastic swan that looked like a planter. . . . Reverend Dawn wasn't much of a housekeeper.

Her voice said, "You got the villa through a real
estate agent. They showed you pictures of different
ones. . . ."

"Right again," Harry said.

He felt her hand touch his shoulder and rest there
and he looked up, but she was behind him.

"You didn't pay cash, though, for the villa."

Harry smiled. "No, not that time. I had to transfer
enough from a Swiss bank to one in Rapallo, estab-
lish myself there to make the deal, you know, and

have money for living expenses. I bought a car, too, a Mercedes." He said, "That could be the unfinished business. I have to do something about the car."

He heard her say, "Maybe," as her hand left his shoulder and he watched the light reflecting on the ceiling dim and heard the rattle of venetian blinds being closed, her voice saying, "But I don't think the car's the reason you're drawn to Rapallo. Where is it exactly?"

"On the coast, not too far from Genoa."

"I'm trying to picture it. I know Italy's shaped like a boot. . . ."

"That's right, so Rapallo'd be up there on the shin, just below where the boot spreads out to cover your knee."

"In the northern part," her voice said. "And you like to travel, don't you?"

"You bet. That's one of the advantages of Rapallo, it's centrally located. Drive down to Rome, couple of hours to Milan. Anywhere you want to go's fairly close."

"Visit other countries," Dawn Navarro's voice said. "Isn't Switzerland right there?"

"Not too far."

"You've been there."

"Yeah, a number of times; it's beautiful."

"Harry, use that lever to tilt back; the footrest comes up."

He eased back all the way.

"How's that?"

"Fine."

"You're comfortable?"

"I could go to sleep."

Her voice said, "Close your eyes, but not too tight, and breathe slowly. I'm gonna count backward, Harry, down to one and then start to regress you. Okay? Here we go. Ten. Imagine all of your muscles relaxing, going limp. . . . Nine. In your face . . . your shoulders . . . down through your body . . . into your legs . . . Eight. You feel yourself drifting into a deeper state of relaxation . . . Seven. But you're completely aware of everything that's happening. . . . Six. You're drifting deeper and deeper. . . ."

Bobby came around back to the kitchen door, Louis following with a roll of duct tape. Through the screen they could see Chip on the other side of the kitchen, by the door that opened into the living room, but couldn't see what was going on in there. Chip, standing with his back to them, blocked their view— until Bobby opened the screen and Chip turned, pressing a finger to his mouth. Bobby went in first, moved across the linoleum to the doorway and shouldered Chip over to make room. He didn't like it. He put on a look Bobby caught but ignored, Bobby watching the fortune-teller standing next to Harry in the recliner, the fortune-teller looking this way now, brushing her long hair from her face with the tips of her fingers, looking this way right at Bobby—checking him out—Bobby sure of it, the woman calm, still looking this way as she said, "Two. You're deeply relaxed, Harry, you feel safe, comfortable." Now she was looking at Harry again. "And one, you're ready to begin. First, though, I'm gonna take your hand in mine and stroke it, okay? You tell me what you feel."

Bobby watched her pinch the skin on the back of Harry's hand, hard, and was surprised Harry didn't jerk his hand away.

She said, "Harry?"

"What?"

"Did you feel anything unpleasant?"

"No."

"Do you want to look at your hand?"

"No."

"Are you willing to talk to me? Yes or no."

"Yes."

"And go back in time? Yes or no."

"Yes."

"We'll go back gradually, Harry, regress you to last year when you were in Italy for a short time. You said your money is over there in a Swiss bank? Yes or no."

"No."

Bobby could see the fortune-teller, frowning now at Harry, didn't expect him to say that. He watched her use two fingers to slide the man's eyelids back and stare at him before taking her hand away.

She said, "Harry, you told me you transferred money from a Swiss bank to a bank in Rapallo. Not all of it, but enough for expenses. Were you telling the truth, Harry? Yes or no."

"Yes."

"So you do have money in the bank over there."

"Yes."

"I don't mean in Italy, I mean Switzerland. Do you have money in Switzerland, Harry? Yes or no."

"No."

Bobby watched her expression, the fortune-teller frowning again, something not working here the way it was supposed to, the woman thinking hard now— look at her—wondering what to do next. Bobby turned to Chip staring straight ahead, said, "This is bullshit," and Chip, annoyed, put a finger to his mouth the way he did before. Bobby spoke in a whisper with some force to it, saying, "Harry's playing with her, man. You don't see that?"

Chip turned his head toward Bobby and said without looking right at him, "Will you shut the fuck up?"

Bobby stared at Chip's profile, the man looking straight ahead now, Bobby wanting to shove him against the door frame, hold him there and tell his bony face the show was over, man, forget it . . . But now the fortune-teller was speaking again.

This Dawn Navarro saying, "Did you tell me you had money in a Swiss bank? Yes or no."

"Yes," Harry said.

"You mean a bank *in* Switzerland?"

"No."

"Where is the bank, Harry?"

"In Freeport, Grand Bahama."

Freeport, where Louis was from, the Bahamian Arabian. Bobby thought of it right away. But now the fortune-teller was looking over here again, brushing her hair aside. Looking at you, Bobby thought. You see that? Sure of it as he watched her turn her attention again to the man in the recliner, lying there with his eyes closed.

Dawn Navarro saying, "How much do you have in the account, Harry?"

"I don't know the exact amount."

"Roughly, how much would you say you have?"

"Close to three million," Harry said.

Chip made a sound like he was letting his breath out. Bobby heard it, watching the fortune-teller, who was looking over here again, he believed smiling at him now, but he wasn't sure.

Chip was gone before Bobby could stop him—while he and Louis were getting Harry ready to travel, covering his eyes and mouth and tying his hands with that silver duct tape. Bobby took Louis into the kitchen to tell him Chip was in too big a hurry; they should wait for dark to take Harry from the house. Louis said this was the way they planned it; all the trees and shit around the house, there was no way anybody would see them. He held up the keys to Harry's car, saying, "You want to get rid of it, or you want me to?"

"You know how?"

"In my youth," Louis said, "I boosted cars, sent them over to Nassau, Freeport, Eleuthera. . . ."

"Freeport," Bobby said, "where the guy has his money. You use to live there."

"That's a fact," Louis said. "I been thinking on it. Do I know somebody knows somebody might work in that bank?"

"You didn't say nothing to Chip?"

"He knows I'm from there."

"Yeah, but you didn't say nothing, did you?"

"Not yet."

"You see a way to get the money?"

"I'm starting to have an idea, yeah."

"We should talk about it before you tell Chip anything."

"You want to cut him out?"

"I say I think we should talk," Bobby said. He took the car keys. "You watch Harry. I'm gonna check on the fortune-teller, see how she's doing."

Louis said, "You don't have time for that."

"For what?" Bobby said. "What do you think I'm gonna do to her?"

They had put Reverend Dawn in the bedroom, out of the way. Bobby opened the door and looked in and there she was sitting on the bed twisting a strand of hair between her fingers. Bobby stepped in and closed the door and she stopped fooling with her hair.

He said, "How you doing?" Giving her a chance to come on to him in some way that women let you know they were interested.

She stared at him, but not with a look he recognized.

"You have my money?"

Bobby almost told her to see Chip; it was on the tip of his tongue. He changed his mind and said, "I'm gonna bring it to you, next week." Giving her another chance to show some interest.

She kept staring at him and maybe it meant something, he wasn't sure. He said, "Are you scared?"

She said, "Should I be?"

Bobby stared and she stared back at him.

"I like your act."

"It's real."

"He was hypnotize, uh?"

"I checked his eyes."

"What does that tell you?"

"They were rolled back. You can't fake that."

"I thought maybe it was too easy, what you got him to say."

"Harry likes to talk about money. He pays cash for everything, even his car."

"You like that car?"

"It's all right."

"Better than your little car. You know how much we gonna get from Harry?"

She said, "Look, I don't want to know anything about what you're doing. I don't even want to talk to you."

"You *see* what we doing."

"I saw nothing. Harry was never here."

"I was thinking you should get more than fifteen hundred."

"I told Chip what I wanted; that's it. And that's all I'm doing for you."

Bobby said, "You sure?"

e i g h t

Sunday, Raylan phoned Joyce from the restaurant in Delray Beach.

"The waiter remembers him. He said Harry had a few drinks, paid for the first one and then ran a tab. The reason the guy remembers him, Harry left his money on the table when he went in to use the phone."

Joyce said, "That's when he called and left the

message. Said he'd call me later, but that was the last I heard."

"The waiter said he kept an eye on Harry's money."

"I'll bet he did."

"No, he said he told Harry, when he was leaving, he ought to be more careful with it."

"The guy he was meeting never showed up?"

"Doesn't look like it. No, but there's a lady hangs around here does tarot card readings?"

Joyce said right away, "*Yes,* he mentioned that," and sounded excited about it. "Is she there?"

"Not on Sunday. The waiter said she sat down with Harry and I guess they just talked. She didn't lay out the cards or anything."

"But she was with him."

"I guess. I don't know how long."

"Can you find out?"

"Listen, Joyce? The waiter said Harry was drinking doubles, throwing them down. I checked with Delray PD and Boca Raton, see if he might've been picked up."

"He would've called," Joyce said, "I'm his one phone call, his bail, his ride home . . ."

"Unless he didn't want you to know he'd messed up again. He could've called somebody else, one of the guys used to work for him."

"It was two days ago," Joyce said. "Where is he? Raylan, he calls me every *day* for something."

Tell me about it, Raylan thought, using his day off to look for a guy he wished would disappear from his life. Joyce, at the same time, saying how much she appreciated his help, sounding so polite, saying if anyone could find Harry . . . He might've said, What if I don't want to find him? But didn't and there was a silence. He was getting used to silences talking to her.

Her voice came on again, Joyce saying, "What if Harry went to see the tarot card lady and she told him . . . I don't know, that he was about to take a trip, go to some exotic place. That would appeal to Harry. I think he might do whatever she said."

"You mean made plans to see her later."

"It's possible."

"Like she told him to go back to Italy, where he wouldn't be bothering anybody."

Joyce said, "I think it's worth following up," sounding so serious, sounding like that all the time lately. "Can you ask around, find out where she lives? Or get her number and I'll call her."

"I have her card," Raylan said. "There's a whole stack of them by the cash register."

Joyce said, "You're way ahead of me, aren't you?"

"I'll go see her, find out if Harry had his fortune told. Maybe, as long as I'm there, have her tell mine, see what's in my future."

"You believe in that?"

"I don't know—maybe some of it."

She said, "Well, you're psychic yourself. You know things no one else does."

It took him a moment to realize what she meant. Still at him. He said, "You want to go around on that again? I knew Tommy Bucks had a gun. I've thought about it since the other night and there's no way I see it any different. I called him out and he knew it. If he didn't pack his suitcase and leave he'd be packing a gun. That was his choice."

"You called him out," Joyce said. "What did you think, you were in a movie?"

It caught him by surprise, because he did see it that way sometimes. The idea of giving the guy twenty-four hours . . .

Joyce said, "What if he told you, sitting at that table, he didn't have a gun?"

She wouldn't let it go.

"Would you have shot him?"

"I don't know if I would've or not. How's that?"

The hell with it, let her think what she wanted.

She said, "All right," in a different tone of voice, quieter. "I won't mention it again."

Was he supposed to be grateful?

Raylan said, "Honey, I shot the son of a bitch and killed him and I'd do it again, the same way. If you have trouble with that, then you don't know me and there's nothing I can do to help you."

She said, after a moment, "I'm sorry," her voice even quieter than before.

Raylan waited, looking out at the Sunday brunch crowd on the terrace, not feeling he had any more to say, and there was a silence.

When her voice came on again:

She said, "Raylan?"

"What?"

"If we knew who owed Harry money, would that help?"

Like that, back to poor Harry.

"It might."

"When I was driving him around, he had names in a ledger he'd check off, with the amounts. Then when he called me from where you are and left the message? He said the guy would have sixteen five for him. The one who didn't show up."

"He mention his name?"

"No, only that he's Puerto Rican."

"I'll call you after I see the tarot card lady."

"Call me at Harry's. I'll go right now and look for the ledger." She said then, "Raylan, I'm sorry. I really am."

He said, "I am, too," without knowing exactly what either of them was sorry about. As soon as he'd hung up, though, he felt a sense of relief.

nine

Harry would say, "Is somebody there?"
He'd wait, feeling someone in the room with him.
"Will you please tell me what you want?"
Nothing. No answer.
So he'd wait. Sitting on a metal cot, a blanket and a
thin mattress, no pillow. His ankles chained and pad-
locked. His hands free. At the time they brought him
here he said, "You're gonna leave the blindfold on?"

No answer. They never said a word to him or to each other, not even in a whisper.

The last voice he heard was the little girl's, Dawn Navarro, asking him how much he had in the Freeport bank. Like being half asleep and hearing it, lying in that chair with his eyes closed, and telling her he wasn't exactly sure, close to three mil. . . . Was that what he said? What he actually had in there was just under two million. Now he wasn't sure if he'd been awake or actually hypnotized. He remembered lying there waiting . . . then all of a sudden realizing a blindfold was being taped over his eyes and he thought it was the little girl doing it, so he wouldn't be distracted. But then there were hands all over him holding him down and tape being pressed over his mouth. They pulled him out of the recliner, got him facedown on the floor, rough hands on him, and taped his wrists together behind his back. The tape covering his mouth touched his nose and he could smell it trying to breathe and turned his head from side to side to let them know, Christ, he couldn't *breathe*. He did hear the little girl, Dawn, heard her say, "What are you *doing*?" yelling it out. *That* was the last thing he heard—not her asking about the bank account—but didn't remember her saying it until he was here in this room and began going over in his mind step-by-step what happened. How he tried to calm down and breathe through his nose and that part wasn't too bad; he could breathe okay if he didn't get excited and start to panic thinking he was suffocating. It was an awful feeling. They sat him in a chair and never said a word to him or to each other or to Dawn, if she was still there. Maybe they'd done the same thing to her and she was sitting right next to him taped up. He heard them moving around on the wood floor that creaked under them and was bare except for an old braided throw rug—remembering the rug from before, when he was looking around at all the clutter. Then for a while there wasn't a sound in the little girl's house, not until he felt himself pulled out of the chair.

Two of them, each taking an arm, brought him out-side, shoved him into the trunk of a car and closed the lid on him. Not his car, his still had that new-car smell. He was afraid again of suffocating, his face against the rough texture of the carpeting. So con-scious of trying to breathe he wasn't sure how long he was in the trunk or what direction they went after making a few turns, maybe to confuse him. Harry believed he was in there over an hour before they stopped and pulled him out—Harry ready to be marched into a woods or a swamp out in the Glades and one of them would say okay, that's far enough. No, they brought him into a house. Harry couldn't believe it. He sensed it was a house, a residence, as soon as they brought him up a carpeted stairway that curved up to a second floor and along a hallway to what he assumed was a bedroom. But then wasn't so sure when they sat him down on a cot with a thin mattress. He did feel deep-pile carpeting on the floor and decided, yes, he was in someone's house and this was a bedroom.

When they pulled the tape from his mouth Harry was so glad to suck in air he didn't mind the pain; it stung like hell. As soon as they cut his hands free he touched his face, his mouth. . . . Then tensed, expecting them to rip the tape from his eyes, but they didn't; they got busy chaining his ankles and he asked about the blindfold, if they were going to leave it on.

No answer.

"You want to tell me what this is about?" He waited and said, "I guess not."

He could feel them around him, two guys, maybe three. Harry was pretty sure who they represented, so he tried again. "Look, you know I wasn't skimming on you guys. The individual now running the crew, Nicky, he told me himself I had nothing to worry about." Harry paused. "Wait. Am I talking to Nicky Testa?"

No answer.

"What're you treating me like this for? What do you want, for Christ sake?"

No answer.

Only the sounds they made fooling with the chains.

He had to get himself calmed down. Thought about it a minute and said, "I didn't quit on you guys. I was put out of business by the U.S. attorney. I get busted again, I do five years straight up and not at one of those country-club joints either. I'm retired, okay? You mind?" Harry becoming agitated.

No answer.

"You people can't talk? What's the problem, I might recognize somebody's voice?"

Still no answer.

"Okay, I'll keep quiet. You guys are running some kind of game on me. Fine, I'll wait. Sooner or later you're gonna have to tell me what this is about." He paused. An obvious reason for being here hit him and he said, "Wait a minute. Is this a kidnapping? Jesus Christ, you better talk to me if it is. You know what I'm saying? I'm a friend of Nicky Testa's. If you guys are smart . . . Or you're part of his crew and he finds out, Jesus, what you're doing . . . ?"

He waited.

"I said I'm gonna keep quiet," Harry said, and did, kept his mouth shut after that, sitting there chained and blindfolded. Minutes passed. He thought he heard them moving around and did hear a door close. Harry listened, pretty sure he was alone before reaching down to find a light chain wrapped around each ankle and padlocked, about twelve inches of chain between his legs and the rest of it extending along the floor. Harry got down on his hands and knees and followed the chain, about eight feet of it, to a metal ring bolted to the floor, through the deep-pile carpeting. He stood up and began to shuffle around, touched the wall by the cot, then shuffled off across the room and banged his shin on another metal cot. He felt along the wall and got as far as an open doorway before the chain stopped him.

He wondered if it was the way he came in. If it was . . . He began to imagine them on the other side of the doorway watching him, some guys he might even know, Harry becoming more sure of it. He said, "You're right there, aren't you, you fucks." He said, "Will you say something, for Christ sake?"

* * *

"Talking to somebody he thinks is in the bathroom," Louis said that first day, watching Harry on the TV screen in the study. "Uh-oh, he's trying to lift up his blindfold."

"He'll learn quick," Chip said.

They watched, on the screen, the door open and now Bobby was in the room, Harry turning toward the sound, getting all the way around as Bobby clobbered him with a right hand—Chip saying, "Pow, right in the kisser"—and Harry stumbled and went down.

"So now he knows," Louis said, "no peeking."

They watched the monitors all that weekend, cutting from the patio to the front entrance to the driveway—watching the driveway more than the other areas now—to the bedroom upstairs, Harry sitting on the cot with his head raised, listening, like a blind man looking around.

Whenever Louis or Bobby got ready to go up to the room Chip would say, "Be sure you don't speak, okay?"

They both went upstairs one time and Bobby said, "He tells me that again, I'm gonna get the tape and shut his mouth with it."

Louis said, "I'll hold him."

They put a plastic bucket in there next to the cot by Harry's feet and he got the idea he was to use it to piss in. So they wouldn't have to run in there every time he had to go.

Bobby said, "Why don't we give him more chain, he can go in the bathroom?"

"That would make too much sense," Louis said. "Then he could go in there and do number two by himself and we wouldn't have to unchain him every time. Last night I took him in there he asked for something to read."

Other things didn't make sense to Bobby. Why take the beds out, put in those little cots? Louis said it was how the Shia done it over in Beirut, the Shia having written the book on how to mind hostages. Louis said Chip wanted to use straw mattresses like he read about in one of the hostage books, but nobody made such a thing.

Food, they'd bring in on a tray and hand it to him: all different kinds of TV dinners Louis chose. The first time they fed him, that Friday night, they stayed to watch Harry dig in blindfolded. He took a bite of the Mexican Medley and said, "What is this shit?" but kept eating, made a mess cleaning his tray. Finishing up Harry wanted to know what was for dessert. When he didn't get an answer or any dessert he said, "How about some Jell-O? If you guys don't know how to make it, go to Wolfie's on Collins Avenue and pick me up some. Strawberry, with the fruit in it. Get some rice pudding, too."

The routine Louis decided on was to feed Harry TV dinners twice a day and snacks in between like cookies, potato chips, candy bars. Louis said the Shia fixed their hostages rice and shit, but no doubt would have given them TV dinners if they had any.

Saturday morning Bobby drove Harry's Cadillac to a bump shop in South Miami to unload it, Louis following in Bobby's car to pick him up. On the way back he watched Bobby counting a stack of bills, his lips moving, but never saying how much he got and Louis didn't ask. Fuck him. He thought since they were alone Bobby would want to talk about Freeport, ask Louis what his idea was to get to Harry's money; but he didn't, busy with his own money, and Louis didn't bring it up.

Coming to Delray Beach, Louis turned off the freeway and headed east toward the ocean. Bobby, looking around, asked where was he going and Louis said to Tom Junior's Rib Heaven, get some takeout, best ribs in South Florida. He said they had other good stuff, too, like conch fritters, collards—man, blackeye peas. Bobby said he didn't eat that shit and Louis held on to the steering wheel.

When he turned off Old Dixie and pulled into a grocery store on Linton, Bobby said, "What you stopping here for?"

Louis said, "Supplies," and got out of the car thinking the P.R. motherfucking bill collector would sit there and wait, but Bobby followed him in the store.

A man and woman that reminded Louis of the Shia, Arab-looking, were behind the counter in front talking to each other in a foreign language, arguing, it sounded like, ugly people. When they looked up Louis said, "How you doing?" He took a cart and started down the nearest aisle, wondering if the woman had dyed her hair orange or was wearing a wig. You saw people like them all over running little groceries and party stores, Arab or something like it.

Louis began picking out snacks from the shelves. He got Oreo chocolate sandwich cookies. He got potato chips, tortilla chips, Cheez-Its, pretzels, a box of peanut brittle, some candy bars, moved on to the cereals, picked out—let's see—Cocoa Puffs, Cap'n Crunch . . . and Froot Loops. Louis went on to the dairy case for milk, picked up six-packs of beer and Mountain Dew—he'd heard had more caffeine in it than any other kind of soda—and a pair of rubber gloves for cleaning the blindfolded man's bathroom. Louis put the groceries on the counter and said to Bobby, looking at the magazine rack, "Since you got all the money, you want to pay for this?" Turning, walking away, Louis said, "I forgot something." He went down an aisle where he thought Jell-O should be and over to another aisle before he found it, all kinds of flavors in color. He took three boxes of strawberry, what Harry said he liked, two strawberry-banana, and an orange. He didn't see any rice pudding, but there were jars of instant tapioca and he took one of them.

Louis stepped over to the aisle that went directly to the counter, seeing Bobby standing there now and, past him to either side, the Arab-looking grocer and his wife with orange hair. They were watching Bobby doing something.

Throwing a package aside after taking something out of it, it looked like.

Raising his hand in the air then as he pulled a yellow rubber glove down over the hand.

Louis saying, Oh shit, to himself.

He kept on to the counter, seeing Bobby pulling the other glove on and then reaching for the grocer as the man ducked down behind the counter to come up holding a gun that Bobby right away took by the barrel and twisted and the man screamed something in his language, letting go of the grip. Bobby kept hold of the gun by the barrel, a big chrome revolver he hit the grocer over the head with, swiping the man sidearm, and the man screamed again holding his head, blood coming through his fingers as Louis reached the counter and saw the man sink to his knees. The woman was screaming in her language—*had* been screaming—and now Bobby reached over to grab her by the hair, got a good hold of it—Louis thinking the orange hair would come off in Bobby's hand, but it didn't. It was her hair. Bobby now dragged her up against the counter. The woman tried to push away and Bobby let go of her hair, seeing her hands on the counter and looking at them closely.

He said, "That's a pretty ring." A heavy gold band with some kind of orange-looking stone set in it. He said, "Let's see you take it off."

Looking right at him big-eyed, hair mussed, the woman said, "I don't speak no English."

Which sounded to Louis pretty good if she didn't. He said to Bobby, "You gonna rob the place then fucking rob it, man, and let's go." He took a paper sack from the counter and started putting his groceries in it.

Bobby wasn't paying any attention to him. He said to the woman, "You won't take it off?"

She said it again, "I don't speak no English."

Louis watched Bobby take hold of her hand and pull on the ring to slip it off, but it wouldn't budge.

Louis watched Bobby reach behind him now and take out his pruners with the red handles, holding the woman's ring finger with the other hand and the woman said, "No, please, please don't, please."

Bobby said, "You learn to speak English in a hurry. That's pretty good."

The woman tried to pull her hand away, crying now, begging Bobby, "Please, please," but he had a good hold on her finger, getting it in there between the curved blades of the pruners, telling her, "I want your money, too. All you got."

Louis picked up the sack of groceries in his arm and turned, expecting to hear the woman scream as he pulled out his shirttail and hurried to wipe off the handle of the grocery cart he'd used. Louis left the store, not looking over at the counter, got in the car, like an oven with the windows closed, turned on the engine, the radio and the air-conditioning up high. After a minute or so he watched Bobby come out of the store counting bills, going through the money quick before folding it over and sticking it in his pants pocket.

When he was in the car he said, "You think I cut her finger off?"

"Never thought you wouldn't," Louis said.

That evening Harry said, "How about some booze? I got a condition that requires two fifths of vodka a day or I become dehydrated and liable to die. I know you don't want that to happen. If you picked me up to whack me out, you'd have done it by now. So you must have another reason, huh? . . .

What do you say? Bottle of Absolut. And a pack of Marlboros."

Nothing.

Fucking creeps.

Harry sat in the darkness of his blindfold—he believed duct tape they'd wound around his head over a thin towel that covered his hair and served as padding over his eyes. Showing some consideration. But now when he told them he needed to bathe and change his clothes:

Silence.

No answer.

Nothing.

Sunday morning he asked how long he'd been here and how long they planned to keep him.

"And why?" Harry said. "You know what it's like sitting here like this, chained, for Christ sake?"

No answer.

" 'No man who has ever passed a month in the death cells believes in cages for beasts.' You know who wrote that, you dumb fucks? Ezra Pound, that's who. Ez was a very dear friend of mine."

Harry waited, he didn't know how long. He didn't hear anything, not a sound, but said it anyway:

"Is anybody there?"

Louis found Chip in the kitchen making himself a Bloody Mary and asked him, "Who's Ezra Pound?"

Chip said, "Ezra Pound," stirring his drink and then pausing. "He was a heavyweight. Beat Joe Louis for the crown and lost it to Marciano. Or was it Jersey Joe Walcott?"

ten

This Reverend Dawn Navarro was a cute girl, younger than Raylan had expected, say around thirty, her dark hair parted in the middle and hanging past her shoulders. She said, "Don't tell me why you're here, all right? The reason might be different than you think and it could confuse my reading."

She sat him on an old mohair sofa, brought over a card table and a straight-back chair for herself, saying she would use psychometry, read him through touch, and once she was seated, placed slender fingers on his coal-miner hands resting flat on the table. Closing her eyes she said, "Do you have a feeling someone wants to contact you?"

"Not that I know of," Raylan said, sitting forward on the edge of the sprung sofa; he had to look up at her in the straight chair.

"I mean from the other side, the spirit world," Reverend Dawn said. "As you came across the yard I saw a presence with you dressed in black, wearing a long cape with folds in it." Her fingers stroked the veins on the back of his hands.

Raylan said, "A presence?"

"Someone who's left this earth plane. I don't mean this particular entity represents death and is after you. No, you're still full of energy, I can tell. I see you working outdoors rather than in an office."

Without telling her anything Raylan said he was outside quite a bit.

Reverend Dawn told him the presence she saw out in the yard with him was a spirit guide, like a protector, to make sure he got here okay. She said they sometimes wore capes like that—the idea, to wrap it around you if need be. She said, "Wait now, whoa, I'm starting to feel another presence," and then smiled, still with her eyes closed. "It's the gray wolf; he came in the house with you."

Raylan looked over his shoulder, to one side and then the other, not expecting to see a wolf but checked anyway.

"He was in the street as you got out of your car," Reverend Dawn said, "and I thought he was just some stray I hadn't seen before. Uh-unh, it's a beautiful gray wolf, another kind of spirit guide. You know the senses of a wolf are very keen. He's telling me, he's letting me know it isn't someone anxious to contact *you,* it's the other way around. You need to talk to somebody, get a certain matter settled."

Raylan said, "A person in the spirit world?"

"No, it's someone close by, though I don't see him yet."

Reverend Dawn Navarro, *Certified Medium & Spiritualist* on her business card, would look up with her eyes closed and shake her head to one side, a quick little move to get her hair out of her face. The way her hair was parted in the middle and hung long and straight made Raylan think of how girls looked back in the days of hippies and flower children. Otherwise she seemed to have no particular style, wearing jeans and a loose white T-shirt. He believed her eyes were green and would check it out when she opened them again. He had already decided she was good-looking enough to be in a pageant or have a job on TV pointing to game-show prizes. The only thing that bothered him about her, looking at her hands resting on his, she bit her fingernails as far down as he had ever seen fingernails bitten.

"Did you know," Reverend Dawn said, "you have psychic powers of your own?"

He thought of Joyce accusing him of it.

"All that energy in you."

"Is that right?"

"You like to help people," she said. "I see you taking someone by the arm."

Raylan didn't comment. Then she didn't speak either, her head raised as though listening for something. The house was quiet, this little stucco place full of old furniture and knickknacks sitting on shelves.

"The message I'm getting," Reverend Dawn said, "there's an individual you're having a disagreement with and you want to get it settled. Now what I'm getting"—she paused—"yes, it could be someone who's gone over to the other side."

Raylan gave it some thought and said, "Did I harm this person in any way?"

She shook her head, eyes still closed. "I'm not getting any kind of vibes like that. I think it's something that was left undone, something that's been bothering you and you want it cleared up. That's the message I'm getting. There was some kind of disagreement between you and this person?"

"Well, there's one I can think of."

Raylan paused and Reverend Dawn said right away, "That's who it is, the first one who comes to mind."

Raylan paused again. "I was responsible, you might say, for his death."

This time Reverend Dawn said, "Oh," and opened her eyes. They were green. "Your fault—you're not talking about an accident, like a car wreck, something you caused."

"Nothing like that," Raylan said. "But see, the thing between us *was* settled. There isn't anything left has to be done."

She kept staring at him now as she said, "You're positive of that?" Not sounding as psychic as she did before, telling him about earth planes and spirit guides. She said, "What about a relative?"

"My dad's over there," Raylan said. "Died of black lung before his time. I'd just as soon leave him rest in peace."

"I mean a relative of the one you had something to do with his passing over," Reverend Dawn said. "A person that might be holding a grudge against you."

Raylan shook his head. "I doubt it."

Reverend Dawn seemed to study him, thinking, making up her mind. Finally then she closed her eyes again and raised her face as though to stare off past him, a really nice-looking girl, while her figure remained a mystery beneath that loose T-shirt.

"The gray wolf is trying to tell me something." She paused and said, "You're a teacher, aren't you?"

Raylan said, "You're kidding," and thought too late, Wait a minute. Before being assigned to Miami he was a firearms instructor at Glynco, a training center for federal agents. He let it go as not important, or not the kind of teacher she meant. With her eyes closed he could stare, look at her closely. She seemed to him too young and attractive to be stuck in this place telling fortunes.

She said, "You *are* in a profession. I want to say *lawyer,* even though I know that isn't it."

Raylan kept quiet.

She said, "Coming across the yard you had your hat off, but as you reached the door you put it on."

"I guess I did, didn't I?"

"You were being . . . I want to say *official,* and

your hat's like a badge of office. You like to set it forward a little, close over your eyes."

"I've had that hat eight years," Raylan said. "I never thought I wore it any special way, I just put it on my head."

Reverend Dawn surprised him this time saying, "You're from either West Virginia . . . No, you're from Kentucky. You worked in coal mines at one time, but haven't done that for a while now, it's way in your past. You still think of yourself, though—not all the time but once in a while—as a coal miner. Don't you?"

"It's what all the men on both sides of my family did," Raylan said. Today he was wearing a blue-and-white sport shirt with sailboats on it and jeans with his hat and cowboy boots, not wanting to give her any idea of what he did for a living.

Her hands moved on his, fingertips brushing his knuckles, it seemed needing only a light touch to read him. She said, "You're looking for someone, a man."

When she paused Raylan said, "If you mean on this earth plane, yes, I am."

"The one you're having this disagreement with."

That wasn't exactly true. He said, "We—"

And she cut him off. "It's not an argument exactly, it's just, there's something about him that bothers you."

"I guess you could say that."

"Well, that bothers me, too, a lot. I won't allow myself to be an instrument in this matter if you intend to do him harm, or anyone else."

"I'd never do him harm."

"But he's on your mind all the time?"

"Not him, no. Someone else is."

She opened her eyes, stared at him and said, "Now you're talking about a woman, aren't you?"

Raylan nodded and she closed her eyes again to get back into it, her expression, he noticed, more at peace.

Reverend Dawn said, "Okay, there's a woman . . ." and said, "Wait a minute, I see another woman. You have a situation here I didn't sense right away, this man being on your mind. Okay, now there're two women. You're married . . ."

"I was."

"I see children, a couple of little boys."

"How are they?"

"They're fine. Living with their mother . . ."

"Ricky and Randy. I wanted to call them Hank and George, after Hank Williams and Ole Possum, George Jones? But Winona got her way, as usual. Yeah, they're with her up in Brunswick, Georgia."

"She divorced you," Reverend Dawn said, "to marry a man she met." She paused. "But he isn't the one you're looking for."

"There was a time I almost went after him."

"Because of your boys, not so much over his taking Winona from you."

Raylan said, "That's right," even though he believed it was Winona's idea to start something with the real estate man who'd sold their house, Gary Jones, and not a matter of her being stolen away.

Reverend Dawn was saying, "You met this other woman."

"That's right, in Miami Beach."

"You and she are close," Reverend Dawn said. "I'll go so far as to say intimate."

Raylan wasn't sure that was still true.

"You shared a frightening experience. . . ."

She waited, but Raylan didn't help her.

"That part isn't too clear, but there's someone else, a man. He stands in the way of you and this woman planning a life together."

Raylan said, "That's pretty good."

"He's an older man."

Raylan waited.

"But not her father."

"You don't see him, huh?"

"Not too clearly."

"I'm surprised," Raylan said. "He was here just the other day, Friday afternoon."

He waited for Reverend Dawn to open her eyes and look at him. When she did she stared without speaking and he was aware of how quiet it was in the house.

She said finally, "What's his name?"

"Harry Arno."

Raylan kept watching her thinking she'd close her eyes as she tried to recall Harry, but Reverend Dawn continued to stare at him, hard, and Raylan had to concentrate to stare back at her, not look away. He said, "Harry's sixty-eight—no, sixty-nine—medium height, grayish hair, lives in Miami Beach. I imagine he told you all about himself. Harry loves to talk."

Reverend Dawn kept staring at him even as she shook her head back and forth, twice.

Raylan frowned and then tried to smile. Was she kidding? He said, "You don't remember him? Harry Arno?" He watched her shake her head again and said, "I wonder if Harry used another name for some reason. How about, did anyone who came here Friday ask you about going back to Italy? Whether he should or not?"

She said, "Oh . . ." this time nodding. "Parts his hair on the right side, which is kind of unusual, and touches it up to cover the gray. Drives a white Cadillac."

"That's Harry." Now Raylan was nodding. "So you did talk to him."

"For a few minutes," Reverend Dawn said, "at a restaurant where I do readings." Nodding again. "He did mention Italy. Has a house there? . . . But I didn't give him a reading, here or at the restaurant. I offered to and he said some other time. He seemed —now that I think about it—in a hurry."

There was a silence and Raylan felt her moving the tips of her fingers over his hands. Almost, he thought, like she was tickling him.

"I could let you know if I see him again," Reverend Dawn said. "You have a business card?"

"I told her," Raylan said to Joyce on the restaurant phone, back there again, "I didn't have one. I just gave her my name."

Joyce said, "But if she does hear from him . . ."

"She wanted the card to find out who I am, what I do."

"Why didn't you tell her?"

" 'Cause I'm pretty sure Harry went to see her and I can't figure out why she'd lie about it."

"How do you know he was there?"

"It's a feeling I have."

She said, "That's *all,* a hunch?"

"Joyce, I ask people questions and listen to how they answer. It wasn't she acted nervous or evasive. What it was, she sounded different after I mentioned Harry. Before that it was all psychic stuff, like she saw a gray wolf in the room with us. But she didn't know why I was there till I asked about Harry."

"There was a wolf?"

"A spirit guide. Reverend Dawn said when I arrived a guy in a black cape walked up to the door with me. Another spirit."

"Reverend *Dawn*?"

"Dawn Navarro. I didn't ask why she's 'reverend.' "

"But you think she's a fake."

"I had the feeling she put on some of it, talking about the spirit world and this earth plane we're on. She did say I was looking for someone, but to clear up a misunderstanding. And she said I was originally from Kentucky. But might've gotten that from something I said."

"Maybe," Joyce said, "Harry asked her not to tell anyone he was there."

"Why would he think anybody'd care? Either he

didn't go see her and took off from here on his own—"

"Why would he?"

"So you'll worry about him. Or he did see Reverend Dawn and she lied to me."

"You think she knows where he is?"

"She might've looked at a tarot card and saw him taking a trip. He liked the idea and made her promise not to tell anybody. Or . . ."

"What?"

"She knows where he is and has some other reason for not telling. What it could be," Raylan said, "I have no idea. How about Harry's ledger—you find it?"

"I have it right here," Joyce said. "All the ones he's checked off are the ones he saw when I was driving him around."

"Any up this way, around Delray Beach?"

"It lists just names and phone numbers, and the amount owed. Some of the ones not checked off have 407 area codes."

"That's up here, Palm Beach County."

"I know," Joyce said. "And the guy who owes Harry the sixteen five? Harry has it written sixteen point five K. His name is Chip Ganz, with Cal in parens, and a phone number with a 407 area code. I could call him, find out if the money was collected."

Raylan said, "Well . . ." thinking about it. "Why don't you give me the number. I'll find out where Ganz lives and go see him, unless you hear from Harry. It won't be for a couple of days, though, we're pretty busy."

"What if I don't hear from him?"

"Let me know. I'll have another talk with Reverend Dawn."

"What does she look like?"

"The way girls used to look twenty years ago. Long, dark hair parted in the middle. Thin . . ."

"How old?"

"Maybe thirty."

"She's *young.*"

"Nice-looking, but bites her fingernails."

"You want to see her again, don't you?"

"I may have to," Raylan said.

e l e v e n

Dawn phoned Chip's pager as soon as Raylan was out of the house, no wolf following him now, Raylan putting on what seemed his official hat as he walked from tree shade into sunlight, cocking the brim low on his eyes, and Dawn thought, He knows you're watching. Okay, Mr. Raylan Givens, I'm gonna keep watching. Pretty sure he'd be back in the next couple of days.

Waiting for Chip to answer his pager she looked for a fingernail to bite on.

Sundays he was never home. He'd stroll one of the beaches or a mall or visit a Huggers Gathering in the park and try not to get hugged while he mingled and looked for runaways. Chip's favorite kind were young girls who'd left home pissed off at their dads and feeling betrayed by their moms; they came to Gatherings homesick, would get caught up in the flashing peace signs and Huggers saying "Love you" with dopey grins and pretty soon the little girls would be dosing on acid.

The time Chip held a Gathering at his home Dawn stopped by to see what it was all about. There were Huggers all over the patio and what used to be a lawn that extended to the beach; Chip's New Age pals and their girlfriends, about forty people, most of them hairy, pierced, tie-dyed and tattooed earth people and born-again bikers. They came in rusting-out vans and pickups with their beer and dope and got high while cops cruised Ocean Boulevard past the PRIVATE DRIVE, KEEP OUT sign, and while Chip moved among them grinning, showing his movie-star teeth he'd had capped in another time, before his life went in the toilet.

Dawn had the tip of her left thumb between her teeth, gnawing to get a purchase on the nail and thinking about Raylan again, a cowboy in a shirt with sailboats on it driving off in a dark green Jaguar she knew wasn't his.

The phone rang.

Chip said, "This is important, right?" With his

deadpan delivery he thought was cool. "Taking me away from business?"

"Where are you?"

"Dreher Park, West Palm; I'm picnicking."

"Let's see," Dawn said, closing her eyes, "the girl you're with has stringy blond hair, cutoff jeans, she's from Ohio and hasn't had a bath in a week."

"Indiana," Chip said, "she's a little Hoosier. Nasty kid, hates her parents. I dropped acid in her eye and she sweetened up some."

"About sixteen?"

"Going on thirty, but dumb."

"Her folks," Dawn said, "don't even miss her."

"What're you, a mind reader? I told her dad up in Kokomo, Indiana, I'd let him know where to find his little girl for five big ones. He goes, 'She isn't worth near that much,' and hangs up on me. What we're doing, you understand, we're negotiating. I call him back. 'Okay, twenty-five hundred and I'll see no harm comes to your little girl. All you have to do is wire the cash.' I give him the name I use and he hangs up on me, again. I'm thinking, What kind of a father *is* this guy? When I call back I'll talk to the mom. Jesus, parents these days . . ."

"Try the mom for fifteen hundred," Dawn said, "so I can get paid. Your new guy, Bobby? He said he'd bring it next week, and I'm sure he'll come, but it won't be to pay me."

Chip said, "You call to chat or what?"

"A guy came by for a reading," Dawn said. "It turns out he's some kind of federal agent and guess who he's looking for?"

Chip said, "What do you mean *some* kind of federal agent? He show you his I.D.?"

"He didn't have to, except he doesn't look anything like, one. He's forty-three. When he was younger he was a coal miner."

"You check his fingernails?"

"He walked in, I thought he was a farmer, or maybe a rancher. He looks like a cowboy, that rawboned, outdoor type. Wears cowboy boots and a hat with a curled brim."

"The Marlboro man," Chip said.

"Yeah, except he's real."

"And he's looking for me?"

"Actually your name didn't come up. He's looking for Harry Arno."

There was a silence before Chip's voice came back on the line. "What reason did he give?"

"Are you kidding? The man was here Friday and hasn't been seen since."

"But why is this guy looking for him?"

"I just told you."

"I mean, you say he's a federal agent, is he investigating Harry's disappearance or he's a friend or what?"

Dawn wasn't sure, so she said, "What difference does it make? He thinks Harry was here."

"How could he?"

"I guess someone remembered seeing us together, at the restaurant."

"What'd you tell him?"

"That he wasn't here."

"He buy it?"

"He's thinking about it," Dawn said. "I hope I get my money before he comes back."

"What's that supposed to mean?"

"If I'm arrested for some dumb stunt you're pulling, I want to be able to make bail."

"There's no way this guy can possibly get onto us, so be cool," Chip said. "You thought he was a *farmer*?"

"I told you, he's got that outdoor good-guy look. Even has crow's-feet when he squints."

"But he was wearing, what, a snappy blue suit and wing tips with the hat? That's how you made him, huh? I mean why do you say he's a fed, not some local cop?"

" 'Cause that's what he is," Dawn said. "I'll give you something else to think about. Not very long ago he shot and killed a man and did it deliberately, at close range. What I'm saying is he intended to kill the guy and he did."

Again the silence before Chip said, "Come on, he told you that?"

"I felt it in his hand," Dawn said. "The one that held the gun."

twelve

Late Tuesday afternoon Louis was relaxing in the study, feet on the cocktail table chest, watching Oprah on the big screen giving the audience some cool intro shit about the guests she had coming on next. The surveillance picture in the corner of the screen showed the front drive, or where it was supposed to be in all that vegetation. Oprah wasn't doing much of anything at the moment, so Louis pushed a button on the remote to put the back of the house on the screen, the patio, and Bobby Deo out there with his fine Latino shirt off pruning shrubs. Louis had to watch him because it made no sense, the man working when he didn't have to. Louis pressed a button and was now looking at the hostage room, Harry Arno sitting on the cot, his head wrapped up—always sitting, never lying down, a man his age. Chip was suppose to be in there checking on him. . . .

No, he was coming into the study, looking at the TV screen before sinking down on the sofa, next to Louis.

"How's the houseguest doing?"

Chip said, "Turn it down, will you?" Sounding like he was irritated about something. The man picked lint off his clothes, something always bothering him. Louis would have some hip-hop going on the CD player, Digable Planets, and the man would come in saying, "Turn that goddamn racket off. Jesus." He liked Neil Diamond and such. Old Sammy Davis Junior CDs, the candyman can, that kind of shit.

"Harry hears the faintest sound," Chip said, "he goes, 'Is somebody there?' "

So the man wasn't irritated especially, he just wasn't Oprah-minded. Louis said, "I know what you mean. Four days the man's been saying it. 'Somebody there?' His voice getting to sound pitiful."

"That's the idea," Chip said, "get him to the point he's dying to hear a human voice." Chip paused, his gaze on the TV, on Oprah and her sad-looking white women guests. "What's this about?"

"I believe they gonna tell how breast implants fucked up their lives."

The Chipper, not too interested, said, "The time comes I *do* speak to him, Harry will be more than receptive, agreeable to whatever I tell him."

"He won't have much choice but agree," Louis said, watching Oprah listening to a woman talking about her implanted ninnies, Oprah's eyes concerned without it taking away from her stylish look. "He'll agree to what you say, but then he has to do it, has to produce."

"I'm not worried about that," Chip said. "Harry's a manipulator, it's one of the reasons we picked him. Anyone who can scam the wiseguys and get away with it . . . He's a conniver. You can say the same thing about the other people we want, the S&L guy. They live, in a way, by their wits. Someone said that about me once, that I lived by my wits . . ."

Louis let the man talk, the sound of his voice laid in among the TV voices, until Louis heard words that sounded familiar and he said, "What?"

"I said it's time we picked up Ben King." Talking about the crooked S&L man now. "He's sitting there waiting, can't go anywhere, can't leave town . . ."

"Not suppose to anyway," Louis said, "with that bond set on him."

"It has to look like he took off," Chip said.

"We keeping that in mind."

"Not like he was abducted."

"No need to worry your head."

"So when're you gonna do it?"

"Pretty soon."

"They bring him to trial he's going away. Then it's too late."

"What that S&L man done with money don't belong to him," Louis said, "they be in court a month shuffling papers around."

"Why can't you just tell me when you think you'll do it?"

"I said soon, didn't I?"

Man could drive you crazy. Louis had to ease up in his mind so as not to take the man by his neck and shake him. He said, "Me and Bobby been dry-running through it. We close now, so don't keep talking about when. We watch the man's house, watch him come and go, watch him play golf . . . It's gonna happen. I give my man Bobby Deo a head bob and we gone. You know Mr. Ben King has to play golf alone? Nobody wants to associate with him." He watched Oprah up in the audience finding ladies with implants and fucked-up lives, Oprah not needing anything planted underneath that brown suit she had on. Chip even was quiet now, watching Oprah with him.

Quiet for a minute, then saying, "Why don't you go help Bobby?"

Listen to the man.

"It's your house, why don't you? I'm watching your property." Louis used the remote to switch the video from Harry to Bobby, pruning away, to the front drive, what you could see of it. Louis thinking if the man had anything going for him, any kind of grit to him, he wouldn't say why don't you go help Bobby, he'd say get your ass out there. Bobby was right asking did they need the man. They needed the man's house more than they needed the man. He'd gone out yesterday looking for runaway children to scam the parents and came back with reefer. So the man smoked while they tended to the houseguest asking was somebody there.

Louis saw the car the same time the man did, Chip saying, "Jesus Christ!"

The car showing in all that shrubbery choking the drive, approaching Bobby Deo's car parked in the foreground of the picture. The man saying, "Get Bobby," and Louis jumped. Punched his thumb on the remote to take Oprah off and put the car on the screen big, what looked like a Jaguar. Chip had the chest open now to get out the shotgun, saying, "For Christ sake, go!"

Louis stood there not moving on purpose, watching the man looking at him. He said, "Be cool," and it seemed to take off some of the man's edge. Louis turned then, walked out of the study.

Raylan almost passed the driveway looking at the PRIVATE DRIVE sign, KEEP OUT, the words spray-painted on a board. He saw the house number on the mailbox just in time, braked hard and turned into the drive:

Like a road through a tropical forest, cracked pavement full of weeds, the roof line of the house showing back in there, red tile against the sky; sea grape on both sides brushing the car, different kinds of palm growth he didn't know the names of. Until coming to Florida, Raylan thought he knew trees and plants, but tropical growth was something else and there was so much of it. He came to a stop at the front end of a Cadillac parked in the drive facing out, and thought of Harry's as he saw the grille, but this car was black.

Raylan got out and walked past the Cadillac toward the house, seeing more of its white shape through the trees. Then, right in front of him, seeing a guy step out of the growth to stand waiting. A guy with no shirt on holding a machete.

Raylan walked toward him through sunlight and touched his hat brim to set it lower on his eyes. He said, "You got your work cut out for you," looking around at the vegetation. "You cleaning up this whole place?"

The guy didn't move, standing there with his machete.

He said, "It needs to be cut back and start over."

A Cuban or P.R. accent. No shirt, but wearing what looked to be his good pants and came to work in a Cadillac. Raylan loosened his hat and set it again, looking around at the growth. "There plants here I'm not too familiar with. Is that some kind of palmetto there?"

"Yucca. Over there, that's saw palmetto."

Wearing his good shoes, too. Snake or lizard under the film of dust.

"I recognize the oleander and hibiscus. Is this periwinkle?"

"Yeah, what they call it here."

"What's that tree growing all over the place?"

"Gumbo-limbo. It has to be taken out."

"You're busy, I don't want to hold you up," Raylan said. "I'm looking for Mr. Ganz. Is he in the house?"

"Mr. Ganz?"

The guy frowning at him now, shaking his head.
"I don't know any Mr. Ganz."

"He doesn't live here?"

"I never saw him."

Shaking his head again.

"His name's on the mailbox out front. Isn't this the
Ganz place?"

"Yeah, Ganz, sure. I work for Ms. Ganz."

"That his wife?"

The guy shook his head. "His mother."

"Well, is she home?"

"She don't live here. She's in a place in West Palm
Beach, staying there, you know, so somebody can
take care of her."

"She's in a nursing home?"

"Yeah, that's what it is, for old people. I go see her
to pay me, but she don't know who I am. You understand? She's old, has something wrong with her head,
like she forgets who you are. So when she don't know
me this time, she don't pay me and I have to go
back."

"You see her every day?"

"Two times, I just start to work here. You looking
to buy this place?"

"Why, is it for sale?"

"I don't know that."

"What's the name of the nursing home?"

"I forget."

"But you go there."

"Yeah, it's by the hospital, that street there."

"Flagler?"

"Yeah, I think that's it. Listen, I got all this work to do, okay?"

Raylan watched the guy turn and walk away, a pair of pruners on his belt at the hip, the same place Raylan carried his gun.

Chip said, "What's he doing?"

"Nothing," Louis said. "He's standing there."

"Well, why doesn't he leave?"

"He's looking the place over."

Louis had sent Bobby out front and got back to the study quick to keep an eye on Chip, watch how he behaved in this situation, somebody coming to the house. The man looked like he'd froze, his eyes stuck to the TV screen, the video of the front drive on big. Bobby wasn't in the picture now, he'd walked off, but the dude in the suit was still there.

"I make him to be a real estate man," Louis said. "Come to see you want to sell the house. Got all dressed up in his suit, his dude hat, wearing it like he knows what he's doing, or wants you to think he does."

Right then Chip said, "The *hat*." Sounding at the moment excited, like he was remembering something he'd forgot.

Louis looked at him. "Yeah? What?"

Chip didn't answer, staring at the screen.

Louis looked at it to see the dude walking away now, past Bobby's Cadillac to his car. The dude doing all right for himself to be driving that Jag-u-ar.

"He's leaving." Louis watched the car back out of the drive, disappear, then looked over at Chip to see the man still watching the screen. "He's gone, Chipper, the show's over."

It brought the man back to life saying, "Jesus, that was close."

"Close to what? You saw Bobby talk to him, send the dude on his way?"

"I thought he might come up to the house."

The man looked to be still edgy, rubbing his hands together, scratching his arms.

"Why would he come to the house? He don't have no business here. Bobby told him nobody's home; what he said he'd tell anybody came. He's cleaning up around the place and don't know shit otherwise. With that blade in his hand. You think the dude's gonna argue with him?"

Bobby came in the study then, sweaty, still holding the machete.

"Told the dude you just the help around here, don't know shit, huh?"

"Who was it?" Chip said. "What did he want?"

Louis said, "Was a real estate man, huh?"

"I ask him," Bobby said. "He didn't say."

Chip said, "Will you tell me, for Christ sake, what he wanted?"

"You," Bobby said. "I told him you not here. So he's gonna visit your mommy now, then maybe come back. What do you think?" Looking right at Chip. "You ever see this guy before?"

Chip said, "No," shaking his head.

But didn't seem that sure about it, edgy, or like he was thinking of something else. Louis watched him walk out of the study, the man not telling where he was going.

Louis asked it. "What you think?"

"If we have to watch him, too," Bobby said, "it's more work."

"I know what you mean. We got to keep the man out of sight."

"Tie him up in a room," Bobby said, "if we have to."

"Why you say the dude may come back?"

"I think he's a cop."

"He didn't show you nothing."

"No, it was the way he checked me out," Bobby said. "Like a cop trying to be a nice guy."

"So if he comes back?"

"We wait and see."

Chip phoned Dawn from his bedroom.

"You said the guy wore a hat."

She said, in almost a whisper, "I happen to have a client with me."

"Just tell me, for Christ sake, what it looked like."

"I did. Like a cowboy hat, the way the brim was shaped. But not one of those big ones like the country music guys wear."

Chip sat at his desk in the bedroom staring out a window at dark shapes, the sun gone from the yard. He heard her say, "Turn a light on so I can see you," and felt himself jump. He heard her say, "You called him the Marlboro man and I said, 'Yeah, except he's real.' Don't tell me he came to see you . . . please."

"Somebody did. Bobby spoke to him."

"Chip, if you get me involved in this . . ."

"It's not the same guy. I just wanted to make sure."

Her voice said, "Chip . . ." as he hung up the phone.

thirteen

When Raylan introduced himself to Ms. Ganz, she looked at his I.D. and his star and said, "Thank God. I call the police every day and you're the first one to come."

The old lady sat in a wheelchair, cloth straps around her like a seat belt to hold her in. One of the nurses had told Raylan Ms. Ganz was eighty-five and she looked it except for her blond hair, a white wine color, he realized must be a wig. There was the wheelchair and an oxygen machine by the bed, otherwise this room—with Lake Worth out the window and Palm Beach across the way—reminded Raylan of a hotel suite he'd gone into one time to make an arrest.

He said, "Ms. Ganz, you call the police?"

The old lady looked past him at a nurse, a big black woman, coming in with roses, dozens of white roses in a vase she placed on a dining table full of magazines and photos in silver frames. Raylan watched her pick up the vase of roses already sitting there, the flowers barely starting to wilt, to take out with her.

Ms. Ganz said, "Victoria, are those from Warren?"

Victoria said yes ma'am, they were, and left.

"Victoria's from Jamaica," the old lady said, and smiled, looking at the roses. "From Warren."

Her husband's name. The woman living in the past.

"Every week he sends me four dozen roses."

Raylan said that was nice, flowers made a room . . . it made the room cheerful. Ms. Ganz said the flowers had been coming every week for as long as she'd been here. Raylan didn't ask how Warren Ganz worked it, being dead. He stepped over to smell a rose, show some interest, and had to look at the framed photographs then, all of the same woman, Ms. Ganz at different ages. Ms. Ganz in big hats, Ms. Ganz by an old-model Rolls in a big hat, with a man and a small boy, the woman wearing a big straw summer hat in that one and holding flowers. It made Raylan think of her property so overgrown and was about to ask if she'd hired a yardman, but she spoke up then.

"Will you talk to them, please?"

He turned to see her looking up at him, helpless in her chair. "Talk to who?" Raylan said.

"I can't take much more. Will you tell them to stop it?"

He couldn't help feeling sorry for her, poor old lady in her curly wig; tied up. "You say you call the police?"

"Every day. First it was my underwear. I ask Victoria, I ask Louise, I ask Ada, 'What in the world is happening to my underwear?' They say oh, I'm imagining things. I put my underwear underneath the bed wrapped in newspaper. They found it. They've stolen my underwear, my good shoes, a lovely pin my grandmother gave me when I was a little girl, all my towels I brought from home, my piano—"

"Your piano," Raylan said, "you had it here?"

"Right there by the window. That's how they got it out. My friends here, they used to come by every day and ask me to play. Their favorites were 'Indian Love Call' and 'Rose Marie,' different ones Jeanette Mac-Donald and Nelson Eddy sang together. I have the records, too. 'Oh, Rose Marie, I love you. . . .' I woke up from my nap, I couldn't believe it. Two colored men I know are Jamaican, because I see them around here, were picking up the piano and shoving it through the window. I said, 'Put that down this minute.' They paid no attention. Oh, I was mad. I raised Cain around here. I said, 'Didn't *any*body see them? My God, they marched off with my piano right down Flagler Avenue in broad daylight.' Not a person here said yes or no, but you could tell they knew about it."

Raylan nodded, trying to show interest. He said, "By the way, Ms. Ganz, did you hire a man to do yard work?"

"Something's going on," the old lady said, "and I think it's that Victoria who's behind it. She's another one of the Jamaicans."

"I'll speak to her," Raylan said.

"Would you do that? I'd be so grateful."

The old lady's eyes shining with hope, or just watery; Raylan wasn't sure.

"If she denies it," Ms. Ganz said, "tell her she's a lying fucking nigger. That's what I do."

He asked Victoria about the yardman, Cuban or Puerto Rican, said he came by to see Ms. Ganz and get paid?

"She tell you that?"

"The yardman did."

"I saw a person like that come to see her last week, but I didn't speak to him myself. It used to be people came to be paid by her; a plumber fixed something, another one for the air-conditioning. Not so much anymore."

"She ever go home?"

"She used to, when she first come. Go home for a few days."

"She said some guys stole her piano?"

"Yes, steal her underwear, her shoes. She goes crazy when nobody believes her. I go in there, some-

times she tries to hit me with her cane, call me something I won't say to you. You understand this woman
never had a piano long as she been here. The roses?
She send those to herself, two hundred dollars a
week, a standing order, they have to sign the card
'With love from Warren.' "

"Her husband," Raylan said. "I imagined Ms.
Ganz was the one doing it."

"Not the husband," Victoria said, "suppose to be
from the son, Chip. But that's as hard to believe as
the dead man sending them. Chip don't spend ten
cents on his mother. You know Chip?"

"Not yet," Raylan said. "Tell me about him."

fourteen

It was dark now and they kept the house dark except for the study where there were no windows. When Bobby Deo came in from outside he said to Louis, "You see him?"

It straightened Louis, sitting on the sofa, the shotgun next to him. "He come back?"

"Quiet this time, no lights on."

Louis said, "Man, I didn't see a thing. Got it on the full screen, too. But you can't see shit out there at night with that cheap-ass camera, even with the spot. He get out and look around?"

"Came up to the house, he takes a look in the windows. Looks all around before he leaves. Walks to the back, looks at the swimming pool, looks in the garage. . . ."

"You put your car in there."

"Yeah, well, he's seen it now. Gonna want to know what it's doing there at night."

"You mean if he comes back," Louis said. "What you tell him, you're the caretaker." Louis thought about it and began to nod saying, "Yeah, the dude looks in the window, don't see any furniture, looks at the scummy swimming pool. . . . You understand what I'm saying? The dude can *see* nobody's living here."

"Yeah, but my car is there," Bobby said.

"Man, I just told you, you the caretaker. You watch the place nobody breaks in. You sleep in the kitchen and must not've heard him outside. I'm saying *if* he comes back. See, then you ask him for some identification. You want to know who the fuck he thinks he is coming around here at night, you trying to sleep."

Bobby was nodding like he agreed, but then said, "I don't know about this guy. Is he looking for Harry?"

"See, I wondered the same thing," Louis said, "on account of Chip owing Harry and here Harry is right upstairs. So we think, 'Oh, he must be looking for Harry.' You understand what I'm saying? But all the dude say he wants is to talk to Mr. Ganz. Am I right? The dude, it might be wants to sell the man something, like he can give him a deal on aluminum screens, some shit for the house."

"So he comes at night," Bobby said, "to measure the windows."

"What I'm saying," Louis said, "we don't *know* what the dude wants outside of he wants to talk to Mr. Ganz. But now he sees Mr. Ganz ain't here. Nobody is."

Bobby was nodding again, only this time he said, "Why do you call him Mister?"

"Does it bother you?"

"I don't know why you do it. You don't work for him."

"We go back," Louis said. "He use to come over to the casino in Freeport when I was back there awhile dealing blackjack. One night he cashes in big, gives me a five-hundred-dollar tip and hires me to bodyguard him now and then. I been living here, learning how to be African-American, going back and forth when I felt like it; but now I come to stay. And now I'm being *me,* you dig? See, mostly he was going down to Miami then, playing high-stakes poker with the big boys and some of them had bodyguards, so he wanted one, too. Wasn't bad at cards. He start losing, his mama would pick up his IOU's, keep her sonny from getting his legs busted. See, then I went away and didn't hear from him till I come out and he start to call me, ask how I'm doing. I come here to see him? Everything's different now, his mama's gone, he's selling off the furniture, and he lay his idea on me, how we gonna be millionaires."

"Without him doing any the work," Bobby said.

"I told you he don't know shit. Tried falsifying bank loan applications one time and drew probation. Otherwise the man's cherry."

"But we say okay, whatever he tells us."

"Going with his idea, yeah."

"He says let Harry sit there two three weeks, nobody talk to him. We say okay and we sit here watching the TV."

"What you saying," Louis said, "you don't think we should wait."

"I don't see what good it is. Kidnap a guy and give him time to wonder what's happening to him. For what?"

"We didn't kidnap him," Louis said, "we took him hostage."

"You like to think of it that way? It's the same thing," Bobby said, coming over to the sofa, standing so close Louis had to bend his head back. "You get caught, you go to prison, man. He's four days up in the room, that's enough. We should talk to Harry now, tonight, tell him what he has to do."

Louis said, "Get to it, huh?" wanting to think about it, but knowing he didn't have time. It was him and Bobby for the time being and he'd have to go along. So he said, "I don't see the good of waiting either, just 'cause the man say to."

Bobby said, "Let's go do it."

And that was that.

What they'd do, go upstairs and Louis would check on Harry, see if he had to go potty, while Bobby went to Chip's bedroom to get him, the man last seen staring out his window burning herb.

* * *

As soon as Louis opened the door Harry's voice in the dark said, "Is someone there?" Same as he always did.

"Goddamn it, say something!"

Yelling it. Bobby was right, this man was ready to be talked to. Louis went in past him to the bathroom and turned on the light. The window in here and the two in the bedroom were covered over with sheets of plywood nailed to the window frames. Louis looked at Harry in the light from the bathroom, sitting on his cot, the towel and silver tape wrapped around his head, the man not moving a muscle, listening hard for sounds.

The same way the hostages in Beirut must've sat listening, not knowing shit where they were at, why they were being held, nothing.

Chip had read all about the hostages, seen them on TV when they were released, read a book one of them wrote and came up with the idea he told to Louis. Pick up any one of these rich guys he had on his list and hide him out for a while.

Louis had said at that time, "You talking about *kid*napping?" The same thing Bobby said when he was told about it. Like the man was crazy.

The way Chip saw the difference: "Kidnapping, you hold a person for ransom. What I'm talking about, we don't call anyone, like the guy's wife, and say pay up or you'll never see your husband again. We wait, and after a while we ask the guy what his life's worth to him."

Louis, that time, still didn't see the difference. He

said, "But everybody knows the man's been kidnapped."

And Chip said, "No, the guy's disappeared. No one knows if something happened to him or he took off or what. All the time they're looking for him we've got him hidden away. Okay, once the guy's no longer in the news, nobody's talking about what happened to him, we pick up another guy from the list and do the same thing, chain him up blindfolded . . . like the real hostages, they were kept like that for months, some of them even years."

Louis knew it was some Muslim brothers over there did the job. Being Abu Aziz for a moment instead of Louis Lewis, he said, "I believe was the Shi'ites. You don't mess with those people." He asked Ganz where he was going to hide his hostages and the man said he hadn't worked that part out yet. This was before deciding his house was as good a place as any; the house itself was hidden away and hardly anyone he knew ever came by.

"This kind of setup," Chip said, "only dealing with the hostages, you don't have to warn anyone not to call the cops. Once the guy's missing they'll look for him; but remember, we're not asking for ransom money, so there's nothing to tie us to the hostage."

"So how do we score?"

"First," Chip said, "we take time to prepare the guy, get him in the right frame of mind. For weeks he sits in a room and never hears a human voice. He knows somebody's bringing him food, taking him to the can, but nobody in all that time says one fucking word to him. See, then when I do speak to the guy he can't believe it. Jesus, someone's actually talking to him. But all I say that first time, I ask him, 'What's it worth to you to get out of here?' "

Louis liked that part. "Yeah?"

"Couple of days go by, I approach him again. 'Have you decided?' You bet he has. How much do we want? Name it. Then it's like negotiating, coming up with a figure we both agree on, something we know the guy can manage. We have to, you know, be realistic."

"He pays, we let him go?"

"I guess. The guy's never seen us. Take him out in the Glades and leave him."

"What if he don't want to pay?"

"He doesn't have a choice," Chip said. "First we agree on the amount. Then he has five days. . . . I tell him, 'You have five days to come up with a way of paying us that we like.' I tell him, 'And it better be the best idea you ever had in your fucking life, I mean foolproof, because if we don't like it, if we're not absolutely sure it'll work, you're dead.' So it's strictly up to him. In other words we don't have to work anything out, the guy does it. And he's the kind of guy who knows how to move money around, a guy with hidden resources, like that savings and loan guy. Goes bankrupt, can't pay his depositors, but he's sitting on an estimated thirty mil. Right now he's out on bond. Another guy on the list, everybody knows he launders drug money, gets it cleaned and pressed, puts it in a land development deal and the feds haven't been able to touch him. There're all kinds of guys like that around, I mean right in South Florida."

"The hostage," Louis said, "can't think of a good idea, he gets shot in the head, huh?"

"If that's how you want to handle it. There're other ways might even be worse."

"Like what?"

"You didn't hear about the guy," Chip said, "wakes up in the middle of the night, his wife's got his dick in her hand?"

"What's wrong with that?"

"She's standing across the room with it. Cut his dick off with a butcher knife while he's sleeping."

Louis made a face. "Man, that's the worst thing I ever heard of."

Chip said, "See?"

It was in the news when they first started talking about taking hostages. Chip said he was kidding about threatening the guy that way. He said no, if the guy refused to cooperate, or came up with an idea of paying them they didn't like, Louis could take care of the guy any way he wanted.

Letting him do the heavy work.

Louis unlocked Harry's chain and brought him into the bathroom, Harry turning his head to say, "I only have to take a leak." So Louis put him in position. When he was going, looking down at the toilet blindfolded, Harry said, "Speak to me, will you? Tell me what time it is. Christ, what day it is. You don't want to do that, fine, but say *some*thing."

Louis felt like whispering in the man's ear and see him jump, but couldn't think of anything good. He took Harry back to his cot and locked his chain again to the ring bolt in the floor, Bobby and Chip standing in the hall now looking in. Bobby motioned and Louis came out. As soon as he closed the door Chip started in.

"This guy, this fucking bill collector, tells me he wants to change the plan I spent more than a year working out. He gets a bug up his ass 'cause he's tired of sitting around."

"We already decide," Bobby said.

Louis took Chip by the arm saying, "We gonna talk, let's step over here," and brought the man away from the door. Saying to him now, "We wouldn't be here it wasn't for you." Louis keeping his voice quiet, soothing. "We not changing nothing, we just want to get it moving."

Chip was turning his head from Louis to Bobby. "Go along with your prison buddy, is that it? The cons taking over?"

"Hey, come on," Louis said, "it's cool."

"He's stoned," Bobby said.

"Yeah, feeling good, huh?" Louis said, getting close, in the man's face now. "You like that ganja." Louis's gaze moved to Bobby. "Gets some of his herb at his mama's nursing home, from one of them Rasta fellas work there." Now he was looking at Chip again, the man staring back at him with big eyes. "Listen to me now. We all going along with it. Me and Bobby Deo and my man Mr. Ganz. Understand? Harry, I can tell, is strung out ready for us, so we gonna do it, get to the money part."

Chip shrugged and had to move his feet to keep his balance. He said, "This is the way you want it?" Being cool now since he didn't have a choice. "Fine. I'll go in and put the bug in his ear. 'Harry, what's it worth to you to get out of here?' "

"Go home to his loved ones," Louis said, placing his hands on Chip's shoulders. "Except one thing worries me. You made bets with Harry on the phone, didn't you? Many times, called him about every week."

"I'd speak to one of his sheet writers."

"Yeah, but you talk to him, too."

"Once in a while."

"See, you go in and talk to him now, he could recognize your voice. Man like Harry, being careful, he knows voices. Same as with Bobby. Bobby's spoken to him, the reason he come here. So he could know it was Bobby to speak to him."

"You're gonna do what you want," Chip said.

"Listen to me. What I'm saying is I'm the one should talk to the man," Louis said. "One, he don't know me; but two, I know Freeport, Grand Bahama. Man, I'm *from* where his money's at. Soon as he told Dawn I began to think, Do I know somebody works at his bank? I told you that. You my man, Mr. Ganz. What I want you to tell me is go in there and say your words, set the man up just like you was saying it."

Harry raised his head, the way he always did.

"Is somebody there?"

Louis closed the door before turning the light on. He walked over to the cot and sat down. Harry, feeling it, turned his blindfolded head toward him.

"Will you say something? Please?"

"I'll make you a deal," Louis said.

"Jesus, anything."

"We do some business. Just me and you. We don't tell nobody else, not a soul. You understand what I'm saying? Just me and you."

fifteen

Wednesday, Raylan brought his prisoner, the man barefoot and handcuffed in bathing trunks, through the parking structure and into Miami Beach police headquarters by way of the sally port in back. Check your weapon through a window slot and they close the outer door before opening the inner one to the holding-cell area.

Lt. Buck Torres was there waiting.

"I thought finding them in bed asleep was the way

to do it," Raylan said. "Get 'em sunbathing's even better, no surprises under the covers. Buck, we have here Carl Edward Colbert, escapee from the West Tennessee Reception Center, down for armed robbery and assault with a deadly weapon, a pitchfork."

Torres, looking up at Colbert, said, "Man, he's a size."

"Yeah, but sunburnt. All you have to do is touch him and he minds. If it's okay with you," Raylan said, "I'll leave him here till I can arrange transportation, have him shipped back. Carl, how about packed in ice, would you like that? . . . Carl isn't talking; he's lost faith in his fellowman. A buddy of his, guy works at one of the hotels on the beach, turned him in to avoid getting brought up for harboring."

Torres said, "You could've taken him over to Dade, they got more room there."

"Yeah, but I wanted to ask you something," Raylan said, "you being a good friend of Harry's and all. He's disappeared."

Torres said, "Again?"

"Last Friday he was to meet a guy collected on some old bets for him—this was up in Delray Beach. The guy never showed up. Harry left the restaurant and that's the last anyone's seen of him."

"Friday," Torres said. "Maybe he went back to Italy, decided he liked it."

"Harry wouldn't leave without making a big production out of it. He goes to the bathroom, he calls Joyce and tells her. She checked with Harry's travel agent; he said Harry hasn't gone anywhere that he knew of. I was thinking one of Harry's sheet writers might know who did the collection work, but I can't find any of those guys around."

"No—we closed Harry down, they left," Torres said. "Let me think a minute. If Harry couldn't find a certain guy, he'd call me to check, see if he was in jail. As a last resort he'd hire a collector. I know once in a while Bob Burton helped him out. Burton's a skip tracer—you know, a bounty hunter, always working. He'd do a collection for Harry as a favor. There was another guy, a bounty hunter, went up on a manslaughter conviction. . . ."

"Harry told Joyce the guy was Puerto Rican," Raylan said, and right away saw Torres nodding.

"Bobby Deogracias—that's the guy—they call him Bobby Deo. This one, man, I'm telling you is dirty. It used to be we find a guy shot in the head and it looks like an execution? We bring in Bobby Deo. We knew he worked sometimes for the wiseguys, Jimmy Capotorto, when he was around, but we could never close on him. He did that kind of work and he went after fugitives," Torres said. "Same thing you're doing."

"How about that," Raylan said. "You think he's the one?"

"Could be. How much was Harry trying to collect?"

"Sixteen thousand five hundred."

"That kind of money, yeah, it could be Bobby Deo, it could be anybody. He tells Harry no, the guy didn't pay him and keeps it."

"But he called Harry and told him the guy *did* pay, and to meet him in Delray Beach."

"So he changed his mind. All that money in his hand? What's Harry gonna do, call the police? Listen, if it was Bobby Deo—anybody hires a guy like that deserves to get ripped off. Harry realizes too late he should've known better, so now he's feeling sorry for himself. You know how he is. Underneath all that old-time hip bullshit he puts on he's a baby. Hides out so we have to look for him."

"Wants attention," Raylan said.

"Loves it. He'll give it a few more days. You don't find him, he'll get tired of hiding and come out. Ask him, 'Where you been?' He'll say, 'What do you mean, where've I been?' He doesn't show up by this weekend I'll give it to Missing Persons."

"I think you're right," Raylan said. "But I still wouldn't mind talking to Bobby . . . What's his name?"

"Deogracias. I remember seeing it on a Corrections release report when he got out. DOC'll have his address. But whether it's any good or not . . ."

"I appreciate it," Raylan said. "You might run a trace on Harry's car, brand-new Cadillac. See if it might've turned up abandoned."

Torres nodded. "I can do that."

"And you might run a name for me," Raylan said, "while we're covering the bases. A Dawn Navarro?"

Raylan walked into the cool, tiled lobby of the Santa Marta on Ocean Drive, South Beach; salsa, mambo, some kind of Latin music coming out of the bar. Raylan crossed to the desk clerk, a good-looking young Hispanic in a dark suit, hair shining, rings on his fingers, and said, "Excuse me."

The desk clerk was busy working a computer behind the reception counter, his hips twitching to the Latin beat. He didn't answer Raylan or look up from the screen.

Raylan said, "I was here one other time. . . ."

The desk clerk tapped some more keys and then looked at the computer screen to see how he was doing.

"You might recall I was with a group," Raylan said. "Bunch of fellas had DEA written big on the back of their jackets?"

He had the desk clerk's attention now, the guy looking right at him.

"We had search warrants, but you didn't want to let us in any the rooms. You recall that? So we busted down some doors, found who we wanted and took you with us when we left. Remember that time? You give me any shit, partner, I'll run you in again, handcuffed and shackled. What I want is Mr. Deogracias's room number."

The clerk hesitated.

Raylan let him.

The clerk said, "Four oh eight."

"Is he in?"

"I don't think so."

"I called, some guy answered the phone."

"That would be Santo."

Raylan said, "Much obliged."

*   *   *

A girl wearing a green Harley-Davidson T-shirt and short white shorts opened the door, barefoot. Cute, but needing to comb her hair and maybe take a bath.

"I called a while ago," Raylan said, "asked for Bobby Deo and some guy said he didn't speak English and hung up on me."

The girl turned her head and yelled, "Hey, Santo!" Looking back at Raylan she leaned her shoulder against the door frame, one bare foot on top of the other, and it reminded him for some reason of high school girls back home. She said, "I like your hat," and even sounded like those girls, this one acting coy, giving him a look.

A man's voice said, "Who is it?" and a young Hispanic guy wearing sunglasses appeared out of the bedroom where a radio was playing Latin riffs, a little guy about five-six with his pants open, sticking in his shirttails.

The girl turned her head again. "He's looking for Bobby."

"What's he want him for?"

Raylan saw the guy as one of those tough little banty-rooster types as the girl was saying, "What am I, your fucking interpreter? Ask him yourself." She moved away from the door in time to the music coming from the bedroom. Raylan took a step inside, glanced around to see a mess of clothes thrown on chairs, towels, newspapers, beer cans on the coffee table. He looked at Santo.

"I want to ask Bobby if he did a job the other day for Harry Arno. Is he around?"

Santo zipped up his pants, pulled his belt tight around his waist and buckled it, taking his time.

"Who is this Harry Arno?"

"How come," Raylan said, "you can't answer a question without asking one?"

"It's the way they are," the girl said. "They think you can't trust anybody that isn't like them. Where're you from anyway?"

"Right here," Raylan said, getting his I.D. out and showing his star, "with the United States Marshals Service. I'm not looking to give anybody a hard time. Okay?"

Santo said, "Bullshit," to the girl. Or it might've been some word in Spanish, Raylan wasn't sure. There wasn't any doubt about the guy's manner, though, turning his back, walking out to the balcony to stand looking off. Some pose.

"These guys work at being a pain in the ass," the girl said. "I told you, it's the way they are. Sometimes I don't know what I'm doing here."

Raylan said, "I was gonna ask."

"They become sociable when it gets dark, they dance like crazy." She began moving in a kind of mambo shuffle to the radio. "We go to clubs in Hialeah."

Santo, on the balcony, stood hunched over the metal rail leaning on his arms. Raylan walked out there to stand next to him, thinking all he'd have to do was lift the guy up by his belt and ask again where Bobby Deo was.

Instead, his gaze settled on Ocean Drive and the strip of art deco hotels in their pastel colors that looked to Raylan like big ice-cream parlors. Hotels with cafés fronting on the street where the trendies stayed in season and girls with string bikinis stuck in their bums came cruising by on Rollerblades; young guys hotdogged on skateboards and photographers posed skinny models out on the beach, their outfits taking weird shapes in the wind. Except that right now it was between the hurricane season and the tourist season and the crowd roaming South Beach were locals and bush-league trendies. It was still a show.

He heard the girl behind him and said, "It isn't anything like back home, is it? Wherever that might be."

She said, "It sure ain't, it's fun."

"Santo here your boyfriend?"

The banty rooster stirred as the girl said, "God, no, I'm with Bobby, when he's here."

"Where can I find him?"

Santo, turning his head, said, "Melinda, you don't have to tell him nothing. You hear me?"

She said, "Hey, fuck off. Okay?"

Raylan turned to her standing in the doorway. "I only want to ask him about this friend of mine, if he's seen him."

Santo said, "Yeah? What do you show your badge for?"

Raylan said, "Why don't you stay out of it, partner?" and looked at the girl again, Melinda. "You know where he is?"

"He's working. He won't be back for, I don't know, a while."

"I don't have to see him in person, if you have a phone number where I can reach him."

He waited.

She said, "I might have it someplace."

"I'd really appreciate it. This friend of mine, Harry Arno? I'm hoping Bobby knows where he is."

"Bobby was working for him?"

"Yeah, they're friends."

Santo, turning his head again, said, "I never heard of no Harry Arno."

Raylan said, "How far's it down there to the pavement, forty, fifty feet? Keep looking at it."

He turned to see Melinda going into the living room and put his hand on Santo's shoulder.

"Nice talking to you."

She was bent over the desk now looking at notes, scraps of paper by the phone. Raylan came up next to her. "Will he give you any trouble?"

"Who, Santo? He touches me Bobby'll kill him." She straightened saying, "Here it is. He called me once and gave me the number. You want me to write it down for you?"

Friendly because they had something in common, their accents and, maybe, because there were moments when she was homesick and he reminded her of some farm town or coal camp way off the interstate.

"I'd appreciate it."

He watched her write the area code, 407, but couldn't make out the rest of the numbers.

"You say Bobby's working. What's he do?"

The girl looked up at him, maybe a little surprised.

"He's a gardener."

Raylan said, "Oh." And said, "He is, huh."

"A master gardener. Bobby learned grounds beautification when he was up at Starke."

Raylan took the piece of notepaper she handed him, folded it without looking at the number and thanked her.

She said, "I sure like that hat."

At the door he touched the brim to her. He would think about this girl, remind himself to check on her in a week or so, see how she was doing. In the hall he stopped to unfold the notepaper the way a poker player might look at his hole card the first time, sneaking a peak and hoping.

And there it was. The same number Joyce had given him for Warren Ganz.

He used the pay phone in the lobby to call Torres.

"It's a small world," Raylan said. "I've already spoken to Bobby Deo without knowing who he was." And had to explain that. "Now I'll have to have another talk with him. What about Harry's car?"

"Hasn't shown up."

"You get a chance to check on Dawn Navarro?"

"Nothing in the computer. Who is she anyway?"

"Certified medium and spiritualist, she's a psychic, hangs out at a restaurant in Delray, the place where Harry was supposed to meet Bobby Deo."

"She knows Harry?"

"Says she talked to him for a minute. I've got her down as the last person to see Harry before he disappeared from the face of the earth."

"Or went down to Key West to get drunk in peace. You think she knows what happened to him?"

"She knows *some*thing she's not telling me."

"Dawn Navarro," Torres said, "she sounds like a stripper. She lives in Delray?"

"Nearby."

"You're working out of the Palm Beach County Sheriff's Office, for Christ sake, talk to the people up there, ask around. If she's been up on any kind of charge somebody there will've heard of her. Check with Crimes Persons. I have to tell you how to do your job?"

"I appreciate it," Raylan said. "Listen, you don't happen to know anything dirty about a guy named Warren Ganz, do you?"

"Good-bye," Torres said and hung up.

sixteen

Starting out, Chip had pictured a damp basement full of spiders and roaches crawling around, pipes dripping, his hostages huddled against the wall in chains. He wanted it to be as bad as any of the places in Beirut he'd read about.

He told Louis and Louis said, "Where we gonna find a basement in Florida?"

All right, but the living conditions had to be miserable, the worse the better. They could certainly find a

place infested with bugs, those big palmetto bugs.
Maybe a shack out in the Everglades.

Louis said, "We gonna be out there with the hostages and the bugs? And the different motherfucking
kind of swamp creatures out there like alligators? We
already got ants upstairs in the room."

All right, then some place with concrete-block
walls. Drive in steel staples and hook up chains with
two-inch links, the kind they used over in Beirut.

Louis said, "I don't know nothing about any steel
staples or how you drive them into concrete. Chains
with two-inch links—how you bend a chain that size
around a man's ankle? Bicycle chain's what you use,
the kind you chain your bike to a post with so nobody
gonna steal it."

Chip said they'd feed their hostages cold rice and
mutton, hard stale cheese. . . . Spill the food on
purpose, the way the guards did over there, and make
them eat it off the floor. He favored leaving overripe
bananas in the room, out of their reach, the smell
becoming worse each day.

Louis said, "Worse for anybody has to go in there."
He said, "Where we gonna get mutton around here?
The same place we get the straw mattresses? Spill the
food—who cleans it up, me or you?"

When he brought in cookies and potato chips and
stuff, Chip wanted to know if they were holding a
hostage or having a house party.

Once they saw they'd have to use this place, Louis
said, "Chipper, there's no way to treat hostages like
they did in Beirut in a five-million-dollar house in
Manalapan, Florida."

* * *

This morning, Thursday, Louis said, "Almost a week now I been taking the man to the toilet. Have to unchain him, wait for him to do his business and chain him up again."

"In Beirut," Chip said, "the hostages had ten minutes in the morning to wash up, wash their clothes, brush their teeth when they had toothbrushes, and take a dump. Ten minutes. If they didn't have to go right then but had to go later on? They had to hold it till the next morning."

Louis said, "We ain't over in Beirut and I ain't a Shia. I ain't even trying to pass no more as Abu the Arab, am I?"

He went upstairs and added ten feet of bicycle chain to the end hooked to the ring bolt. As he was working on it Harry said, "Are you the one?"

Louis kept his back to the video camera mounted high on the wall, like in a bank. Hunched down over the ring bolt he said, "What if I wasn't? Man, you keep your mouth shut 'less I say something to you. All right, what I've done, you can feel your way into the bathroom now by yourself."

"I appreciate it," Harry said.

Louis looked up at him sitting blindfolded on the cot. "Man, you beginning to smell."

"What do you expect?" Harry said. "I haven't washed in . . . how long's it been, a week?"

When Louis came down to the study again, to Chip pushing buttons on the remote, the man trying to look eagle-eyed staring at views of his property, Louis said, "Harry needs to wash hisself and shave.

He can't do it with that blindfold around his head.
How'd they manage over in Beirut?"

Mr. Chip Ganz, the authority on hostage-living,
didn't say anything right away. Louis saw he had to
think about it.

"Well, there were different ways. The guy that was
there the longest, they moved him around a lot."

Louis said, "Blindfolded?"

"Yeah, they put a cloth over his head and taped it
on, the same way we did. They'd say, 'Death to
America' and give him a slap."

"So they spoke to him."

"They'd say things like, 'No move, no speaking,'
but he didn't know them, so he wouldn't recognize
any of their voices."

"Didn't you tell me this man read the Bible, he
played chess?"

"He made the chess pieces out of tinfoil some of
the food was wrapped in."

"How could he do that, you say he was blindfolded
all the time?"

"I meant when the guards came in the room. If
they caught the guy trying to peek out under his
blindfold, they'd beat him up."

"So the hostage could take the blindfold off if the
Shia wasn't around."

"Sometimes; it worked different ways," Chip said.
"Harry has to be kept blindfolded because he knows
us."

Louis said, "I'm gonna look around the house, see
if I can find something the man can slip over his head

when we in there and slip off when he needs to clean hisself up."

"What do you mean, something he can slip on and off?"

"Like take a mask and tape up the eyeholes."

"This Bobby's idea?"

"Be cool," Louis said and turned to leave.

"Wait. Where is he?"

"Bobby? Getting dressed. We going to see if Mr. Ben King's ready for us."

"Are you serious? You're gonna pick him up in broad daylight?"

"I told you about it. We'll see how it looks." He turned again toward the door.

"Louis."

He stopped and looked back.

"Last night you said you knew someone at the bank in Freeport, where Harry has his account."

"I said I'm from there, so I *might* know somebody."

"You said you'd mentioned it to me before."

"Didn't I?"

"Louis, why do I get the feeling you and Bobby are into something you don't want me to know about?"

The man was maintaining on reefer, Louis could tell, so he'd seem to be relaxed.

Louis said, "I tell you things and you forget is all."

"You're changing the whole setup, to the way you and Bobby want it."

"What you mean, like the blindfold? Man, we new at this hostage business. Have to see what works here and what don't."

"Louis, what's going on?"

The weed making him think he was cool and knew things.

"Ain't nothing going on you don't know about," Louis said, turning again to the door. "I'll see you."

Chip's voice raised as he said, "You put a blindfold on Harry he can slip on and off . . . Louis? You know sooner or later . . ."

Louis was already out the door.

He went upstairs to the bedroom Bobby was using that used to be Chip's mama's room, dark in here with the dark furniture and the heavy rose-colored drapes almost closed. Sunlight came through the narrow opening, across the rose bedspread and the rose carpeting to where Bobby stood at the dresser looking at himself in the mirror. He had on his black silk pants and lizard shoes, no shirt, and was gazing at himself with his arms raised, muscles popped, twisting his ponytail into a knot.

Louis said, "You getting ready?"

"We have time," Bobby said to himself in the mirror. "What's going on?"

"The man thinks we're planning shit against him."

Bobby said, "Who knows, huh?"

He watched Louis, in the mirror, open the door to the closet and begin pawing through the woman's clothes.

"You looking for something to wear?"

"I won't know what I'm looking for," Louis said, "till I find it."

*   *   *

The phone rang.

On the table next to the sofa where Chip was sitting on his spine staring at the television screen: the front drive on, the hidden driveway. He had made up his mind to go out, give Louis the watch and get away for a while. He thought of Palm Beach and the Au Bar, where he used to hang out, back in the days when his credit cards were good.

The phone rang.

They were spending the money Harry had on him for food. Guy with all his dough, a hundred and seventy-six bucks in his wallet. But now the credit cards . . . Why hadn't he thought of them before? They weren't doing Harry any good. The credit cards could come in handy.

The phone rang.

He pushed a button on the remote and was looking at the patio now, the pool and the sweep of weeds that used to be a lawn extending to palm trees and sky, clear blue. A path through the bushes beneath the trees led to the beach. At one time he thought of the ocean here as part of his property.

The phone rang.

He had to get out for a while. Not go to a bar— take his clothes off and walk down to the beach and look at the ocean, smoke another joint to clear his mind, see everything enlarged . . .

He didn't answer the phone because he wasn't supposed to be here, but then, without thinking, as it was ringing again, he picked it up.

Dawn's voice said, "Chip?"

"Hey, I was about to call you."

"I'll bet."

"Really, I have your money."

"I'll believe it when I see it."

"Don't get pouty on me. Meet you in Delray?"

"Why don't I stop by?"

"Honey, you don't want to come here, not just yet. If you get my drift." He liked that. And liked the silence on the line, Dawn pulling in, reconsidering, seeing she'd better not be so fucking aggressive. He said, "I'm gonna be out and around. Why don't we meet at Chuck and Harold's for lunch? Twelve-thirty?"

She said, "Chip? You'd better be there."

Threatening, with nothing to back it up.

He told himself to be nice and said, "I'll be counting the minutes," and hung up. He wouldn't show and tomorrow he'd put her off again, think of an excuse. Busy for the next few days doing something, he'd tell her, she would definitely not want to know about. He said out loud, "Okay? You told me you didn't want to know anything, and if I tell you then you're involved in whatever it is, right? Hey, you're already involved. So quit your bitching."

Send Bobby to see her. . . .

Saturday go to a Huggers Gathering and try to scrounge up the fifteen hundred. Find a runaway whose daddy misses her.

He should've asked Dawn about the guy, the dude in the hat, what he was like, what they talked about.

He pushed a button and was looking at the front drive again, Christ, thinking about the guy and there he was, in his suit, the hat, coming through the trees toward the house.

Ganz hurried out of the study to the front hall, started up the stairs and yelled as loud as he could, "He's back! The guy's back!"

seventeen

Raylan saw them as soon as he came around the side of the house past the garage: Bobby the gardener and a black guy sitting at the table on the patio, their shirts off, getting some sun and reading the newspaper. Both of them holding open sections of the paper, reading away.

It took Raylan all of a moment to realize they knew he'd come back and were putting on this show for him.

There were sections of the paper and a white shirt on the glass-top table; but not lying flat, Raylan noticed, something under there. Maybe their gardening shears, or the machete the guy had the other day.

"I see you got yourself some help," Raylan said to Bobby Deo. "What you need for this job is a crew."

Both of them had looked up and were watching him now, coming across the patio.

"I noticed your car in the garage, figured you were around somewhere. You taking a break?"

The one he knew was Bobby Deo had on his good pants again and his reptile wing tips, shiny clean. The other guy was wearing cream-colored pants and sandals.

Bobby Deo said, "Yeah, we resting."

"I don't blame you," Raylan said, taking time to squint at the sky and reset his hat on his eyes. Looking out at the scraggly date palms and sea grape lining the property he said, "What I don't understand is why you're doing this instead of your collection work."

He turned now to face them.

"There's a lot more money in getting deadbeats to pay up, isn't there?"

Bobby didn't answer. The two of them sat there staring at him.

Raylan said, "You'd like me to get to the point here, wouldn't you?"

The guy still didn't answer.

"Okay, maybe you can help me out. I understand you do collection work for a friend of mine, Harry

Arno. Is that right?" Raylan waited, watching the guy
making up his mind.

Finally Bobby said, "Sometimes."

"I'm told you worked for him last week."

"Where you hear that?"

"From another friend of Harry's. He told this
friend you made a collection for him and he was suppose to meet you in Delray Beach. Harry waited and
called this friend when you didn't show up."

Bobby said, "You heard that, huh? Who told you I
was here?"

"Your buddy Santo."

"Yeah? How do you know to ask him?"

Time to identify himself.

Raylan held open a leather case to show his star
and I.D. "It's what I do, find people, fugitives on the
run. I'm United States Deputy Marshal Raylan Givens, Bobby. I do the same thing you used to do, only,
I bet, for a lot less money." Raylan put on a slight
grin, showing he thought it was funny they had this in
common.

Bobby didn't grin back.

"Let me ask you something," Raylan said. "When
you track down a guy who skipped, he ever offer you
money to leave him alone?"

"That what you want?"

"Wait now," Raylan said. "You think I'm looking
for a payoff?"

"What it sounds like."

"For what? Not ask you questions?"

"Forget it."

"All I asked was if a fugitive ever offered you money."

"Sometimes."

"More than you'd make bringing him in."

"Always."

"You ever take it?"

Bobby shook his head.

"Why not?"

"I wouldn't do it."

"You mean it would get around and you'd be out of business," Raylan said, "which you are now anyway. No more skip tracing since that fall you took. Or, you're saying you wouldn't do it 'cause you're a straight shooter. I believe that, Bobby. So tell me how come you didn't meet Harry in Delray last Friday, one o'clock?"

"Something came up, I couldn't be there."

"But you'd made the collection."

"No, I told Harry the guy can't pay him."

"The guy," Raylan said. "You mean Warren Ganz."

Bobby shrugged and Louis spoke up.

"You see that sign out front where you drive in, say 'keep out'? That means you, man. This is private property, so leave."

Raylan turned to him. "Who am I talking to?"

"You talking to *me*. Who you think you talking to?"

Raylan said, "You want to get in this? Tell me who you are and what you're doing here with this guy. Couple of gardeners—you put your good clothes on to clear brush. Sit here for my benefit like you're taking a break? If you're not working here then you must be trespassing. So I'll have to cuff you and take you in."

"I *live* here," Louis said.

"Maybe I'll take you in anyway."

"For what?" Louis sounding surprised now. "Man, I'm the caretaker. He's staying while he does the work and I help him out some."

"What's your name?"

"Louis Lewis."

"You putting me on?"

"It's my *name*. You want me to spell it for you?"

"Where's Warren Ganz?"

"Down in the Keys someplace, been gone all week."

"When's he coming back?"

"Didn't tell me."

Now Bobby said, "When I came here to collect, he was leaving. He said go see his mother, she'd pay me. So I go see her at the home—"

"They're talking," Louis said, "Bobby tells her he's a gardener and she hires him to clean the place up."

"Yes, but first," Bobby said, "she tell me no, she won't pay the debt, even for her own son. So I call Harry, I say maybe if you try—you the one her son owes—you can get her to pay you. He say to meet him and we can talk about it. But I never went there."

Like they were getting their stories straight.

Raylan said, "You told Harry about the mother?"

"I did. Told him how she is, how you don't know

what she's talking about sometime. Like when I go to get paid for my work."

Bobby shook his head, resigned, before looking up at Raylan with sort of a frown, interested.

"You went to see her the other night, didn't you?"

"I spoke to her," Raylan said.

"Yeah? How was she?"

"Older than she looks," Raylan said. "We talked."

"About what, her piano? Then you talk to a nurse and she tell you the old woman don't have a piano? You ask about her son, the nurse tells you he never comes to visit? Then you come back here and sneak around look in the windows?"

"Woke me up," Louis said. "I almost call the police, tell 'em there's a prowler, man could be armed and dangerous, so shoot the motherfucker on sight. You mean that was you?"

Louis waited until Raylan, giving them a look but no last words, walked off around the corner, back the way he'd come, before Louis said to Bobby, "Hold up your hand."

"What?"

"Man, put your hand up in the air."

Bobby raised his right hand above his head and Louis came out of his chair to reach over and slap the hand saying, "Yeaaah, we done it, man. The dude's gone off scratching his head wondering what happen to him."

Bobby smiled, not giving it much.

Still, it was the first time Louis could recall ever seeing the man smile, Louis smiling with him, sitting down again. He said, "There's no way the dude can say any different than what we told him. You see a way?" He pushed the newspapers off the table and picked up the shotgun he'd laid there underneath, with the machete. Then looked at Bobby again. "Do you?"

"Do I what?"

"See how the man can believe anything but what we told him?"

"I don't know what he believes," Bobby said. "I have to think about it. The first time, he act like a cop trying to be a nice guy. Now we know he's a cop, so he don't have to act nice." Bobby speaking with a thoughtful tone. "Comes here looking for Harry. . . . Why would they send a U.S. marshal, a federal cop?"

"Nobody sent him," Louis said. "Didn't you hear the man say he's a friend of Harry's? Hasn't seen him in a few days, so he ask around, follows some leads, decides to check on people owe Harry money. See if they've seen him, that's all." Louis looked toward the house and raised his voice to say, "Hey, you suppose to be down in the Keys."

Bobby turned to see Chip in the sunroom, watching them through a pane of glass. He said, "Leave him in there."

"Scared to come out," Louis said. "Look at him," and said, "Come on, man, the coast is clear."

"I told you leave him in there," Bobby said, his tone getting Louis's attention. "We have to think about this guy—what's his name?"

"Raylan something," Louis said, "believes he's a

cowboy. Got the hat, the boots. I wouldn't mind a pair like that, black with the tan wing tips?"

"Had his coat open, thumbs in his belt," Bobby said. "You see that? Ready to draw his gun. I always wonder what that would be like, two guys facing each other with guns."

"Like in the movies," Louis said.

"Yeah, but it could happen," Bobby said. "This guy isn't going away."

eighteen

Whenever Raylan thought of Reverend Dawn he'd see her facing him from across the table with her eyes closed, her long hair parted in the middle. He'd see her eyes open then to look at him with her calm expression. He'd see her hand come up to move her hair away from her face, using the tips of her fingers in a delicate kind of gesture, and he'd notice the way she bit her nails down.

Raylan was anxious to have his fortune told again,

see how he was doing, and was on his way from Warren Ganz's home to Reverend Dawn's when the beeper message stopped him. He followed up to hear a female voice in the Sheriff's Office detective bureau asking if he'd meet Sergeant Lou Falco in the parking lot of a funeral home on Federal Highway in West Palm. As soon as possible.

Shit. He knew Falco, Falco was okay, but how long would this take? It sounded like a stakeout.

Raylan found the funeral home, 1940s moderne painted white with round corners and glass-brick inserts. He got out of the Jaguar and into an unmarked Crown Vic, a gray one, saying, "How do you work surveillance when everybody knows this's a police car?"

"I'm waiting for a guy," Falco said, "who's coming to see what his brother looks like with embalming fluid in him. The brother is sitting on his front steps, a guy gets out of a car, pops him three times, gets back in the car and drives off. Maurice has to know who did it, but won't talk to us. So maybe, you know, when he sees his brother laid out . . ."

"Maurice," Raylan said. "That's the name of one of the guys tried to jack my car that time." He saw Falco nodding.

"Maurice Woody. You see them once you know you'll see them again. Maurice is why I asked you to come. The other one's Faron, the dead one."

"Wears his hair in cornrows?"

"Yeah, that's Faron."

"They must've made bond."

"Ten thousand each. They promised their grandma

they'd never get in trouble again and she put her house up as collateral. The brothers were out five days when Faron got popped."

"Maurice was there?"

"In the house."

Through the tinted windshield they watched a car coming along Federal toward the funeral home. As it passed Falco said, "You know Maurice. I was thinking when he gets here if you went in with me . . . You heard about Faron so you stopped by . . ."

"Offer Maurice my sympathy?"

"Talk to him in his bereavement, shoot the shit."

"Offer a plea deal on the car-jacking?"

"You could mention it. See if he'd like to trade, give us who did his brother."

"There isn't a state attorney in Florida," Raylan said, "would go for a deal on car-jacking. You know that."

"Yeah, but Maurice doesn't."

"He'd have to be awful dumb. The guy's in and out of the system."

"So? We don't know his I.Q. He might go for it. We were hoping," Falco said, "to put them at a robbery in Delray, a mom-and-pop grocery store, right after they got out. Use it to leverage Maurice into cooperating. We showed their pictures, the woman said no, it wasn't them, so . . ." Falco was silent, watching the street, before saying, "It was like these two guys spur of the moment decide to rob the place. They go through the store picking out what they want and put it on the checkout counter—snacks like pretzels, potato chips, a couple of six-packs, and Jell-O."

Raylan said, "Jell-O?"

"Yeah, all the party stuff and a half-dozen boxes of Jell-O. The store owner pulls a gun and gets creamed with it, thirty stitches in his head. The one guy wants a ring the woman's wearing but can't get it off her finger. So—listen to this—the guy takes out a pair of snippers and is gonna cut her finger off. The woman begs him, please let her try, and luckily she gets it off. The guy looks at the ring up close like he's appraising it and gives it back to her, doesn't want it. But if she hadn't gotten it off . . . They left with their groceries and about eighty bucks. Early Saturday, before noon."

"The guy had snippers on him? Like tin snips?"

"I think more like the ones you use for gardening."

"Pruners."

"Yeah, for trimming bushes."

"Both guys were black?"

"The woman thought so but wasn't sure. They're Lebanese, the couple, only been here three years."

They sat there not saying anything for a while, watching cars go by on Federal, Raylan seeing Bobby Deo with the pruners on his belt that first time, in the front yard with the machete, Bobby the gardener. You wouldn't call him black, though he could be and the woman wasn't sure. But if it was Bobby and the other guy, Louis, what would they be doing holding up a grocery store for snacks and six boxes of Jell-O? Raylan tried to remember the last time he'd had Jell-O. At lunch in Miami Beach. With Harry? . . .

He thought of Harry and right away began thinking of Dawn again, Dawn with her eyes closed, her eyes opening, looking at him, and he said, "I've been meaning to ask around, I wondered if anybody in Crimes Persons knows a Dawn Navarro. She's a medium, like a fortune-teller."

"Reverend Dawn the psychic," Falco said. "Sure. What's she doing now?"

"I'm trying to find out what she knows about a missing person."

"Ask her. That's right up her alley."

"How do you know her?"

"From a homicide investigation, couple years ago. I was with Tactical then and there was a question she might need protection."

"If she testified in the case?"

"Even before, if she got too close to our suspect, a guy we believed had killed a woman in Boca. Beat her to death and then dropped her off a balcony ten stories up. We find out the woman was one of Dawn's regulars, Mary Ann Demery, a widow, fairly well off, saw Dawn at least once every week for a reading. So we talked to Dawn about different guys Mary Ann knew, who she was seeing. . . . There was one guy in particular we had high on our list." Falco stopped. "Oh, you have to understand it looked like a suicide. Only we knew it wasn't, and without telling Dawn *any*thing, not a hint, she knew it, too. On her own, no help from us. We took her up to Mary Ann's apartment and she reenacted the scene, how the guy hit Mary Ann with a brass bookend—it was like a modernistic bull, a bright gold color. Dawn looked around the living room and couldn't believe it wasn't there. See, we'd already established the bookend as the murder weapon and were holding it as evidence, traces of Mary Ann's blood on it. Dawn tells us the guy hit Mary Ann with the bookend *before* dropping her from the balcony, and that was exactly the way we saw it."

Raylan watched a car coming. "How'd she know?"

"What do you mean *how*? She's psychic. She sees things without actually seeing anything."

"She identify your suspect?"

"She was tuned in to the woman, the way Dawn explained it, and saw what happened to her but not the guy doing it. She felt his presence, said he smoked pot."

"Maybe she picked up on something you said."

"Listen, she told us things there was no way she could've known about."

"Why does she call herself Reverend?"

"From some kind of spiritualist group she used to belong to. We checked her out, she's okay."

"She ever give you a reading?"

Falco didn't answer, watching the car now, a white T-bird making a U-turn to pull up in front of the funeral home, Falco saying, "There he is. Bet you anything it's Maurice. No parking, so that's where he parks. Probably stole the fucking car." They watched Maurice get out—wearing the crocheted cap Raylan recognized—and Falco said, "We'll give him a few minutes with the family, his mother, his grandma and some aunts."

*   *   *

They came up on either side of Maurice standing at the blond-wood casket, the women in dark dresses and hats watching from rows of empty chairs, silent. Raylan looked down at Faron's closed eyes, his corn-rows, his folded hands resting on a floral necktie and white shirt. He remembered telling him that being dumb didn't mean you had to get shot.

"I understand," Falco said, in a hushed voice, "he got hit with hollow-point three-eighties. You were lucky, Maurice, you know it? That could be you lay-ing there." Falco paused. "Didn't your dad go the same way? Died of gunshot when you were a little kid?" Falco paused again. "Is this like a family tradi-tion, Maurice? If it is, I think you should end it."

There was a silence.

Raylan waited.

Maurice didn't move, standing with his head bowed, holding his skullcap in both hands at his crotch.

"The man next to you," Falco said, "you remember him?"

Maurice didn't answer or look up.

"You tried to jack his car and found out too late you picked the wrong guy." Falco leaned in to look past Maurice at Raylan.

So Raylan said, "How you doing, Maurice?" with the feeling that was it, all he had to offer. He waited, not expecting an answer and didn't get one.

"This man's in a position to maybe help you out," Falco said. "Put in a good word when you come up for sentencing. You know what I'm saying, Maurice? If you can see your way to cooperate, tell us who did

Faron." Falco paused. "I've got an eyeball witness who puts you at the scene. Saw you come out of the house. . . . Just give me a name." Falco paused again. "What do you say?"

What Maurice said, head still lowered, not looking at either of them, was, "Why don't you cut the bull-shit and lemme pray over my brother?"

Coming out of the funeral home Falco said, "Ass-hole. Try to help, that's the kind of cooperation you get."

"He wants to do it himself," Raylan said.

"That's right, and the next time we come here Maurice is in the box."

They crossed the lot toward their cars, Raylan thinking, hesitant about a question he had for Falco and then asked it.

"Lou, have you ever had to kill anybody?"

"Once. Well, two guys, actually. The end of a chase we got them coming out of their car."

"How'd you feel about it?"

"You sound like the psychologist I had to see. I told her what I felt was a tremendous relief."

"You get sick?"

"Nauseated, yeah. Every cop I know who had to shoot . . . it happens, you don't feel good."

"You didn't have a choice."

"None," Falco said. "You carry a gun you have to be willing to use it. And I'll tell you something: it's a lot to fucking ask of anybody." They reached their cars, parked next to one another, before Falco said, "You ever use your gun?"

Raylan, now, was looking at Falco over the top of his car. "Twice, two different times."

"You put them down?"

"Yeah."

"Then what're we talking about? You know when you have to shoot and you're the only one who does. Don't let anybody give you any shit about it, either." Falco turned to open his door. "I'll see you."

Raylan unlocked his car and looked up again. "You didn't tell me, on that homicide, you get a conviction?"

Falco, on the other side of the Jaguar, turned to Raylan. "We never even had enough for an indictment. I still think he did it. Kind of guy acts innocent but you know is dirty? Mixed up in bank fraud, heavy gambling, always in over his head . . ."

"So Reverend Dawn didn't help much."

"She tried. She had an idea if she touched him . . . She goes, 'Let me touch him and I'll tell you if he did it.' We didn't know what she was talking about. Touch him—where? But she was right about how the woman was killed, so we decided okay and set it up. Put a wire on her and got them to meet at the Sheriff's Office."

"What happened?"

"Not much. Dawn touched him, held his hand. . . . I guess she didn't get the right kind of vibrations. She said as far as she could tell, he didn't do it. Their conversation's interesting, though, you ever want to hear the tape."

"You let him go on Dawn's word?"

"We couldn't quite put him at the scene and his mother alibied him out. Guy named Warren Ganz."

Falco started to turn.

"Lou?"

"What?"

"I know his mom."

All the way down 95 to Delray Beach in midday traffic, Raylan looked at what he knew as fact, hoping something he hadn't thought of would jump out at him. Okay:

Ganz owes Harry a lot of money. Harry sends Bobby Deo to collect. Bobby tells Harry to meet him, he has the money, but doesn't show up. Instead, Harry happens to run into Dawn Navarro who, it turns out, happens to know Warren Ganz—from when he was a suspect in a homicide and she touched him. Harry disappears. And now Bobby Deo, ex-con, former bounty hunter, is hanging out at Ganz's house with a guy named Louis Lewis—however you spell it, check him out—while Ganz happens to be somewhere in the Keys.

What did all this tell him, if anything?

That Harry might be dead.

It jumped out at Raylan and there it was, whether he liked it or not. The idea: Ganz hires Bobby to kill him and takes off so he won't be around, have to answer questions.

But, if Ganz was so broke he's selling his furniture, how does he pay Bobby? It would cost him a few thousand at least, hire a guy like Bobby. How does he afford a trip to the Keys?

Say he doesn't. He hides out at home. And that's why Bobby and Louis are hanging around, to answer the door, pick up the phone. . . .

It seemed to make sense.

But now Raylan took it another step, to look at an idea that didn't make sense but jumped out at him anyway. The idea that if Harry wasn't dead, hadn't taken off but wasn't around anywhere, Harry could be in that house. And if he was, Bobby and Louis were there to watch him.

It was a feeling Raylan had, so it didn't have to make sense. At least not right away. The thing to do was let his mind work on it while he wasn't looking.

But when the feeling kept growing on him he had to look at it again—sailing down 95 among semitrailers, tourists in rentals, retirees in white cars that all looked alike. What made him keep thinking Harry might be in that house?

A feeling. Yeah, but more than that. Something Falco had said that made him think of Bobby Deo.

The pruners.

A guy staying at the house who carried pruners, wore them with his good clothes and could've had his pruners with him when he robbed a grocery store. Bobby and Louis. In the store to get snacks and Jell-O. And the last time Raylan had Jell-O . . . It was at Wolfie's having lunch with Harry and Joyce and Harry said he always had Jell-O for dessert, strawberry with fruit in it. Harry said try it and Raylan did—and it was Jell-O all right, no better or worse than it ever was.

If Harry was being held, they'd have to feed him.

But would they ask him what he wanted? Why not? Keep him happy. But what reason would they have to hold him?

Outside of money.

Harry had it and Ganz didn't and Falco said Ganz was dirty—into illegal deals, big-time gambling, bank fraud. . . .

Kidnapping?

If Harry was in there against his will, that's what it was, a federal offense; you could get life. Ganz had the right guy for it, Bobby Deo, who used to go out and snatch fugitives. Bobby picks the place to meet, the restaurant, because Dawn's there. Harry arrives and Dawn sets him up. For her old friend Warren Ganz.

But if it's a kidnapping, how do they score? Who pays? Harry doesn't have a wife. All he has is money.

Raylan looked at it for a minute or so; it didn't tell him anything.

The only thing he saw to do was go in the house and look around. Not with a consent to search, they'd never let him in. You could do it with Colombians because back home they couldn't refuse a search and thought it worked the same way here.

He could call it exigent circumstances, the imminent threat of death or serious bodily harm and break the door down. And if Harry wasn't there get sent to a new assignment like Minot, North Dakota.

The only other way, get a search warrant. Describe the premises in detail, what the house looked like, not just the address. Give the reason for requesting the warrant, also in detail, the probable cause why he wanted to gain entry, what he expected to find and why and show it to a U.S. attorney. Leave out the pruners and the Jell-O; no one would follow that kind of thinking, even though it was something he knew and could feel. If he was lucky and all the U.S. attorney did was put in a bunch of commas, he'd then take it to the U.S. magistrate and stand there while Her Honor read it, while she frowned and gave him a look, said something like, "Mr. Ganz owes Mr. Arno a sum of money, so you believe Mr. Arno is being held against his will in Mr. Ganz's home?" Her Honor would tell him his probable cause sounded like wishful thinking. He wouldn't in a million years get the magistrate's signature.

In the funeral home parking lot he'd told Falco about Harry being missing, the reason he'd met Warren Ganz's mother. Falco agreed with Torres: wait a few days and get Missing Persons on it.

"But what about Dawn?" Raylan said. "You think she really is psychic?"

"I think sometimes, anyway."

"What if she can tell me where Harry is?"

"You mean using her clairvoyance?"

"It wouldn't be enough to get a warrant and take a look, would it? The word of a psychic?"

"You'd still have to show probable cause, get into all that. I'd talk to her though, why not."

"You think, if Harry was kidnapped, Dawn could be involved in some way?"

Falco had stared at him over the roof of the car before saying, "You think she's stupid?"

Raylan wasn't sure that was an answer but let it go.

He said, "You mentioned you put a wire on her, for the meeting with Ganz? I'd like to hear it."

"Anytime you want."

Dawn wasn't at the restaurant and the hostess hadn't seen her all day. She was there yesterday, and the day before; Dawn hadn't said anything about taking time off. Raylan picked up one of her *Certified Medium & Spiritualist* cards and rubbed it between his fingers walking back to his car. It didn't tell him anything.

He did have a feeling she wasn't going to be home, and when he reached the house on Ramona saw he was right. No red car in the drive. He went up to knock on the door and looked at the sign as he waited, at DREAM INTERPRETATIONS, PAST-LIFE REGRESSIONS. Pay to get regressed back to a coal mine and breathe that dust again. Raylan walked around the house looking in windows cloudy with salt mist, careful not to get stuck by palmettos. He looked into dim, dismal rooms, at the old worn-out furniture, the sofa he'd sat in and felt the springs, at watermarks staining the wall where the picture of Jesus and the children hung, and wondered if it depressed her to walk in the house. She could be helping Ganz as a way to get out of there.

Raylan didn't feel like hanging around. He got in the Jaguar and drove up to Manalapan with the idea of staking out Ganz's house for a while, see if anyone came or left . . .

And saw it happening before he even got there, as he came past groomed oleander toward the wall of trash vegetation marking Ganz's property, saw Bobby Deo's Cadillac pop out of the drive and turn north. Two guys in the car.

Now Raylan had to make a decision quick: follow or, with them gone, see about getting in the house.

nineteen

Chip watched Bobby's Cadillac on the television screen until the car was through the shrubs along the drive and out of view. Finally. He'd been waiting all morning for them to leave so he could talk to Harry.

Trying to hurry them along didn't work. "You want to get the show on the road—isn't that what you told me?"

Louis said they'd leave when it was time to leave. Louis dragging his feet, Bobby taking half the morning to get dressed, Ganz smoking weed. This was before the guy in the hat showed up on the patio and spoke to Louis and Bobby. Ganz lit another joint, sucked it down listening to Louis say the man was a United States marshal, with the star, with the gun on his hip under his coat. Could see it when he took out his I.D. But mostly the man was a friend of Harry's, the reason he came. Chip toking, Louis saying the man's seen how it is now, who's who, and won't have a reason to come back. By the time Louis finished Chip was worry-free, zonked on the weed, able to ask deadpan, "A U.S. marshal? He ride in on a horse?" Louis grinned while Bobby sat there with a bug up his ass as usual. Chip thinking, even if it was the same guy who spoke to Dawn, so what?

Wait some more, finally one o'clock before Louis said it was time and they left, the program now back on track in spite of interruptions, shit happening, revising the timetable, his two helpers thinking they knew more than he did. Why argue? If they wanted to speed up the program, get it done, fine. Chip thinking, telling himself, Go with the flow, man. Saying, You cool? Yeah, you're cool. He felt it, full of his old confidence, in control. . . .

Pushed a button on the remote, to switch the picture from the front drive to the hostage room upstairs, and stared at the picture for several moments —at the cots, the chains on the floor, trash, boxes of snacks—before he realized, Christ, Harry wasn't there.

Ganz came up out of the sofa.

* * *

The black guy had stood behind him the whole time while he cut the blindfold off with scissors, so Harry didn't get a look at him. All he knew for sure, it was the same guy who'd said the other night, "We do some business. Just me and you." Harry had thought at the time the guy was putting on a Bahamian accent so his voice wouldn't be recognized. This time the guy said, "Go on in the bathroom and clean yourself up. Man, you smell ripe." And Harry realized what the guy had was the trace of a Bahamian accent, maybe left over from when he was a kid. The guy stood close breathing on him, saying, "There's a toothbrush in there, a razor, I believe anything you need." The guy who wanted to do some business being nice to him. Making a play, it sounded like, to cut out the other guys—Harry pretty sure now there were three of them. He said, "I can't take a shower with these chains on."

"Do the best you can," the black guy said. "Take a whore bath. You know what that is?"

"Before you ever heard of it," Harry said.

The guy handed him a bathing cap to use as a blindfold, with instructions when to put it on, didn't say anything about doing business, and left. Harry washed up and shaved; next thing would be to talk the guy into a shower and promote some clean clothes. He looked around his cell for the first time, the room bigger than he'd thought; looked at the windows covered with plywood and shuffled over to see if he could work the sheet free, but it was nailed onto the window frame.

Later on, Harry was coming out of the bathroom

when he heard the key turn in the lock. The door swung open. Harry saw the look on the guy's face, a different guy . . .

What Chip saw was the blindfold gone, something else covering his hair that Harry reached up and stretched down over his eyes: a rubber bathing cap, white with a yellow flower design that Chip's mother used to put on when she swam in the ocean, years and years ago. He could see her wearing it.

Harry raised his arms as though to protect himself, saying, "I didn't see you, okay? Honest to God, I didn't. The other guy said it was okay to take it off when I went to the bathroom or if I was alone, but cover my eyes if anybody came in. I swear I didn't see you."

Chip said, "But you saw the other guy."

"No, I didn't, he was behind me. He told me to put the bathing cap on—it's tighter'n hell and hot. Pull it down over my eyes I can't see a goddamn thing."

Chip said, "He tell you what you have to do?" and watched Harry lower his arms before he spoke.

"What do you mean?"

"Didn't say anything about getting out of here?"

Harry hesitated again. "No. Was he suppose to?"

"Sit down."

He watched Harry stoop to pick up the chain and shuffle to the cot, used to moving this way. When he was seated, Ganz walked over and sat down next to him.

"Have you decided?"

"I don't know what you mean."

"What it's worth to you to get out."

"Name it," Harry said. "Whatever you want, if I've got it."

"How about three mil?"

"You kidding? I don't have that kind of money."

Chip said, "You sure?"

"I know how much I've got put away, about two and a half, two hundred fifty thousand plus some interest."

"Where is it?"

"In the bank. Barnett branch on Collins."

"What about in the Bahamas, in the Swiss bank?"

"The Bahamas?"

"Freeport. You forgot about that one. What I'm gonna do," Chip said, "is give you one day, twenty-four hours, to come up with a way of drawing all the funds out of the Bahamas account and giving it to us, in cash. I mean, of course, without anyone else knowing about it. If I don't like the idea, Harry, you're dead. You pay up, you go home. So it better be the best fucking idea you ever had in your life."

Harry said, "Do I get my car back? It's brand-new."

He heard the guy say, "That's what you're worried about?" And felt the guy's hand on his shoulder, pushing on it as he got up from the cot, the guy saying, "Twenty-four hours, Harry," and a few seconds later heard the door open and close and the key turn.

Harry waited. He said, "You still there?" He waited again, a little longer, and said, "You still

there, asshole?" and peeled up the edge of the bathing cap.

He tried now to picture the guy from the glimpse
he got of him, no one he'd ever seen before, but a
type: Miami Beach, there were hundreds of those
skinny middle-aged guys around with tans, retired,
nothing to do; they sat on benches in Lummus Park
watching the models getting their pictures taken. But
this one—in a place right on the ocean, carpeting
that had to run seventy, eighty bucks a square yard
easy, expensive fixtures in the bathroom, a marble
floor . . . Did the guy live here? He didn't sound
like a wiseguy, he sounded like a guy trying to act
cool. Giving him twenty-four hours to come up with
an idea—that was bullshit. If they knew he had an
account in the Bahamas, all they had to do was get
him to transfer the money from his account to their
account. Open one—what was hard about that?

Harry ate an Oreo cream cookie thinking: They
start out with this great idea, how to score a bundle.
Propose a deal, dress it up. If it works and they get
the money they let you go. He believed they would,
otherwise why bother with a blindfold? But the black
guy had his own proposition, cut the other guys out,
and if he did he'd have to kill them. So that's the kind
of people you're dealing with, Harry thought. Some
guys with an idea who most likely never tried it before, felt their way along without knowing shit about
what they were doing. So you don't know either,
Harry thought. It could come apart for any number
of reasons: not trusting each other, or one of them
tells somebody else, the wrong person, the cops enter

the picture and these guys panic . . . Harry thinking, The cops should be on it by now anyway, for
Christ sake. What were they doing? Buck Torres,
he'd know you're missing. Joyce would call him first
thing. It got Harry excited. But then he thought, No,
she wouldn't call Buck, she'd call Raylan . . . Well,
that was okay, get the cowboy on his trail. But would
he have his heart in it? That fucking cowboy might
just as soon you stayed missing.

No, he'd get on it. Wouldn't he?

What Raylan did was drive along Ocean Boulevard
looking for vacant property, someplace he could park
and cut through to the beach. As a last resort he
could go up to the shopping center by the Lantana
bridge and park there; he didn't think it was too far,
maybe a mile. He watched his odometer. At six-
tenths of a mile he came up on a bunch of Australian
pines, big and scraggly, bent from years of wind off
the ocean, the trees lining an empty lot of scrub
growth. It looked good. He'd leave the Jag here and
approach Ganz's place from the ocean side. Take his
boots off to walk along the beach.

Chip was back in the study keeping watch, the hostage room still showing on the TV screen: Harry
Arno, without the bathing cap, sitting on his cot eating a cookie . . . eating another one, digging into
the package of Oreos again, Jesus, biting into another one. It made Chip hungry to watch. Not for
cookies, though, popcorn. Nothing hit the spot after
smoking weed like hot buttered popcorn laced with

garlic salt. Thinking about it he had to swallow. Sit here and shove handfuls of popcorn into his mouth while he kept watch. He remembered there was a big jar of Newman's Own popcorn, unopened, in the kitchen and it gave him a good feeling. He preferred Paul Newman's to Orville Redenbacher's, though Orville's wasn't bad. It was nice to be a little stoned and know the situation was in hand. Watching Harry the bookmaker eating Oreo creams. Chip grinning now—hey, shit, look at him, still eating. An Oreo wouldn't be bad . . . Or peanut brittle—there was a box of it in Harry's room, right there, on the floor. Jesus, peanut brittle, he could taste it. That's what he needed, something sweet. First scan the grounds, then go upstairs and get the peanut brittle. Fuck Harry, he had his cookies. Chip pushed a button on the remote. Nothing going on out front. Now the back of the property . . .

And Chip felt himself jump, the same way he'd jumped ten minutes ago when he looked at the room upstairs and didn't see Harry. What he saw this time, out beyond the patio, was the guy in the hat again, the U.S. marshal, by the trees at the edge of the yard, the guy pulling on his boots, looking toward the house and now coming this way past the pool, coming across the patio, the guy in the hat and dark suit in full view now, close, filling the screen, looking up as he approached and now he was out of the picture, beneath the video camera mounted above the French doors.

The phone rang and Chip reached for it.

It was in his mind he didn't want the guy to hear

any sounds from inside the house and had the phone in his hand before he realized his mistake. What he should've done, let the guy hear the phone ring and no one answer. . . . It wasn't too late to hang up. He started to when he heard, "Chip?" and thought he recognized the voice but wasn't sure.

"Who is this?"

"Who do you think?" Dawn said.

"Listen, I can't talk to you right now."

"Someone's there?"

Chip watched the TV screen, the empty patio, wanting the guy to appear again, see him walk away. All the doors were locked; he'd made sure of that after Louis and Bobby left. The guy wouldn't break in—he couldn't, he was a federal officer, for Christ sake.

"Chip? I'm at Chuck and Harold's. . . ."

"I know—something came up, I couldn't make it."

"You don't have my money, do you?"

"Tomorrow, how's that?"

"You're stringing me along. . . ."

"No, I called, you'd already left," Ganz said.

"I'll check my machine."

"I didn't leave a message. Listen, I wondered, has that guy been back?"

"What guy?"

"With the hat."

"No."

"You said he was a fed, some kind of federal cop."

"Yeah?"

"How'd you know?"

"I guess the same way I know he's looking for you

now. He hasn't found you yet, but he's getting close."
Dawn paused and Chip waited. She said, "He isn't by
any chance there right now, is he? Outside, looking
around . . . ?"

"I haven't seen him."

"You mean you haven't spoken to him," Dawn
said.

The front door chimes rang in the hall.

Chip switched the picture on the screen from the
patio to the front entrance and there he was, waiting,
touching his hat as he looked up at the video camera,
Dawn's voice saying, "But you *have* seen him. Chip?
Tell me the truth, aren't you looking at him right
now?"

He didn't answer.

"Chip?"

He was watching the guy, watching him turn finally
and walk off the front stoop, gone, out of camera
range, and Chip switched the picture to the driveway.
Nothing. No sign of him. Chip thinking, He's gone
around back. And Dawn's voice came on again.

"Chip? He knows we know each other."

"How could he?"

"It's what he does. He finds out things."

"All right, let's say he's on it. But you haven't seen
me. Listen, I'm not even here. Louis told him I'm
down in the Keys, doesn't know when I'll be back."

"He's talked to Louis," Dawn said, "but not to
you. Is he still there?"

"He left."

"But you saw him."

"For a minute," Chip said. "Not even that." He

felt alert but was thinking in slow motion, trying to hold a conversation and make sense, sound convincing without saying too much, Christ, with a federal U.S. marshal creeping around outside. It was hard, it required nerves of fucking steel. He put the patio on the screen—empty in a glare of sunlight—and said, "Look, you don't know anything, so there's nothing you can tell him, is there?"

"You mean what I might've gotten from you."

"Exactly, since I haven't told you anything."

"But what about what I know," Dawn said, "without anyone telling me? I'm not going to prison, Chip, for fifteen hundred dollars I don't even have."

Chip said, "Jesus Christ." He said, "Wait." But she'd already hung up.

He sat listening now, staring at the empty patio. He wanted to smoke another joint and wanted something sweet, hungry again, and wanted to go to the bathroom. He thought of going through the house, the living room, the library, to look outside, all around, but didn't want to leave the study and be in rooms with windows. He didn't know how long he could sit here. Or what to do when he heard the sound coming from the sunroom—a rapping sound, four times on a pane of glass—and felt his neck become rigid.

Raylan had taken another walk around the house. He pressed close to the French doors now, hands at his face to block out his reflection looking in at the white-covered furniture and the door across the sunroom that was closed, but showed a line of light beneath it. He reached up and rapped his knuckles against glass, hard, watching the door inside the room, wanting to see it open. He waited a minute before stepping back, and now thought of taking off his hat, putting his fist inside and punching it through a pane of glass. Reach in then and open the French doors, walk over to the door with the light showing underneath and yank it open.

He thought of doing it knowing he wouldn't. He could cut official corners to call a man out, give him twenty-four hours to leave the county, but couldn't walk in a man's house unless invited, or else with a warrant and bust down the door.

It was the way he was raised, to have good manners. Though a situation one time in particular had set it in his mind as something more than etiquette, back when they were living in a coal camp and the miners struck Duke Power: Raylan walking a picket line most of the year, his dad in the house dying of black lung, and company gun thugs came looking for Raylan's uncle, his mom's younger brother, living with them at the time. They came across the street, five of them, a couple with pick handles, and up the walk to where his mother stood on the porch. He remembered she was having trouble with her teeth and they ached her that day. The gun thugs said they wanted to speak to her brother the agitator, set his thinking cap on straight for him. She told them he wasn't home. They said they intended to look in the house, and if she didn't move out of the way they would help her. Raylan came out the screen door to stand with his mother and remembered her eyes, the way she looked at him like she'd given up hope. Though it was not in her voice when she told them, "You don't walk in a person's home 'less you're invited. Even you people must believe that. You have homes, don't you? Wives and mothers keeping house? This is our home and I'm not inviting you in." They shoved her aside and hit Raylan with the pick handles to put him down; they went through the house and out the back, empty-handed.

Her words hadn't stopped them. No, what they did was stick in Raylan's mind—her words, her quiet tone of voice—and stop *him*, more than twenty years later, from breaking into this man's house.

Walking away he had a strange thought. What if he wrote Harry a letter and sent it to this address?

twenty

"**H**ow can this guy be a crook," Louis said, "he does everything the same always."

"They no different than other people," Bobby said. "I learn that skip tracing. Get to know the guy's habits, he's yours."

They sat in Bobby's black Cadillac on South County in Palm Beach, the golf course where Ben King played every afternoon on both sides of the road. They were waiting for the S&L crook to finish the first hole and cross the road in his golf cart to play number two, the guy always alone. "Thoughtful of him, huh?" Louis said. Nobody wanting to play with him now, associate with a man up on charges to defraud, embezzle, and maybe a few other things, out on a half-million dollars' worth of bail put up by three different bondsmen.

They had parked by the clubhouse to watch him tee off. "Still having trouble with that slice," Louis said. "But he's all right. First three holes, you any good at all, they no such thing as a bad lie."

Bobby said, "You telling me you play this course?" his tone saying *bullshit.*

"I caddied here when I first come over, skinny little boy, the golf bags bigger than I was."

They pulled around to South County to watch Mr. King approach the green and putt out the first hole.

"There he is," Louis said now, "marking his card. I bet you the man cheats."

They watched him get into a green golf cart and cross South County in front of them.

"Man's big," Louis said. "You notice? Must go two hundred and I bet thirty pounds. What do you say?"

"About what?"

"How much he weighs."

"I don't give a fuck what he weighs."

"Man takes up the whole cart," Louis said, "going with pink and white today. The cigar, the sun visor— wants you to know he's a big important mother- fucker, why he smokes the cigar all the time. Chip say he stole money right out of his own company, put it in land deals, put it in offshore banks in the Cay-

mans. Sold mortgages he didn't even hold to different banks. How you expect to get away with shit like
that? Stole money out of trust accounts, like old retired people had their money in? Wiped them out.
Chip say, 'I think of my poor mother, if it ever happened to her.' What he's thinking, there wouldn't be
no money for her to leave him. It's why he wants this
S&L man," Louis said, his gaze following the green
cart. "And off he goes."

Once King was across South County, Bobby put
the Cadillac in drive, crept up to the next intersection
and turned left into a private road, this one narrow
and shaded dark with tall pines lining both sides.
"Hole's a three-hundred and fifty-six yard par four,"
Louis said, looking at it right there on their left. "Go
up about halfway. You see those bushes out there,
with the red flowers?"

"Hibiscus," Bobby said.

"They put them every hundred and fifty yards so
the gentlemen know where they at, what club to use."

"Here he comes," Bobby said, looking at his outside mirror, the green cart approaching along a path
close to them, on the other side of the pines.

"Sliced it again," Louis said. "I been counting on
his slice, keep him over on this side of the fairway.
See, but he underclubbed it. The shot plays longer'n
you think. The man oughta know better."

"How far was his drive?"

"About one-eighty. He won't be on in two, and
that's good, how we want it. Let's see where his second shot goes." Louis turned to look back through an
opening in the trees. "He's lining it up. Slice the

motherfucker, will you, please, so we don't have to go out on the fairway?" Louis waited, still turned in the seat to watch. And smiled. "Man is stuck with that vicious slice. You see it?"

"It's right up there," Bobby said, "in the trees. I didn't see it go through."

Louis had turned to look ahead, not smiling now, but pleased and anxious. He said, "Thank you, Jesus, for delivering this big-ass millionaire to us. Where is he . . . he coming?"

"Pretty soon," Bobby said. "He's in his cart."

"I love it," Louis said. "You ready? Soon as he gets up to the ball."

Bobby had his hand on the door handle. He said, "Anytime."

And Louis frowned at him. "You not ready. Wait." Louis hunched over to open the glove box. He brought out two Browning .380 autos and handed one to Bobby, who racked the slide while Louis went back into the glove box for the ski masks Chip had bought out of a catalog. The pistols Louis had bought off jackboys in Riviera Beach, cheap, the jackboys dealing in arms they stole and had plenty. The idea originally, one for Louis and one for Chip, but now Bobby had the man's while the man smoked weed and watched TV. Now Louis was ready.

"Man, put your ski mask on."

Bobby said, "Fuck the ski mask, it's too hot. I'm gonna hit the guy before he has time to see us." He opened the door and got out.

Louis sat there making up his mind—wear the ski mask or don't wear it—watching Bobby outside now in the trees, Bobby anxious, huh? So anxious he almost got out of the car without a piece. Louis opened his door. Okay, no ski masks—shoved them back into the glove box and felt the roll of silver tape. Man, so anxious himself he almost forgot it. Once out of the car he told himself to be cool. Understand? You a pro, man. You know what you doing.

He saw Mr. Ben King two trees away in deep shade, a big pink-and-white shape bent over his lie. Changing his mind then, using the clubhead to tap the ball away from the tree. Tapping it again to improve his lie. Louis moved up behind Bobby in the tree shade, about twenty feet from the pink-and-white man, watching him taking a practice swing now. The clubhead brushed against pine needles on the backswing and the man looked over his shoulder. He saw them, or saw something to make him turn around and now he was facing them, the cigar in his mouth, standing straight up staring at them. So they moved toward him. Bobby, holding his piece against his leg, said, "How you doing?" as friendly as Louis had ever heard him.

The man wasn't buying it. He said, "What do you want?" When they kept coming he said, "This is a private course. Get the hell off, right now."

There was nothing left to do but go for him, Bobby ahead of Louis as Louis told the guy, "Turn around," brought up his piece to put it on him and said, "You hear? Turn the fuck around."

The man was turning, yeah, but getting ready to swing his golf club, but then hunched his shoulder as Bobby got to him and clubbed him over the head with his piece, the barrel part, chopped him, the man's sun visor coming down on his face, the cigar gone. But the man didn't drop like in the movies when getting hit over the head knocks the person out; Louis had never seen it happen in real life and he had seen people hit over the head with guns and heavy objects. The man was staggered, but still trying to swing his golf club at Bobby. Louis took the man around the neck as Bobby was about to chop him again and twisted, bringing the man over his hip and they both went down, the man's thick body struggling against him, Louis trying to tussle him still while holding his piece and the fucking tape in his hands, Bobby saying, "Let me hit him good," Louis saying to hold the motherfucker, will you? and Bobby stepped on the man's wrist, reached down to take the golf club from him and shoved the grip end against his mouth, twisting so it would go inside. Louis sat on him now, laid his piece on the man's chest so he'd have two hands to tear off some tape, then had to pull the man's sun visor up off his face. So now they were looking at each other eye to eye, Louis feeling the man memorizing his face, every fucking line of it, before he stuck the tape over the man's eyes. Bobby pulled out the golf club and Louis stuck a piece over the man's mouth.

Bobby said, "Some golf carts . . ."

Louis looked up. Three hundred yards away a foursome was teeing off. Time to leave. He said to the blindfolded man, "You coming with us. Hear? So don't give us no trouble. Stand up."

Bobby put his piece in the man's face and cocked it. He said, "You give me any more shit, you dead."

They brought him through the trees to the car, taped his hands behind him quick, put him in the trunk and got out of there.

Up to Royal Poinciana and across the bridge to West Palm.

Louis said, "We should've wore the ski masks."

Bobby said it again, "Fuck the ski mask." Like saying he didn't care the man had seen them.

Louis had to ask himself what he thought about that. What it meant.

The last time the door opened, about a half hour ago, someone came in, didn't make a sound, didn't touch him, was in the room no more than ten seconds and out again, Harry thinking whoever it was had maybe left another snack; it wasn't time for a meal. He took off the bathing cap and looked at the floor, looked at the trash on the other cot. . . . His peanut brittle was gone. These fucking guys, these creeps, one of them gives you a treat and another one steals it.

This time he knew right away it wasn't just one guy. Harry had his bathing cap down over his eyes as soon as he heard them at the door. He sat on the side of the cot hunched over, arms resting on his thighs. He heard one of them making kind of a grunting sound, maybe in pain. He heard something hit the wall opposite him and a groan and a voice say, "Goddamn it, take it easy." A deep, kind of loud voice. Harry raised his head and almost asked if he had a cellmate, feeling surprised and a lift along with it, wanting to say something, and was glad he didn't. One of them put a hand on his head and pushed him back; he had to grab the edge of the cot to keep from hitting the wall. He heard the chains then, rattling, and heard the same deep voice say, "The hell you doing, chaining me up? What is this? Will you tell me, for Christ sake, have I been kidnapped? If that's what this is, guys, you have to get in line. There're between four and five hundred people say I owe them money." There was a silence then, except for the sound of the chains. Harry waited, listening inside the hot rubber bathing cap. Now he heard the voice again. "What're you doing? . . . Jesus Christ, you're tearing my skin off." It was quiet then. Harry imagined the voice belonged to a guy who was maybe his age, maybe a little younger, but a big guy, robust, heavyset. He imagined them ripping tape from the guy's eyes and blindfolding him with something else. How about another bathing cap? Harry could see himself and the guy sitting here like a couple of aquacaders waiting to go on. He heard the guy's voice again say, "Which one are you," quieter this time, "the colored guy or the spic?" Harry shut his eyes inside the bathing cap and right away heard the smacking sound, the guy getting punched in the face, and another voice, with an accent, saying, "I'm the spic." Harry heard him get smacked again and the Latino voice say, "You want to fuck with me, man? You gonna have a hard time here." Harry heard a low voice, a murmur, not the words, and then the Latino voice saying, "What's the difference? They gonna talk to each other." Then a silence, Harry thinking: Two of them, the black guy, the one who'd spoken to him and gave him the bathing cap, and the Latino. Then another voice saying, "If that's how you want it, I don't give a shit what you do." The thin, middle-aged guy with the hair, he'd caught a glimpse of before, Harry sure that's who it was. A few seconds later the door slammed closed. Harry waited. Now he heard the black guy say, "You want me to tell him?" The Latino voice said, "Go ahead," and the black guy said, "Mr. King, we want you to think on how you gonna get us some money, the bottom line being three million. If we like the idea, then all you have to do is get it. We don't like the idea, you get shot in the head. Dig?" The deep voice said, "I don't have three million, I don't have a dime, I'm bankrupt. You know how to read? I've been all over the papers, the past month." The black guy said, "You broke, then you get shot in the head. You want to think on it some more? Maybe you have money you forgot about." The deep voice said, "If you put it that way, I might. . . ." The black guy said, "We gonna let you think on it." Harry waited. He heard the door open and the black guy again, saying, "Don't touch the blindfold. Understand? Take it off, you get shot in the head."

Harry waited again, hearing only the guy's chains rattling, and pulled off his bathing cap.

King sat across his cot in the trash—wrappers and empty containers—head and shoulders against the wall, chin down on his chest. The towel covering his head—silver tape around it—showed traces of blood and there was blood on his shirt. He had on black-and-white golf shoes.

Harry cleared his throat and saw King's head raise.

"I'm Harry Arno. Your name's King?"

The guy didn't answer, surprised or maybe thinking it was some kind of stunt, take him off-guard. But then he said, "Who are you?"

"I just told you, Harry Arno. I been here . . . What day is it?"

"Thursday. You chained up?"

"Yeah, but I can take my blindfold off when they're not in the room." He watched King sit up and begin picking at the tape. Harry said, "I wouldn't do that. They like to keep you in the dark for a while, I think to get you disoriented."

"Where are we?"

"Someplace on the ocean."

"That tells me a lot."

"You know as much as I do," Harry said. He didn't care for the guy's attitude. Still, if they were going to be together . . . "You were playing golf, huh, when they picked you up?" The guy didn't answer, busy working on the tape, and Harry thought, No, he wears the golf shoes for tap dancing. Ask a stupid question . . . He watched the guy pull the towel and the tape from his head and Harry recognized him right away, Ben King, his picture in the paper lately, the S&L crook, dried blood in his hair, looking this way now.

"Who're those guys?"

"I just met them myself seven days ago," Harry said, "but I haven't seen them yet." He held up his bathing cap. "I have to put this on, anybody comes in."

"I saw them," King said. "I won't forget them, either."

The wrong attitude.

"I'd put the blindfold back on," Harry said, "if I were you," knowing King wouldn't do it, the type of hairy-assed individual he was, used to having his way.

"How long have you been here?"

See? Didn't even listen.

"This is my seventh day," Harry said.

"How much they want from you?"

"All they can get."

He saw King becoming interested in him.

"Yeah? What do you do?"

"I'm retired," Harry said, not feeling a need to confide in this guy, this crook. He began to wonder how the black guy was going to work his scam, whisper things to him with King in the room. It was something to think about. But if the black guy could cut out his partners to deal with him one-on-one, he could do the same with King.

"You ever play the Breakers," King said, "the ocean course?"

Harry shook his head. "Never have."

"I was on a straight par four," King said, "lining up my approach. If I got anywhere near the pin I was going for a bird. . . ."

Louis took Chip to the kitchen to make drinks, but mostly to get the man away from Bobby. Louis got out the ice, put it in three glasses and poured Scotch, telling the man, "The way you *see* something work in your head, don't mean it can work that way when you go to do it. Understand? Bobby say they gonna be talking anyway, comparing their situations, asking each other if they gonna pay and how much, all that shit."

"They ought to be in separate rooms," Chip said.

"That's right, but what you have is this cheap motherfucking video system, a camera in the one room. I told you I wasn't gonna keep running up and down the stairs, check on the room don't have the camera. Man, a cut-rate operation like this, you play it as you go."

"Bobby's got money," Chip said.

"You want to ask him for it?"

Louis saw the man thinking of something else, sipping his drink and thinking.

"I have to pay Dawn. She called, she's getting goosey."

"You want me to talk to her?"

"It was on my mind—you and Bobby got back and I mentioned it to him. He's gonna go see her?"

"Want to scare her more'n she is, huh? Well, Bobby's the man." Louis picked up his drink and the one for Bobby.

Chip said, "The marshal came back."

Louis paused. "He see you?"

"Rang the bell, went around and knocked on the patio doors."

"I want to know did he see you?"

Chip shook his head.

"We can talk about it afterwhile," Louis said. He

turned and led the way from the kitchen across the hall to the back study, the TV room.

Bobby was standing, watching the screen. He said, "Look at this."

Louis turned to the screen with a drink in each hand. "Yeah? You said they be talking."

Bobby said, "That's all you see? I told him don't take off the blindfold. He has it off."

Louis said, "No, *I* told him don't take it off."

Chip said, "This's what happens you start changing things."

Louis said, "I knew we gonna have trouble with this one."

Bobby said, "No, we're not," and walked out of the room.

Chip said, "Where's he going?"

"Gonna beat him up," Louis said. "Want to watch? Be good if the man fights back, huh?"

Louis's eyes held on the screen; he didn't look at Chip or hear him say anything. What Louis saw, waiting for the door in the hostage room to open:

Ben King sitting hunched on his cot and Harry Arno, the bathing cap off, sitting hunched on his, the two hostages facing each other, Ben King doing the talking, gesturing, the man taking his left thumb in his right hand—look at him—like you grip a golf club, taking a short swing now, showing Harry—the man, blood in his hair, blood on his shirt—telling Harry about his golf game. It's what he was doing. Wait. Looking up now. Harry looking up and putting his bathing cap on quick and then sitting back, and here was Bobby in the room, Bobby from behind going to Ben King, Ben King starting to push himself up from the cot, Bobby grabbing him by the hair to raise his face and punch him, what it looked like, but it wasn't happening. Right there Chip said, "Jesus!" loud, because Bobby's right hand was behind him, coming out from under his Latino fiesta shirt with a piece Louis hadn't seen before, not the Browning, one that looked like it, an automatic that size Bobby put in Ben King's face, King all eyes seeing it, mouth coming open, and Bobby shot him. They heard the sound of it like somewhere in the house far away. Louis watched Bobby turn and look up at the camera, his face on the screen with no special kind of expression, like saying to them, hey, nothing to it, and now he was gone. Louis saw Ben King lying dead across his cot in the trash, blood on the wall, man, blood all over it, Harry Arno sitting there made of stone with his bathing cap on.

Louis looked at Chip staring at the screen.

"You wanted Bobby Deo, you got him."

Lay it on the man, then go speak to Bobby. He was in the mother's bedroom now, the show over, but still holding the piece when Louis walked in and turned on the light. Louis stood watching him, not saying anything just yet, wanting to hear what Bobby had to say.

Nothing. Laying the piece on the dresser, he looked over at Louis and Louis said, "What you got there?"

Bobby seemed to shrug, subdued after killing a man. He said, "A Sig Sauer. I've had it."

"You had it at the golf course," Louis said. "I see you getting out of the car without a piece . . . but you had that on you, huh? Have it on you all the time. You wanted to shoot the man right then, didn't you? Out on the links. Why was that, you hadn't shot anybody in a while?"

"I didn't like him," Bobby said.

"I got that impression."

"You the one told him don't take off the blindfold. Didn't you say, or you shoot him?"

"In the head," Louis said. "Laying it on to make my point."

"Well, you tell them what you gonna do, man, you have to do it. You know? Or else don't say it."

"I do the telling and you do the shooting, huh?"

"I could see already it was a waste of time with him. He wasn't gonna pay us nothing."

"What about the mess you made?"

Bobby said, "Harry can clean it up," still subdued, like he was tired or didn't care.

But when Louis said, "Harry, the witness, heard the whole thing. You gonna shoot him too?"

Bobby got his attitude back, put on that macho shit saying, "If I have to."

It hooked Louis. He said, "You mean if you want to." He watched Bobby shrug like, yeah, that was cool, and Louis said, "What you gonna do with the man's body?"

"Dump him in the swamp. You want to help me?"

Louis walked over to the dresser; he picked up the piece Bobby had told him was a Sig Sauer and hefted it.

Bobby said, "Light, uh, for a .45? Eight shots."

"You think that's enough?"

"I can have one, nine millimeter, holds twenty in the magazine, if I want it. Five hundred."

"Go to war with a piece like that," Louis said. "How 'bout I help you to the car with Mr. King? You take him to the swamp, wherever you take people, and I'll get Harry to clean up the room."

Bobby gave him his shrug.

"Want the room nice," Louis said, "for the next guest. That is, if you like him."

Bobby gave his dead-eyed look now, no expression. The man's problem, he had no sense of humor.

Louis said to Harry, sitting on the cot with him, "You didn't see nothing, you didn't hear nothing."

"It was loud," Harry said. "Jesus."

"I bet it was."

"I had the bathing cap on."

The man seemed numb.

"I know you did. Like doing time, man, you don't know nothing going on around you, even right in the cell you're in. So don't think about it no more. You never saw the man. . . . You listening to me?"

He watched Harry's bathing cap with the yellow flower nod up and down, the man sitting straight, like afraid to move.

Louis sat thinking for a minute, looking at Mr. King's stain smeared on the opposite wall, then looked away as he realized he was staring at it. He said, "Harry, go on in the bathroom and stand at the mirror—you be away from the camera—and pull your blindfold off." He had to say, "Go on," before Harry picked up his chains and shuffled in there. Louis followed him.

Louis stood behind Harry, taller, looking over the man's shoulder to see his face appear, red marks on it from the bathing cap, eyes bloodshot, with the pitiful expression of a man who didn't know shit what was happening to him.

Louis said, "Harry, what you see behind you, man, is your salvation. Me. I'm the only way you gonna get out of here alive. I want you to see what I look like 'cause we partners now. Understand?"

He watched Harry's head nod up and down without much change in his eyes.

"You gonna do whatever I tell you, huh?"

Harry nodded.

"We get out of here, you gonna take a trip to Freeport with me." Harry waited and Louis said, "Aren't you?"

Harry nodded.

"And since we partners, we get there you gonna move half your money from your bank account to my bank account." Louis paused. "Go on, nod your head."

Harry nodded.

Chip was back on his weed, moving like a man underwater to sit down on the sofa, stoned as far as you could go without losing it. He looked up at Louis fooling with the remote and said, "He killed him. Just like that." As if Louis hadn't been here to see it.

"That's Bobby's way," Louis said, "you fuck with him."

"He's going to see Dawn tomorrow."

"That's a bad idea," Louis said.

"I told him he didn't have to, I'd call her. He said he wanted to talk to her anyway, get his fortune told."

"It's still a bad idea," Louis said.

twenty-one

Friday morning Raylan called Reverend Dawn from Miami, gave his name, told her he was there last Sunday for a reading, had stopped by yesterday and was anxious to talk to her again.

She said, "I know."

Her voice calm, telling him—the way Raylan heard it—she knew who he was and what he wanted to talk to her about. She didn't try to avoid him. When he asked if he could come by this morning, she said as long as he came an hour or so before noon; she'd be leaving then to go to the restaurant. So Raylan got in the Jaguar and headed up 95 in the traffic, the lanes both ways, north and south, strung with cars and pickups, vans, semis, motor homes . . . Otherwise it was a nice sunny day and Raylan felt ready for it. He had on his dark blue suit, the air-conditioning turned up high.

Yesterday afternoon he had stopped by the Sheriff's Office to run Louis Lewis on FCIC, the state computer, and found he had spelled the name right. Lewis comma Louis. Also known as Ibrahim Abu Aziz. Date of birth—Louis three years younger than Raylan. A notation said: Born in Freeport, Grand Bahama. Black male, black hair, brown eyes. Six feet tall, 165 pounds—if they ever had a fistfight they'd be evenly matched. Scar, right arm, not specific. No FBI number. Early charges of importation of marijuana nolle prossed, temporarily dismissed for some reason and never brought up. Grand theft, auto, nolle prossed. Here we go:

A 790.01, carrying a concealed weapon. A 790.16, discharging a machine gun in public, and a 790.19, shooting into or throwing deadly missiles into a dwelling. Which sounded like a drive-by. Convicted on all counts. His sentence wasn't on the sheet—or all the hustles he got away with that Raylan read between the lines—but Louis must have done a few years' state time.

So Raylan's three suspects were all felons: Warren Ganz, one-time homicide suspect convicted of bank fraud and placed on probation; Bobby Deo, suspected killer for hire, convicted of manslaughter; and Louis Lewis, minor felon until brought up on gun charges and convicted. The question that remained in Raylan's mind: which one was in charge? It would appear to be Ganz. But could he handle two ex-cons? Raylan didn't know enough about Louis Lewis to make a valid judgment, so he saw Bobby Deo as the one to look out for.

Later on he picked up Joyce and they went to Joe's Stone Crab for dinner. At the table he told her everything he knew to date and his theory that Harry could be in Ganz's house—even though, he admitted, it didn't make much sense.

It did to Joyce. She jumped at the idea, wanting to believe Harry was alive and not buried in a swamp. Raylan had to tell her why he couldn't go in to investigate without permission or a search warrant, and this was the part that didn't make sense to her. If he had no trouble shooting a man seated at a table with him in a restaurant, why couldn't he walk into someone's house?

He said to her, "Why don't you take my word for it?" tired of trying to explain distinctions, the gray areas in what he did for a living.

They picked at their crab claws pretty much in silence after that. He asked why she didn't try the mustard sauce. Joyce said she preferred drawn butter. Would she like another beer? No, she was fine. How about a piece of key lime pie?

He said to her, "We're sure polite, aren't we?"

Joyce didn't bother to answer.

*   *   *

This morning Raylan stopped by the Sheriff's Office to listen to the tape Falco had mentioned, off the wire Dawn was wearing when she met Warren Ganz.

Falco set it up in one of the squad room offices, saying the conversation had taken place right out there—Falco pointing through the glass wall of the office to a row of chairs—Ganz thinking he'd been brought in again for questioning. "You understand this was Dawn's idea," a way she could touch Ganz, their prime suspect in the murder of the woman in Boca, and find out if he did it or not.

Falco started the tape and sat down with Raylan. This was what they heard:

> *Ganz:* You waiting to see the lieutenant?
>
> *Dawn:* They want to ask me about Mary Ann Demery, the lady who committed suicide? I'm Dawn, a friend of hers.
>
> *Ganz:* No, you're not. I'm her friend, you're her fortune-teller.
>
> *Dawn:* If you say so.
>
> *Ganz:* What's going on?
>
> *Dawn:* What do you mean?
>
> *Ganz:* You sit down and shake my *hand*? What're we gonna do, get cozy here? You read my mind and I confide in you?
>
> *Dawn:* I already know things about you.
>
> *Ganz:* Is that right? From Mary Ann or you look in a crystal ball?

"Dawn doesn't answer," Falco said.

Ganz: You read palms?

Dawn: I can. I don't usually.

Ganz: Here, take a look. Tell me what you see and maybe I'll confide in you.

Dawn (following a long pause): You're egotistical.

Ganz: Where do you see that?

Dawn: Your index finger's longer than your ring finger. Most people, they're the same length.

Ganz: Amazing.

Dawn: You have trouble paying bills.

"You'll notice he doesn't deny it," Falco said.

Ganz: Which one's my life line?

Dawn: This one, curving down.

Ganz: All the way to my wrist. That's good, huh?

Dawn: The length doesn't mean much.

Ganz: What do you see?

Dawn: A lack of energy.

Ganz: Don't you see anything *good*?

Dawn: Well, your fate line—you're ambitious, you know what you want. The line's a bit ragged though.

Ganz: You want me to confide now?

Dawn: If you like.

Ganz: What if I tell you Mary Ann didn't commit suicide, she was murdered?

Dawn: How do you know?

Ganz: It's why we're here, isn't it? I'm a suspect and they want to know what you *feel* about me, or however you get your messages. If you're any good you know I didn't do it. But what if I tell you I know who did?

"The guy isn't dumb," Falco said.

Dawn: Do you?
Ganz: Let's say I know, but I can't tell the people here. Let's say for personal reasons I can't afford to become implicated in any way, the idea I was close to a woman who was murdered. Okay?
Dawn: You want *me* to tell them who did it.

"She isn't dumb either," Falco said.

Ganz: You go in there, you tell them you laid out your magic cards or you touched something Mary Ann gave you . . . Listen to me telling you how to do it. You're the pro, you see things, right? You turned over a card and there he was. Or you closed your eyes, went into your clairvoyant mode and you actually *saw* what happened, the guy picking Mary Ann up and throwing her off the balcony. You hear her scream as she's falling. The guy looks down, he turns, and that's when, clairvoyantly speaking, you see his face. You describe the guy to the cops and they go looking for him. Overnight you're famous, the clairvoyant who cracked a murder case.
Dawn: Get my picture in the paper . . .

Ganz: In the paper, in magazines, you're on talk shows. Before you know it they're lined up to get a reading. Will I ever meet Mr. Right? Is my husband fooling around on me? Pretty soon you have a syndicated column in newspapers. . . .

Dawn: What if they find out the guy I describe didn't do it?

Ganz: Then you're fucked. You were gonna go in there and put it on *me,* and if it turns out I did it, you're a star. You want to work this mental telepathy shit to make a name for yourself. Okay, go ahead, try it. Only I'm clean, I wasn't anywhere near Mary Ann's place that night. As I said before, if you're any good, if you know what you're doing . . .

Dawn: You said Mary Ann screamed as she was falling.

Ganz: Wouldn't you?

Dawn: She was already dead.

Ganz: They told you that?

Dawn: I told *them.*

Ganz (after a pause): Are you always right?

Dawn: Often enough. You want a quick reading? I won't charge you.

Ganz: Sure, go ahead.

Dawn: Give me your hand. *(long pause)* You make a good first impression, you can turn on the charm when you want to, and can talk people into doing things they'd rather not. At least some people. You could make a lot of money in sales, but you'd have to work and that's out of the question. So you live by your wits and a high opinion of yourself, for what it's worth, and so far it hasn't proved to be worth much at all.

"She's got him down cold," Falco said.

Ganz: But I know what I want and I'm ambitious. You saw that in my palm, right? When we're through here, what do you say we have a drink?

"I think they had that drink," Raylan said, watching Falco reach over to push the rewind button, "and got to be pretty good friends. She tell you right away it wasn't Ganz?"

"She said she didn't think so, but wanted to meditate on it. A couple days later she said she was positive he didn't do it."

"After they got to know each other," Raylan said.

Falco was nodding. "That was taken into consideration. We know she thought the guy had a lot of money, living in Manalapan."

"Anyone tell her he didn't?"

"Not that I know of."

"Why was Ganz your main suspect?"

"We didn't like anything about him, the guy's shifty. We know he'd borrowed money from the victim, we see cancelled checks in the amount of two grand, twenty-five hundred, that add up to over twelve thousand. He says he paid her back in cash, if you want to believe that, this born fucking loser—we know he owed bookies in Miami. The theory was, he's in deep, he asks Mary Ann for another loan and she turns him down. The guy's desperate, frustrated, they get in a violent argument and he creams her with the bookend, this brass modernistic bull."

"The one Dawn identified as the murder weapon," Raylan said, "without having seen it."

"Right, it was being held as evidence. She did see the other bookend on the shelf; there were two of them. We said, 'You mean that one?' She goes, 'No, the one that was used has blood on it.' "

"Wasn't it wiped clean?"

"No prints, no, but minute traces of blood around the base, this wood block the bull's standing on."

"What about Ganz's prints?"

"All over the apartment. Listen to this, even on Mary Ann's checkbook. The only other prints belonged to the cleaning woman. That's another reason we leaned toward Ganz; there wasn't anyone else, unless some guy walked in off the street."

"None of Dawn's prints around?"

"Not that I recall."

"Wasn't she ever a suspect?"

"We checked her out. There was no reason to think she had a motive."

Raylan gave that some thought before saying, "The two guys that robbed the grocery store, you haven't picked them up, have you?"

"Not that I've heard, no."

"I think I know who they are."

"Like you happen to know Ganz's mom?"

"In a way, yeah," Raylan said. "I want to take them federal. If I don't, they're yours."

twenty-two

Dawn Navarro was wearing a skirt today, a white one that ended a few inches above her knees, and a pale green sleeveless blouse. Raylan, on the mohair sofa, liked the skirt a lot. He thought she'd bring the card table over as she did the last time. Not yet, anyway. She stood in the middle of the floor, about ten feet away and said, "Well now. What can I do for you?"

The skirt showed her figure; she wasn't as slim as

Raylan had been picturing her. He said, "Just out of curiosity, do you have to have a license?"

"First," Dawn said—making that move, tossing her head and brushing her hair aside with the tips of her fingers—"you should know I'm a Sagittarian, born with a Grand Trine in the center of my natal chart. You have that, it almost demands the life I've taken up."

Raylan watched her sway just a little from side to side, moving from one foot to the other in flat white slippers that looked sort of like the kind toe-dancers wore. He noticed the way her hips moved.

Dawn saying, "When I was two years old I knew my dad wasn't my real dad; I wouldn't let him pick me up and everybody thought that was bizarre. I had dreams about things that came true, premonitions; I even experienced astral travel. One time when I was seven, a few days after my grandmother died, I saw her sitting in the living room. She was wearing a housedress and a white wool bed jacket over it. I went to the kitchen and told my mother. She didn't believe me till I described the bed jacket, white wool with little pink ribbons and the store tags still on it. My mother turned white as a sheet. She brought a box from her closet and took out the exact same bed jacket my grandmother was wearing. It was a birthday present, but she died just before. She would've been sixty-three. My mother had never shown the bed jacket to anyone and knew I hadn't seen it. Yet I described it, even the store tags still on it."

Raylan said, "What's astral travel?"

"Leaving your body. Finding yourself somewhere else."

He believed he should let astral travel go and said, "Did your grandmother say anything to you?"

"Yeah, she did. She said let's keep in touch. I talk to her every once in a while. She used to smoke three packs of cigarettes a day."

"You always made a living as a psychic?"

"I did nails and hair studying to be a beautician, but I hated it. I used to run around and get a little crazy sometimes. That was my Sagittarius rising, with Mars on aspect. I'm thinking seriously now of becoming an acupuncturist; it's a wide-open field. You want a cold drink?"

"Not right now, thanks."

"You asked me a question before," Dawn said. "Yes, I'm a licensed psychic, clairvoyant, astrologer, spirit medium and character reader. The license fee is two hundred and twenty-five dollars, while so-called faith healers and exorcists don't have to pay a dime. I'm also an ordained minister. After studying with several distinguished teachers and ministers— Marlene Locklear you might've heard of?—I was ordained into the Spiritualist Assembly of Waco, Texas."

Sounding to Raylan like she was reciting from memory.

"And I do aura readings. Yours doesn't look too bad—a nice blue tone, just a faint red showing around the edge. How do you feel?"

"Pretty good."

"Can you imagine having harmony in your life?

Between yourself and others you don't always get along with?"

"I get along with most everybody."

"Even the ones you arrest?"

Raylan smiled, just a little. "I don't worry about them; they have to get along with themselves." He crossed his legs, getting comfortable on the sprung, stove-in sofa, his right hand touching the brim of his hat lying next to him.

"That's a protective move," Dawn said, "crossing your legs. It closes off energy points in your body. You have to share your energy with me, your vibrations. I can't tell you anything about yourself that you don't want me to know."

He kept his legs crossed and she came over, moved his hat to the round arm of the sofa and sat down next to him.

"You don't want the table this time; you feel you sit too low and have to look up at me. Put your hand on your knee. Are you right-handed?"

"Mostly."

"Good."

She put her hand over his. He saw the nails bitten down and felt the tips of her fingers brushing his knuckles. He kept watching her hand.

"Have you seen Warren Ganz lately?"

Her fingers continued to move on his.

She said, "While I was standing there, you were trying to picture me without my clothes on."

Raylan said, "I was?"

She turned her head to him and smiled. Then looked at her hand again, no longer smiling, moving her fingers over his. "You have feelings, emotions, about a personal relationship you're trying to let go of, so you can allow something new in your life." She turned to him again. "I haven't seen Chip in months."

"Have you ever been to his house?"

"A few times." She said, "The feelings you have are almost gone, but still on your mind, because the relationship seems like a good idea to you."

"You haven't seen Chip, but you've spoken to him."

She nodded.

"About Harry Arno."

"You work very hard," Dawn said, "and you're open and optimistic, the way a child is, and that's a good way to be. You think everything you do will turn out just fine, and it usually does."

"Harry was here, wasn't he?"

"We spoke about Italy," Dawn said.

"Here, in this room?"

"Yes."

"You denied it last Sunday."

"You didn't identify yourself. How do I know who you are? I *did;* but since you never told me, I had no reason to trust you." She looked at her hand and said, "The relationship . . . you try to balance the feelings you have about it with your work and it's hard, so . . . Well, you have to face the consequences of your action, whatever you decide."

"How old are you? You mind my asking?"

"I'm twenty-six. You thought I was older. It's okay, I don't mind." She said, "You know Harry had a feeling he should go back to Italy, even though he wasn't happy there."

"Harry isn't happy anywhere."

"I felt that," Dawn said. "He wants to be a big shot. Someone once said, 'The personality and the ego scream, while the soul whispers.' You know that already. I felt that Harry didn't want to hear what's good for him or be told what he should do. Still, he needs somebody to take care of him."

"You saw him again?"

"No."

"Not since last Friday."

"You have a sense of confusion, what to do, because you're not admitting to yourself what you really feel. You want to get married and have a family, and to do that you need a younger woman who doesn't mind that you carry a gun and killed a man with it. You want to know if I've been checking up on you. I haven't. I know you're a federal agent of some kind. You came here Sunday looking for Harry as a friend and you believe now you're getting close to finding him."

"Am I?"

She didn't answer.

"If he's dead," Raylan said, "I can't help you."

Dawn turned to look at him, touching her hair.

"Do I need help?"

"You know better than I do." He felt her trying to look into his mind and said, "You want to know if you can trust me. You're not getting the right vibrations or what?"

"They're mixed, different kinds," Dawn said, and

looked down at her knees. "You like my skirt, don't you? It's like the one Susan Sarandon wore in *Bull Durham*. When she was showing Kevin Costner how to bat? I saw it on video and went out and bought this skirt."

"I remember it," Raylan said.

"The woman in the relationship," Dawn said, "has it together, she's a nice person, but she can sometimes be tough. You feel she's emotionally hardheaded because she doesn't understand your intuition, why you know things."

"How old is she?"

"You're testing me," Dawn said. "I already told you, she's too old to have babies, something you want, what you miss, having those two boys you hardly ever see." She paused, looking at her hand, and said, "You're not hung up on material things, financial security."

"What about you?"

"I get by. I always have."

"You'd like to move," Raylan said.

"That's true, I would."

"Why don't you?"

"I'm thinking about it."

"How much did Chip pay you?"

She kept staring at their hands.

"For setting Harry up." Raylan could feel her fingers moving. "For getting him to come here." He reached over to touch her face, raising it, and she was looking at him again.

"He hasn't paid me anything."

"He still owes you?"

"You're trying to find out things without threatening me," Dawn said, sounding a little surprised.

"You know where you stand. You're right in the middle, poised between good and evil," Raylan said, hearing himself starting to sound like her and knowing he would never have said it to anyone else. "One misstep either way could get you in a lot of trouble."

She said, "Now you're threatening me."

"Uh-unh, I'm pointing out what you already know. What I have in mind—you could tell me what you know, using your gift for seeing things, that you haven't actually seen or been told."

"You're saying, so I won't be a snitch," Dawn said. "I understand. Like, do I know if Harry's dead or alive."

Raylan waited.

"He's alive."

"You're sure."

"I'm positive."

"Is he okay?"

She nodded. "That's all I'll say about him. What else? Chip. You want to know where you might run into him when he isn't home or down in the Keys."

"You're a mind reader," Raylan said. "Turn your psychic powers on that one, if you would."

"It sounds like you're putting me on," Dawn said, "except I know you're not."

Raylan watched her look away to stare off and then close her eyes.

"He's in a park, walking across the grass to where the Huggers are having one of their gatherings. It's tomorrow, Saturday. It's always Saturday or Sunday;

he goes just about every week. A sign on a tree says WELCOME HOME. They're giving each other peace signs, hugging, saying they love each other. Chip's hugging, even though he hates to. He holds his breath when he hugs, so he won't smell the person. He goes over to where the heads are hanging out at the dope tree. Chip's looking to score either pot or acid he'll use on some poor, unsuspecting teenage girl."

Dawn paused again. This time she opened her eyes and looked down and he felt her fingers moving on his.

She said, "The first time I touched your hand, this one, I knew it had held a gun and you'd killed a man with it. I can feel your hand holding it again."

"Am I aiming at somebody?"

"You have your back to me. There's another person there. . . ."

"You see who it is?"

"It's not real clear. First I see your back, then another person's back. It could be two different times I'm seeing at once 'cause they're the same kind of situation."

"When is this happening?"

"I don't know. It's not clear at all."

Raylan waited. He watched her frown and then shake her head. He said, "You see Chip with the Huggers, trying to score either pot or acid to use on some poor teenage girl. . . ."

Dawn looked off again, closing her eyes. "Some little girl who's run away from home. They come to gatherings all the time, runaways. Chip will talk to her, kid around; he'll get her to toke or trip and find out all about her—where's she from, why she doesn't get along with her folks. . . . Then he'll call them and say he's found their little girl, and if they'll pay him a certain amount for his trouble, he'll tell where she is. It's like one out of four will wire the money to him, under a different name he uses."

"What is it?"

"Cal. I don't know the last name. I've never seen him go to Western Union to pick up the money. He uses a fake I.D."

"Why do the parents believe him?"

"He tells them things he could've only learned from their little girl."

"How does he get Harry to pay?"

Dawn said, "You're sneaky, aren't you? I don't know anything about that, or if there's anything to know. Believe me, I don't."

Raylan watched her look down at their hands.

"Because you don't want to know? You can shut it out?"

She seemed to be concentrating and didn't answer.

Raylan said, "You want to hear what I think I know? You can nod your head if I'm right."

Dawn said, "I see the person in your relationship, she's standing with her back to you, looking out at the ocean. I see you touch her. You want her to turn around."

Raylan was staring at Dawn's profile: head slightly lowered, her dark hair, soft-looking and with a nice scent, falling past her shoulder, bare in the sleeveless blouse.

Dawn saying, "You're looking at me now wondering . . . You want to know something about what I'm wearing, or not wearing, but you don't think it would be right to ask."

He watched her head begin to raise.

Dawn saying, "Someone else I'm thinking of . . ." and paused and said, "Someone I'm thinking of because he's coming . . . No, because he's already *here.*"

Dawn turned to him, so close she was all eyes and it startled Raylan—he didn't hear anything, not a sound. She was out of the sofa now, going to the door by the time he'd turned half-around to look toward the window and through the palmetto leaves, see what was out there:

In the street, a car parked nose to nose with his, a black Cadillac sedan.

twenty-three

Bobby knew the dark green Jaguar. Seeing it as he approached the fortune-teller's house he had to make up his mind in a few seconds: keep going and come back later or stop.

He stopped. Because he knew from the way the feeling came over him all of a sudden and keyed him up, this was the time. Better than if he'd planned it. His chance to meet the cowboy face-to-face and see what it was like.

When he was getting ready to leave the house he had told Chip, who didn't want him to come here, "You like me to scare her? Okay, that's what I'm gonna do." Chip asked if he was going to hurt her and he said, "Why would I do that?" Chip asked why was he bringing a gun. In a brown paper sack some food they bought for Harry had come in, a small sack. Bobby demonstrated. "I hold it up, she thinks the money you owe is in here. I say to her, 'You want it?' She says yes. I bring out the gun instead of money and she sees, man, she can get paid one way or the other, so she better not talk to nobody. Is like a surprise, so it scares her more than if I hit her a few times and she thinks about it later, when she's alone, and gets mad. You got to watch out for women that get mad at you." Louis said yes, that was right, and wanted Chip to tell about the woman who had cut off her husband's dick while he was sleeping; but Bobby wasn't going to stand there listening to stories. He folded over the top of the sack telling them, "This is the way to do it, surprise her."

The sack with the gun was next to him on the seat.

Bobby watched the door of the fortune-teller's house open. Now the United States cowboy marshal, Raylan, appeared. There he was, like it was planned: wearing his suit, his hat, the boots Louis liked—they were okay—and with his coat open. He's not leaving, Bobby thought, and waited a few moments.

He's not coming to you, either. He's going to stand outside the door like a fucking bodyguard. Meaning the fortune-teller had talked to him, so now he was protecting her. If it was true it gave Bobby another reason to get out of the car and do it. Or he could shoot him from here, not even get out. But it wouldn't be face-to-face the way the cowboys did it and he wanted to see what it was like.

He was glad he'd brought the Sig Sauer, his own gun he was used to and knew the feel, and not the Browning. He slipped it out of the sack, racked the slide, cocked it and slipped it back in, careful not to tear the brown paper. Okay, he thought, are you gonna do it? Yes, he was ready now. Then get out of the fucking car and do it. Bobby got out of the car with a smile to greet the cowboy.

"Man, every time I turn around . . ."

The cowboy stood there.

"You not talking today?"

It didn't look like it.

Bobby came away from the car. "You know this lady, uh? Gonna get your fortune told?" On the front walk now, he held up the paper sack in his right hand. "I got something I want to give her."

"She isn't home," Raylan said.

Bobby nodded toward the red Toyota in the drive. "Her car's there."

"She still isn't home," Raylan said.

"Maybe she's asleep, or she's taking a shower."

"When I say she isn't home," Raylan said, "it means she isn't home."

With that cop way of talking.

He had his thumbs in his belt, the same way he had posed before. Bobby could see his shirt, his dark tie, but couldn't see his gun back in there on his hip. The distance to the cowboy, Bobby believed, was about twenty meters. He wanted to get closer, but not too close.

"I think she's home and you don't want me to see her," Bobby said, taking a step, then another; one more and now he was where he wanted to be. He held up the sack. "Man, I just want to give her this."

"What is it?"

"A gift—what do you think?"

"If it's money, she doesn't want it."

Bobby was holding the sack in his left hand now, underneath. All he had to do was unfold the top— take one second—and slip his hand in.

He said, "Money? What do I want to give her money for? I don't owe her no money."

He believed he was ready.

But now the cowboy was coming down the walk toward him, saying, "I'll tell you what. You can give it to me and I'll see she gets it."

This was the moment, right now. But Bobby hesitated, because this wasn't the way it was supposed to happen, the guy so close, standing only a few feet away now. He had shot guys as close as you can get, but not standing up facing like this. He had never seen it done in the movies this close. It wasn't the way to do it. If the cowboy knew what was going to happen he would've stayed by the door, giving them some room—but he didn't know. He'd know when he saw the gun come out of the sack and he'd try for his —that was the idea, how it was supposed to work— but he didn't know that yet.

Saying now, close, "What's in there?"

"It's a surprise."

"I'll tell you what you do," Raylan said. "Keep it. She doesn't want any surprises and I don't either. You aren't to come around here anymore or phone Reverend Dawn or bother her in any way. Tell your friends Louis and Chip they're to leave her alone."

With the cop way of talking, but calling her Reverend. Was he serious?

Bobby looked at the eyes in the dark of the hat brim looking back at him and thought, Yes, he's serious; and wondered if maybe this guy did know what he was doing and had done it before, even this close, even with his gun on his hip, or wherever he had it today.

"Was there something else?" Raylan said.

Bobby's fingers were on the folded opening of the sack.

"You gonna show me what you have . . ." Raylan said.

Bobby hesitated.

"Or back off and get out of here?"

The guy knew.

Bobby was sure of it. He hesitated again, wanting so bad to do it, but the moment passed and he knew it and let his breath out, giving the cowboy a shrug. He said, "You don't want her to have this gift, okay, forget it."

At his car, opening the door, Bobby looked back wanting to say something, but knew it was too late. Raylan the Cowboy hadn't moved. He stood there watching like all the fucking cops who'd ever told him to go on, get moving, had stood watching until he was gone.

* * *

Raylan closed the door and turned to Dawn, still at the window. He said, "Are you having a vision?" Her expression—she looked like she was off somewhere, maybe doing some astral traveling.

"When you die," Dawn said, "you see your whole life all at once, like in a flash."

"I've heard that," Raylan said.

"Did you know he had a gun?"

"It crossed my mind."

"In the paper *bag*." She sounded amazed, awed. "He was gonna kill me."

Or scare you, Raylan thought. But he liked this frame of mind she was in and said, "It seemed his intention. They haven't paid you yet, have they?" When she hesitated, he said, "Just say yes or no without giving me a reading, okay?"

"They haven't paid me anything." She seemed to be still in her mind, or someone else's, until she looked at Raylan and said, "He could've shot you dead."

"He'd have had to pull his weapon to do it," Raylan said.

"He had it in his *hands*."

"Yeah, but you need your mind set on it, too, pull on a man you know is armed. I doubt Bobby's ever done that. What I'd like to know," Raylan said, "is why they had Harry come here. They could've picked him up off the street. What'd they want you to do, get him relaxed and talking? Harry's a talker, he'll tell you anything you want to know."

"All they told me to do," Dawn said, taking her time, "was find out a few personal things about him."

"Like how much money he has? See if he's worth taking?"

"I wasn't in any position to ask *why* they wanted to know. I had no choice."

"Harry tell you where his money is?"

"A bank in the Bahamas."

"What else?"

"That's all really."

"Where did they take him?"

"I don't know. They left, I was in the bedroom."

"But you know where he is," Raylan said. "If you know anything reading minds you know that."

"They said if I told anyone about this I'd be sorry. I was put in the bedroom with the door closed and when I came out they were gone." Sounding now like she was reciting.

"You're waiting to see how it turns out," Raylan said, "before you say too much. But what about Harry? Chip told you nothing would happen to him. Isn't that right? They'd work some kind of scheme to get Harry's money and then let him go."

She looked out the window again, not saying anything.

"You believe Chip so you won't have Harry on your conscience," Raylan said. "Or you believe him because he can turn on the charm when he wants to. Remember telling him that?"

It got her looking at him again.

"You told Chip he could talk people into doing

things they'd rather not. You said, at least some people."

She was staring at him now, her eyes holding tight
to his. Raylan imagined her trying to look into his
mind, see what else was in there.

"So you had a drink with Chip, got to know each
other; you thought he had a lot of money. It looked
like a pretty nice connection, so you helped him duck
a murder conviction."

Dawn said, "Oh, I did? If you know anything about
it at all you'd know I helped the detectives, not
Chip."

"I know about the bookends, the brass bulls," Raylan said. "I know you saw only one on the shelf in the
woman's apartment, where there should've been two.
You decided, nothing to lose, the missing one must
be the murder weapon."

She said, "How did I know there were two?"

"You saw them, when you were up there before."

"But the only time I was in Mary Ann's apartment," Dawn said, "was with the detectives."

"Whether that's true or not, you know bookends
come in pairs," Raylan said. "You say about people
who're alike, they're a couple of bookends. You
guessed, not taking much of a chance, and you were
right. Chip saw why you were doing it and told you,
to get your picture in the paper, become a famous
psychic."

She said, "What's wrong with wanting to do better? I *have* the gift."

Eyes wide open, just a girl trying to get ahead in

the world. For a moment there Raylan actually felt sorry for her. He said, "But if you guessed . . ."

"I didn't. I *knew*."

"Did you know where the missing bookend was?"

"I didn't even think about it."

"You don't know what suits you not to know," Raylan said. "You tell me Harry's okay, but you don't know where he is. Don't you realize that if he's seen these guys and can identify them, they'll kill him? Whether they score the money or not. Don't you know that?"

"He hasn't seen them," Dawn said, turning to the window again. "He's blindfolded."

"That's what you're betting the man's life on, a blindfold? How do you know he hasn't seen them?"

"I just do."

Sounding like a little girl now.

"Tell me where he is."

Raylan waited.

She looked like a little girl: at the window in sunlight, her fingers stroking dark strands of hair. She said, "Right before Bobby came you were looking at me—remember? You were trying to tell, even with all that business on your mind, if I had on a bra." She turned from the window to look at Raylan. "You couldn't decide, could you?"

Raylan said, "You slip in and out of conversations, from one thing to another. . . ."

"You were about to say 'like a snake,' " Dawn said, "and changed your mind."

He watched her come away from the window, past him.

"Where you going?"

"To get ready. I see I'm gonna meet the woman in your relationship."

Each time she took him by surprise like that, he'd try to keep from asking how she knew. Raylan said, "I'm gonna hide you out in Harry's apartment, the Della Robbia Hotel in South Beach. I imagine you already know where he lives. Joyce has a key, so I guess, yeah, you might see her."

"She's dying to meet me," Dawn said, at her bedroom door now. "I'll pack a few things. . . . You go ahead, I want to have my car, case I have to be somewhere."

Raylan said, "I don't know. . . ."

And Dawn said, "Bobby's not coming back. He's home waiting for you."

twenty-four

Chip was going through mail Louis had found in the box on the road and skimmed on his way in with it. Mostly catalogs and junk. What Chip would hope to find was a dividend check he could forge his mama's name on and cash, the checks turning up every now and then. Louis glanced at the front drive on the TV screen, switched the picture to the room—Harry stretched out on his cot—and switched to the front drive again. Louis said, "Bobby should be getting back," and left the study.

A few minutes later he was back with a tray from the kitchen. Chip said, "What's this?" as Louis set a plate of food on the chest in front of him.

"Your dinner."

"I mean, what *is* it?"

"Pork chops done to a crisp," Louis said, going over to the desk with the tray. "Butter beans fixed with drippings and okra done in a tangy creole sauce. The okra, man, you have to stir it and stir it."

"I can't eat that," Chip said, making a face.

Louis was seated now, mouth watering and having to swallow, deciding what his first bite would be. The okra. He took some—mmmmm—and said to Chip, "Your tummy acting up on you?"

"Heartburn," Chip said, touching his chest.

Ever since last night the man had been popping Tums like peanuts, Tums and shots of Pepto-Bismol. He'd taken sick while trying to clean blood from the carpeting, most of it where the S&L man's head had come out of the blanket bumping down the stairs, Bobby dragging the body and not caring he was leaving a trail; the stains still there like rust spots.

"It's that microwave shit," Louis said, "angers your tummy you eat too much of it. I'm gonna cook from now on, fix you some of my favorite dishes."

Chip was watching him. "How can you eat that?"

"Love it. I acquired the taste learning to be African-American; it's part of our culture."

"Nigger food," Chip said, "if you'll pardon the expression."

Louis watched the man go back to looking at mail, Louis deciding not to make something of the disrespect. That was weed talking. The man's nerves were strung tight and the weed helped him sound like he was one of the guys. Push him, he could go over the edge, run off screaming. Look at that—throwing aside the Victoria's Secret catalog without even checking out the cute undies. Louis started eating his dinner, mixing the okra and butter beans together and taking big, heaping bites.

Chip said, "Jesus Christ."

Louis looked up to see him reading a postcard, the man's eyes glued to it.

"There's no way he could know," Chip said. "There's no fucking way."

Louis didn't recall a postcard when he'd skimmed the mail. The man kept staring at it. Louis finally got up, went over, and took it out of his hand. It showed a government building on the front. Louis turned the card over and saw it was made out to Harry Arno at this address on Ocean Drive, Manalapan; it had the zip, everything. The message was short. It said:

> Harry—
> Hang in there.
> Help is on the way.
> Raylan

Louis said, "Hey, shit," grinning, reading it again and then holding the card up to Chip. "You know what this building is? The federal courthouse in

Miami. The message is for Harry, the picture's for us."

Chip said, "You think it's funny?"

"You got to appreciate the man's sense of humor," Louis said. "What's wrong with that?"

"He knows Harry's here."

"How could he? If he *knew,* or like he had good reason to believe it? He'd have been here with the SWAT team the day he mailed the postcard. You understand what I'm saying? The man's trying to get us to jump. Run out the door with Harry and the cowboy's there waiting on us." Louis caught movement on the TV screen, glanced at it, at the black car coming through the shrubs, and said, "Here's Bobby."

"He's the reason," Chip said, "this whole fucking thing is coming apart."

"We still in business," Louis said. "Soon as I get hold of my man in Freeport, make the arrangements, we're out of here in two days, three at the most."

Chip said, "But you haven't talked to him yet."

"If he ain't in jail he'll call me, I left this number. Man has a thirty-six–foot boat."

Chip was looking at the screen, nothing there to see now but bushes. He said, "That fucking Bobby."

"I'll tell you something," Louis said, "he's never been what you'd call a favorite of mine neither."

"I thought you two were cooking something up between you," Chip said, "and you were gonna cut me out, after I come up with the idea, the whole scheme."

"That's your nerves," Louis said, "they cause you to look over your shoulder and imagine things creeping up on you. We cool, huh? Me and you? Thinking back on all the time we been together, we ever have a problem? You always been the man. See, but now we getting to where I can make this deal with Harry work out how we want it to. What you have to do is trust me."

He saw the man blinking his eyes, thoughts running around slow-motion in his head.

"You trust me?"

"Yeah . . ."

"Yeah, but what?"

"That fucking Bobby."

Louis held up his hand. "He's coming."

"She wasn't home," Bobby said.

Like that was all he had to report on the subject. Looks at the plates of food, one then the other, and starts to go. Leaving something out, Louis believed, he didn't want to tell.

Louis said, "Hey, Bobby?" and waited for him to look around. "That's it, huh, she wasn't home?"

Now Bobby was looking suspicious. "You want me to tell you again she wasn't home? She wasn't home."

From the sofa Chip asked, "You stop by the restaurant?"

Bobby shook his head. He started out again as Louis picked up the plate he'd set there for Chip. He said, "Bobby, you going upstairs, aren't you?"

He stopped, but didn't say he was or he wasn't.

Louis walked over and shoved the plate at him. "This's for Harry. Be a treat for him, some home cooking." Bobby took the plate and Louis said,

"Hold it in both hands, you don't drop it." That got Louis Bobby's dead-eyed look, one Louis was getting used to. Bobby walked out and Louis said after him, "You come back, I'll dish you up."

Louis turned to Chip.

"Never wants you to forget he's a mean mother-fucker. The man practices up there front of the mirror, trying different mean looks to use on people."

"All he says is she's not home," Chip said. "What do you think?"

"I'm thinking he might've done the fortune-teller," Louis said, "and he's practicing his story."

"Jesus," Chip said, his nerves showing through the weed in him. "I could call her up and see."

"Don't," Louis said, using the remote to switch the TV picture to the upstairs room, Harry still lying on the cot. "I'll drive over there in a minute, peek in a window."

Louis picked up a pork chop from his plate, got ready to take a bite and held it in the air seeing Bobby on the screen now, his pigtail hairdo, his back in the fiesta shirt moving toward Harry with the dinner plate. Now they were looking at Bobby in profile standing over Harry stretched out on the cot.

"He's asleep," Louis said. "Don't have his mask on." Louis raised his voice to the TV screen, saying, "Harry, pull the bathing cap down, man."

Now it looked like Bobby was saying something. Harry didn't move, eyes still closed. Now Bobby nudged the side of the cot with his leg. Now he raised his foot, put a lizard-skin shoe against the side rail of the cot and gave it a good bump. Harry's eyes opened. Opened wide seeing Bobby at the same time Bobby turned the plate of food upside-down, dumping the chops, the butter beans, the tangy okra all over Harry's face. They watched Bobby come away looking up at the camera, but with no expression to speak of.

"The guy's crazy," Chip said.

Louis watched Harry, sitting up now, wiping the food off him, the man looking dazed, but then seeing a pork chop and picking it up from the floor, studying it close, both sides, before taking a big bite.

Louis took a bite of his pork chop, laid it on the plate and brushed his hands in the air, ready to go. He said, "Well, least Bobby didn't shoot him."

Bobby came up to the Mercedes as Louis was backing the car out of the garage.

"Where you going?"

"Get laid; I'm overdue."

"The guy was there, Raylan? At the fortune-teller's house. He pulled a gun on me, told me to go on, get out of here. I didn't want Chip, the way he is, to know the guy was there, so I didn't say nothing."

"You didn't get to talk to Dawn."

"No, he came out, Raylan did."

"You had your piece in the sack?"

"Yeah, but I never did it that way. What I want to do, man, is meet him face-to-face with my piece right here"—Bobby patted his stomach—"and draw. I know I can beat him."

"Like in the movies," Louis said.

"Yeah, only it's real life. I want to practice doing it with you, so I be ready."

"You want to practice . . . ?"

"Get so I can pull it out quick."

"Man, you crazy. You know it?" Louis took a moment, sitting there with the motor running, Bobby hunched over his arms on the windowsill. "You didn't see her?"

"She was inside."

"You don't know if they talked and she told him anything."

"It don't matter," Bobby said. "I'm gonna kill him." He straightened, stepping away from the car. "You get back, we practice."

Dawn's front door was open a crack. Louis walked in and there she was, coming out of the bedroom, something in her hand. Seeing him, she stopped next to a canvas suitcase sitting in the middle of the floor.

"You leave your door open?"

"I was on my way out," Dawn said and held up her sunglasses. "I forgot these."

Louis moved toward her standing there in a white skirt he'd never seen before, Dawn—with that nice dark hair—looking afraid of him or afraid of something. He held his hands out and now she moved toward him, coming into his arms. She said, "Hold me," and he took her slender body close, tight against him, his fingers feeling the bones in her shoulders, stroking her hair now.

"What's wrong, baby? Got caught in the middle,

huh? Bobby tuggin' at you from one side, the law tuggin' from the other . . ."

"I didn't tell him anything."

"I know you didn't, baby. The cowboy come to see you—then what?"

"When Bobby came, Raylan wouldn't let him in the house."

Calling him Raylan.

"He talk to Bobby, ask him what he wanted?"

"They were outside. Bobby had a paper bag with a gun in it. I didn't see it, but I knew it was a gun."

Louis said, "Bobby take it out, show the marshal?"

He felt her shake her head no, close to him. She smelled nice. "And the cowboy, the marshal, he didn't show his gun either?" He felt her shake her head, again saying no. "Told Bobby to leave and Bobby did, huh? Didn't give the marshal any shit out the side of his mouth?" She said no, still scared; he could feel it the way she clung to him.

Like she clung to him the first time he came here.

Told him what he was thinking: "You're trying to imagine what I look like without my clothes on." And he said, "I *know* you gonna look fine. Let's see if I'm right." He opened his arms and that was when she clung to him the first time—back when she was still seeing Chip but about to break it off, telling Louis Chip talked a good game, but that was all. Louis had caught her when she was tender, in need of loving. She would read him and they'd go to bed and satisfy each other until they were worn out. Fifty dollars for the first reading, on the house after that, once a week or so, Chip never knowing a thing about it. Chip hadn't even seen Dawn in months when Louis thought of using her to set up Harry.

"Chip say you going to the police if he don't pay you."

Dawn said, "I had to tell him *some*thing. I stick my neck out—what've I gotten? Nothing."

"Your ship's coming in, baby, pretty soon now. Tell me what the marshal knows."

"He thinks he knows everything, except where Harry is."

"But can't come up with a probable cause, the way the system works, to get some action going. Else they'd be all over us," Louis said. "I never saw a deal get fucked up so quick—one thing after another. I won't give you the messy details."

"Please don't," Dawn said.

"I should be making my move tomorrow, Sunday the latest. You hear what I'm saying?"

"*Your* move," Dawn said. "You're making plans of your own."

"See, according to my horoscope my reputation for shrewd business ideas is paying off, but it also say romance could suffer. What should I do?"

"Well, for one thing your star pattern is going through a dramatic change."

Talking to him in her fortune-teller voice now while he held on to her, letting her feel he could hold her tighter if he wanted.

"The cosmic dust is just now beginning to settle. The good thing is that during this astrocycle others are extremely open to your ideas."

"I see it happening," Louis said, "starting to put

my ideas to work. Seeing who I want and who I don't want, who's gonna get cut out or left behind. Tell me what you see."

"An empty house," Dawn said.

"Whose?"

"This one."

"Where you gone to?"

"I see myself on a beach."

"Around here?"

He felt her shake her head.

"On an island in the Bahamas. Isn't that where the money is?"

Louis grinned. "You something else."

She said, "Am I going with you?"

"You gonna follow, in a day or so. But tell me where you going now, where you gonna be."

"You won't believe it. Harry's apartment in South Beach. For my own protection."

"You feel you need it?"

"Well, I sure don't want to see Bobby again. I'll call when I get there, give you the number."

"I got all kind of numbers for Harry Arno," Louis said. "What I need to know, if it's true what my horoscope say, about romance could suffer."

"I doubt it."

"Tell me what you feel."

"Well, I feel *some*thing," Dawn said, "pressing against my tummy. It means you haven't lost confidence in your ability to please others."

"I get next to you, girl, I become confident in a big way."

She looked up at him, making a face with sad eyes.

"I have to get going, or Raylan'll be looking for me."

"You call him Raylan," Louis said. "What's he call you?"

"I didn't tell him anything, honest to God."

"I know you didn't, baby."

They sat in metal chairs on the Della Robbia porch making conversation, waiting for Dawn Navarro.

"Harry says these chairs have to be fifty years old," Joyce said. "He never sits out here—doesn't want to look like he's retired. He said the way it used to be, every hotel along the beach you'd see old people lined up in their chairs like birds sitting on a telephone wire."

A guy in his twenties, a grown man wearing shorts down to his knees, no shirt, but gloves and knee pads, went sailing past on a skateboard.

"Harry says the weirdos have taken over and he doesn't like it. You know, maybe he did just take off."

Raylan watched the guy on the skateboard, wondering if this was the high point of his life, weaving through crowds of people in bathing suits and resort outfits—the guy wanting everybody to look at him—skimming past the tables outside the Cardozo, across the side street, where Raylan had walked inside to sit at a table with a man he told his time was up and when the man pulled a gun, shot him. He had thought it was going to happen with Bobby Deo, in front of Dawn's house, but he didn't force it and Bobby, on the edge of doing it, changed his mind. He wondered if he had wanted Bobby to pull his gun and tried to remember what he felt in those moments. There was too much to watch here to concentrate on something that didn't happen. He wondered what he'd do if he saw Bobby now, on the street, Bobby going to see his girlfriend, Melinda. Raylan couldn't picture them together. He liked Melinda for no special reason; he liked her because she seemed natural, full of life. He could stop in while he was down here, ask her . . . what, if she'd seen Bobby? Try to set something up? . . . He didn't want to use her that way. He was thinking, though, she could help him bring Chip Ganz out in the open, and she might go for it. The Santa Marta, where Melinda was staying, was only a few blocks from here.

Joyce said, "I don't think it's a good idea."

"What?"

"Letting her use Harry's apartment."

"It's not her idea."

"I didn't say it was."

"You said 'letting her use it,' " Raylan said, "like she asked if she could."

"How about 'putting her up in Harry's apartment'? Will you accept that?"

"Why don't you think it's a good idea?"

"Harry has nothing to say about it. Don't you have places where you make arrangements to keep people like that?"

"Like what?"

"Witnesses—or whatever she is. Don't you put them up in a hotel room?"

"That's what I'm doing."

"I know what it is," Joyce said, "you don't have

authorization, so you'd have to pay for a room out of your own pocket. That's why you thought of Harry's place."

"He won't even know about it."

"No, but that's why you want to use it—it won't cost you anything."

Raylan let it go. She was looking for ways to criticize him or she was being protective of Harry or—whatever her reason, it didn't matter.

They sat in silence watching vacationers, the fun-seekers, across the street in Lummus Park and out on the beach where you could burn your feet off without shoes getting to the ocean.

Joyce said, "Harry has a lot of nice things in his apartment."

Raylan pictured Harry's living room, looking for nice things. Harry had an imitation-leather recliner, so did Dawn.

"You afraid she might steal something?"

"No, but she could mess the place up. We don't know anything about her," Joyce said. "Does she cook?"

Raylan couldn't recall any cooking smells in Dawn's house. He said, "I don't know."

"That could present a problem."

"You mean if she cooks?"

Joyce, watching people on the street, didn't answer.

"Harry doesn't cook, does he?"

She said, "What's Harry have to do with it?"

"I don't think she'll go in there and start cooking

anyway," Raylan said, "so I'm not gonna worry about it."

"Where is she?"

"She should be along any minute."

"I'll bet she doesn't come," Joyce said.

Raylan's beeper went off. He took it out and looked at it, said, "Excuse me," and went into the hotel.

As soon as he was back, standing by his chair, Joyce said, "She's not coming."

"It was the office," Raylan said. "I have to work a court security detail. Some cartel guy's getting sentenced."

"You have to leave? What about Reverend Dawn?"

"You said you wanted to meet her."

"I did? When?"

That's right, it was Dawn who said Joyce wanted to meet her. Raylan said, "All you have to do is show her upstairs. You feel like it, you can keep her company, sit around and chat."

Joyce said, "You suppose she'd give me a reading?"

twenty-five

Louis put the Mercedes back in the garage and went through the house to the study. Chip was still there on the sofa, the same as when Louis had left, but with expectation in his eyes now, like waiting to hear bad news.

"She wasn't home," Louis said.

"You go by the restaurant?"

"They said she must've gone to read somebody, so we fine, no problem. I get any calls?"

"Your buddy in Freeport," Chip said. "I could barely understand him."

"He leave a number?"

"Said he'd call back."

Louis studied Chip on that big sofa, the man's bones showing he was so thin, with kind of a yellow cast to him underneath his tan, like he might have some slow sickness taking over him, AIDS coming to Louis's mind. He used to wonder if the man was queer or maybe went both ways. Dawn was the only woman Louis knew of the man had been with and Dawn said Chip was never much in bed, went through the motions and got it done. Louis used to worry the man might come on to him sometime, but it never happened.

"You feeling all right?"

Chip gave him a shrug.

"You look like you winding down," Louis said. "Where's Bobby?"

"I haven't seen him."

Louis used the remote to switch the picture from the front drive to the room upstairs—man, tired to death of this security shit. He saw Harry lying on his cot again, his shirt off, food from the dinner plate on the floor.

"Bobby still hasn't shot him," Louis said. "That's good, since Harry's all we got." He saw Chip watching, but not saying anything. As tired of all this as you are, Louis thought. He switched the scene to the patio and there was Bobby standing at the table, his back to the camera.

Louis went out through the sunroom. He walked

toward Bobby, still at the table, Louis saying, "What you doing out in the sun?"

Bobby came around to stand with his hands at his sides, arms loose. Louis recognized the pose. The next thing he saw was Bobby's left hand lifting the front of his fiesta shirt while his right hand went in and dug his gun out of his waist. Bobby held it straight out for Louis to look at that black hole in the muzzle pointing at him.

"You suppose to hold it in two hands," Louis said, "like the dicks in the movies do. Like Mel Gibson and them dudes, Bruce Willis . . ."

"Fuck them," Bobby said. "I got it down, how I'm gonna do it." He put the gun, his Sig Sauer, back in his waist and smoothed his shirt over it. "Can you see it's there?"

"Can't hardly tell. You practicing, huh?"

Bobby said, "Here," turning to the patio table. He had the two Browning .380's lying there. "Take one. Let's see how you do."

"You want me to play with you?"

"I want to know I can beat you." Bobby handed Louis one of the pistols, then drew his Sig Sauer, laid it on the table, and stuck the other Browning into his waist. "I want to try my piece and this one," Bobby said. "See which one I get out faster."

Louis said, "Yeah? Then what? You gonna go look for the marshal? He be in the saloon, man. They always in the saloon, you want to find them. Go through the swinging doors and everybody in the place stop talking."

"I don't have to look for him. He's gonna come back, man, he can't stay away."

"Gonna shoot him right here."

"Get it done. He don't bother us no more."

"What if he beats you to the draw?"

"Then I'm dead," Bobby said. "That's how it works, man. You ready? Stick it in your pants, on the side, where he has his."

Man was crazy.

"The cowboy's is in a holster."

Bobby said, "I don't give a shit. Stick it in your pants, let's go." His gaze moved.

Louis turned to see Chip at the French doors.

"Your friend's on the phone."

Chip followed Louis into the study, wanting to listen without being obvious about it. He stood by the desk, glanced at the TV screen, at Bobby with a gun in each hand, and swung around to Louis.

"Jesus, what's he *doing*?"

Louis looked up from the sofa. He said to Chip, "Hey, I'm on the phone," raised his eyes to the screen with no expression, watched Bobby for a moment and then said, into the phone, "Mr. Walker, my man . . . No, this is my pleasure. Man, I was worried about you."

Bobby was seated now at the patio table, fooling with his gun. Chip looked down at the desk, at Louis's partly eaten plate of dinner, okra and butter beans, Chip not sure if he'd ever tasted butter beans. He heard Louis say "uh-huh" a few times, listening to the guy he called Mr. Walker, then heard him say,

"You did the right thing, man, separate yourself from that nigga. Could've taken you down with him." Chip picked up the pork chop he believed hadn't been touched, hearing Louis saying "uh-huh" again, several times. The pork chop looked good, the fatty part burnt to a crisp, and Chip was about to take a bite, taste it, but stopped. That tenderloin part of the chop was gone; Louis must've eaten it. Louis saying, "You not busy, I got something for you." Saying, "Hey, even if you *think* you busy . . ." Chip put the pork chop down. Louis was laughing now. Chip looked over, knowing that laugh as the one Louis put on to show appreciation and what a nice guy he was. Louis saying then, "No, man, no product. This is a clean run I'm talking about. No contraband, no kind of shit of any kind like that . . . Yeah, right." Chip looked at Bobby on the screen, still at the table, then back to Louis as he heard Louis say, "Three," without saying three what. Now he said, "Yeah, I'm sure." Listened for a while and said, "Let me ask you something first. You know any the ladies work at the Swiss bank? . . . Yeah? That's how you pronounce it, huh, *de Suisse*?" Louis was grinning now as he listened. "Yeah, I thought you might have. Well, depending on how well you know the lady . . ." Chip watched Louis grinning as though he might actually be enjoying himself. "That's right. You know before I even tell you." Louis looked at Chip now as he said, "Listen to me, my man, we talking about fifty grand for a ride in your boat." Louis grinning again, saying, "Yeah, dollars," as Chip thought, What fifty grand? They hadn't even discussed what they'd pay the guy and Louis was offering him fifty thousand dollars. Louis saying, "What you do . . . Listen to me now. You listening? . . . You know the Boynton Inlet? . . . No, man, that's Lake Worth, port of Palm Beach, you too far north. Look at your map. You see the Boynton Inlet and right above it you come to Manalapan. Cut through the inlet, go on up—it's like two miles, you see private docks along on the right side." Louis paused to listen and said, "Man, will you look at your map, please?" Chip waited along with Louis. Now Louis said, "There you go, through the narrow part, yeah . . . I'm thinking tomorrow, Saturday." Chip watched him nodding, saying now, "That's fine with me. Mr. Walker, it's my pleasure. I'll call you there any changes. . . . Yeah, okay then. I'll see you, man."

Louis hung up the phone still smiling a little and looked at Chip.

"Mr. Cedric Walker was in the gun business. Got out right before the man he was dealing with went down."

"You offered him fifty thousand," Chip said.

"Yeah, and that's cheap."

"We don't have fifty thousand."

"We get paid, he gets paid."

"That wasn't what you told him."

"Yeah, well, I will when he gets here."

"What if he won't take us?"

"Man, you got to stop worrying so much."

Chip looked at the screen and then at Louis again, Louis lounged on the sofa.

"You said . . . at one point you said 'three.' "

"I did? Three what?"

"I don't know. That's what I'm asking you."

"I don't recall saying it."

"And right after, you said yeah, you were sure."

Louis shook his head. "I don't know, I must've been commenting on something Mr. Walker said. He's gonna have a lady he knows at the bank look up Harry's account, see how much he has in it. That must've been it, yeah. Mr. Walker asked we talking about a few million? I said yeah, about three. That was it."

"You didn't say 'about three,'" Chip said. "You said 'three.'"

Louis was pushing up from the sofa. "Maybe you didn't hear it right. Maybe you're stoned or you got wax in your ears." He walked past Chip, glancing at the TV screen, Bobby still there waiting. Louis said, "You worry too much for no reason."

Bobby got up from the patio table saying, "Okay, you ready now?"

"What you want me to do?"

"Here, put it in your pants."

Louis took the Browning auto from him, looking at it, racking the slide then, saying, "It loaded?" He snapped the slide back again and a cartridge ejected. "You not suppose to play with a loaded gun, man."

"I want the right feel, the weight," Bobby said. "First I'm gonna try this one, then my own gun. You ready?"

Louis was wearing a loose white cotton shirt and loose gray cotton pants with a tan cloth belt. He slipped the Browning into his waist against his belly, and dropped his arms to his sides.

"Like this?"

"Move it around more to the side."

Louis slid the gun around to his right hip.

"You need a coat," Bobby said. "The guy always wears a coat."

"Come on, man, we just playing."

"I want to see what it looks like," Bobby said. "I'll get you one." He went past Louis into the house.

Louis walked out to the swimming pool that looked like a pond with green scum covering it, the water a murky brown underneath, the sides of the pool turning black, Louis thinking there could be snakes in there, giant beetles and different kinds of ugly shit growing down in the bottom. He felt a breeze and raised his face to it, looking out at the ocean. He believed he could sit all day and look at the ocean, but had never tried it. He believed he'd like to have a boat and cruise around the Caribbean islands in it. Wear white pants, barefoot, no shirt, a red bandanna covering his head. No, kind of a lavender one.

Bobby came back with a black silk blazer hooked on his finger. He held it out. Louis had to come over to where Bobby stood by the table to take it and put it on. The coat fit him and felt good except for the sleeves, an inch or so too short on him.

He watched Bobby backing away now, almost to the edge of the patio. Louis turned to face him, seeing maybe fifty feet between them now. He moved toward Bobby saying, "Man, you too far away."

Bobby backed up some more saying, "Stay there," and Louis stopped.

He said, "Man, this far you have to be a dead shot," brushed the sport coat open with his hand and put it on the grip of the Browning. When he brought his hand away, the coat's skirt fell back in place. "What're you gonna do, count to three?"

"You don't count," Bobby said, "you feel when the guy is gonna draw his gun and you go for your gun."

"Watch each other's eyes," Louis said, "I think is what you do." He stood in a slouch, hip-cocked, arms hanging loose at his sides. He watched Bobby getting ready. "Hey, I spoke to my man in Freeport. He's coming Saturday."

"I don't want to talk now," Bobby said. "Okay, you ready?"

"Ready for Freddy," Louis said, watching Bobby shift around to get comfortable in his pose. "He ask me how many was he picking up," Louis said.

"Man, quit talking, all right? You ready?"

"I'm ready," Louis said.

He saw Bobby's left hand pull up the front of his fiesta shirt, right hand digging for his gun. Louis whipped the skirt of the blazer aside, took hold of the Browning and pulled it free as he saw Bobby's gun rising toward him, Bobby with his legs apart in kind of a crouch, the Puerto Rican gunfighter, putting that black muzzle-hole on him.

"You're dead!" Bobby yelled.

Louis raised the Browning, cupped his left hand beneath the grip the way they did in the movies and fired. Shot Bobby square in the middle. Fired again and put another one in him, Bobby stumbling back now, arms in the air, tripping on the edge of the tiled patio and falling to land flat on his back.

Louis walked over to him. Saw blood covering the man's good fiesta shirt. Saw his chest rising, working hard to suck in air. Saw his eyes open. Louis said, "Mr. Walker ask me how many people was he picking up. I told him three. You understand what I'm saying, Bobby? You ain't going, nigga."

It was like watching a movie. Not a feature film or even a made-for-TV movie. More like a low-budget flick shot on video—way too bright, the sun high above the two guys pointing guns at each other. But very familiar, a scene out of every cowboy flick ever made. Chip smoked his weed thinking, Shit, I've seen this one:

Louis with his back to the camera, a three-quarters rear view—Chip could see the gun Louis was holding —and Bobby facing the camera, his back to the swimming pool. Chip thinking, They're like kids. Nothing else to do, nobody to shoot . . . He used to do this with his buddies. Want to play guns? They'd get out their cap pistols and shoot each other and stumble around taking forever to fall.

When Louis fired, Chip saw the gun jump in his hand and saw Bobby drop his and throw his arms in the air as he was hit and hit again and it knocked him down, Bobby caving in and blown off his feet at the same time, without any stumbling around.

Hey, shit—it brought Chip straight up on the sofa.

He heard the gunfire, faint pops coming from outside, like a cap pistol firing, but Bobby was down, lying there with real bullets in him, and Louis was walking over, looking down at him now and saying something. Louis turned then to look at the camera, held the muzzle of the gun to his mouth and seemed to blow into it. Another familiar bit, Louis mugging for the camera. Now he was dragging Bobby by his feet to the deep end of the pool. He tried to push Bobby in with his foot, but had to get down and shove with both hands before Bobby rolled over the side, gone.

Was Bobby still alive? Chip wasn't sure, but it looked like Bobby tried to grab hold of Louis as he went in the pool.

Louis stood with his hands on his knees looking down at the scummy water. Now he came over to the patio table, laid it on its side and wheeled it by its round edge to the pool, to the spot where he'd dumped Bobby in. Louis let the table fall in the water, jumping back as it splashed up at him. He turned to look at the camera again. With a big smile—Jesus, like a kid—proud of himself and wanting to be acknowledged.

Chip said out loud, "Nice going, man," thinking, Yeah, great; but beginning to have doubts. That took care of a serious problem—Bobby. Or did it?

Coming into the study Louis checked the TV screen, the patio still on big. "Saw me blow him away, huh? That was the famous Puerto Rican gunfighter, wanted to High Noon it and met his match."

"You planned that?" Chip said.

"No, it just came to me. When I was talking to Mr. Walker."

"You said something to Bobby."

"I told him he wasn't going to Freeport."

"He was still alive?"

"Just hanging on. I didn't see a reason to shoot him again. The scum on top the pool like opened up? But the water in there's so putrid, brown like a sewer, what it smells like, too, you stir it up? But you can't see him down there, man's in nine feet of deep shit."

Chip said, "Louis, what about Bobby's money? He had quite a bit, didn't he? What he got for Harry's car?"

He could tell Louis hadn't thought of that.

"Was a wad on the dresser this morning."

"Is it still there?"

He was thinking of it now, you bet.

Louis said, "Lemme look," and was gone.

Chip eased back in the sofa telling himself, Great, no more Bobby Deo, Chip picturing the scene again and wishing he could play it back. He felt a sense of relief, no more Bobby, a big mistake corrected before his eyes. . . . Except that the bottom of a swimming pool wasn't the bottom of the ocean. Not seeing him didn't mean he wasn't there. Someone, sometime or other, would find him. They couldn't say, oh, he must've fallen in; not with two bullet holes in him. Chip didn't want to think about it, but the fact remained, Bobby was still with them.

Louis believed there had to be a couple thousand in the wad Bobby carried around and left on the dresser sometimes, like daring Louis to touch it. The money wasn't there; it wasn't in any of the drawers or anyplace Bobby kept the clothes he'd brought. Looking around, Louis thought of Bobby's lizard shoes; he should've tried them on before pushing the man in. He still had on the black silk sport coat, a gun in each pocket—the Sig and a Browning—he took out and laid on the dresser. The Browning he'd used he'd bury somewhere in the yard; so he left it stuck in his waist when he went downstairs and said to Chip:

"It wasn't there."

Chip had a blank look on his face from doing weed, like he had to think hard of what to say.

"You sure?"

"I looked every place it could be. He must have it on him."

"You'll have to get it," Chip said.

"*I* have to get it. You crazy? Dive in the pool in all that scummy shit?"

"You put him there," Chip said.

Like that was supposed to make sense.

"You the one wants the money, *you* dive in. Just don't breathe, you in there."

"*We* want the money," Chip said, "to pay Dawn. Christ . . . we have to get rid of the body anyway."

"I *did* get rid of it. Go on out and look at the pool, you can't see him. He ain't gonna gas up and float, neither, not with that table on him. The man's the same as gone."

Chip said, "Louis, you know we can't leave him there. He'll smell."

"It already smells; I told you that."

The man had his mind made up, thinking how to do it, saying, "We'll have to get a pump and drain the pool."

Louis stared at him, not agreeing, not angry, not anything, just staring, thinking what he should do was put the man in the pool with Bobby, something heavy like the TV set he was sick of looking at tied around the man's neck. If he didn't owe the man nothing, what was he putting up with the man's shit for?

The phone rang.

Chip reached for it and Louis said, "When you gonna learn? You been smoking, huh?" He walked over to the sofa and picked up the phone from the end table.

"Ganz residence."

A girl's voice said, "Where's Bobby?"

"He ain't here."

"You know where he went?"

"Didn't tell me."

"Well, when's he coming back?"

Louis said, "Girl, I'm busy. Bobby ain't here or ain't ever coming back. So don't call no more. You understand what I'm saying?"

"You understand this?" the girl's voice said. "Get fucked."

They both hung up.

Louis said to Chip, "Some girl looking for Bobby."

Chip said, "Who was it?"

See the patience you had to have with this stoned ofay motherfucker?

"I just told you, didn't I?" Louis said. "Some girl wanted Bobby."

"I meant, what was her name?"

"She didn't tell me."

"Anyway," Chip said, "you know where we can get a pump?"

Louis stared at the man, still not angry or anything, but thinking, Shit, put him in the pool.

twenty-six

There was a poster with the heading HANG 'EM HIGH that showed a famous hanging judge of a hundred years ago, Isaac Parker, against a montage of condemned prisoners on scaffolds waiting to be dropped through the trapdoors.

Raylan would look at the poster, in the lobby of the Marshals Service offices in Miami, and feel good about their tradition. Not the hanging part—they had quit handing out death penalties in federal court—

but the tradition of U.S. marshals as peace officers on the western frontier. Every time he looked at Judge Parker up there in the poster Raylan thought of growing a mustache, a big one that would droop properly and look good with his hat.

Rudi Braga would be sentenced in the central courtroom of the United States District Court for the Southern District of Florida, in Miami. Raylan and three other marshals shackled Rudi's wrists and ankles, brought him down to the basement of the new building, shuffled him through the corridor to the old building and up in the smelly prisoners' elevator to the central courtroom holding cell on the second floor.

An old hand at court support, Milt Dancey stepped out to the hallway for a smoke and Raylan went along to ask him a question. The second-floor hallway was outside and looked down over a railing on an open courtyard with potted palms and a fountain.

Raylan said, "Does a kidnapping conviction always draw life?"

Milt Dancey, smoking his unfiltered Camel, told Raylan that kidnapping, abduction or unlawful restraint carried a base offense sentencing level of twenty-four. "Look it up in the guidelines," Milt said, "it's fifty-one to sixty-three months for the first offense. If ransom is demanded it goes up five or six levels, say to around a hundred and twenty months. And it goes up depending on how long the victim is held or if the victim is sexually exploited."

Raylan admired Milt's use of the word *exploited,*

the way, Raylan was pretty sure, it would appear in the guidelines.

They removed Rudi Braga's shackles before taking him into the courtroom and seating him next to his attorney at the defense table. Raylan and the three other marshals sat behind them, while the rows of spectator seats, like church pews, were nearly all occupied by people who could be friends or cartel associates of Rudi Braga. Watching them was a contingent of full-time court security officers in uniform, blue blazers and gray trousers.

The assistant U.S. attorney present, the one who'd prosecuted the case, was the same natty young guy in seersucker who had seemed anxious to prosecute Raylan following the Tommy Bucks shooting. Seeing him gave Raylan a momentary feeling of sympathy for Rudi, a bald little guy about Harry's age and even resembled him, except Harry had hair. Rudi had been convicted of the unlawful importation and trafficking of a controlled substance, more than 150 but less than 500 kilograms of cocaine, and was facing, according to the presentence investigation report, 360 months to life. This was the reason, Milt Dancey said, for the crowd, nearly all Latins. The sole responsibility of Raylan's group was Rudi. If he tried to run, demonstrate, or threaten the court, "We will assist him," Milt said, "in regaining his composure."

Raylan wondered if the court clerk would have a spare copy of the sentencing guidelines.

Waiting for the proceedings to start, he looked around thinking this was what a courtroom should look like: the ceiling a good twenty-five feet high, gold chandeliers, marble panels on the wall, the windows draped in red velvet, antique-looking lamps on the front corners of the judge's bench. His Honor came in and everyone rose, sat down again and the court clerk called the case number, 95-9809, the United States of America versus Rudi Braga.

It gave Raylan another momentary feeling for Rudi, the whole country against the poor little guy. Then changed his mind about this *rich* little guy— Rudi's attorney up to argue that his client shouldn't have to forfeit his Learjet, his Rolls, his other cars, his boat and his home on Key Biscayne. Milt Dancey said, behind his hand to Raylan, "Near President Nixon's old place." Reverence in his voice.

The discussion went on for a while, the natty young assistant U.S. attorney wanting it all, arguing that Mr. Braga's possessions could not be excluded for the reasons contained in the presentence investigation report, and the judge ruled in his favor.

There was more arguing, the defense attorney requesting a downward departure in the sentence, using the low end of the guidelines, 235 to 293 months at the most, because of Mr. Braga's age. The assistant U.S. attorney argued that the defendant had been involved in criminal endeavors for over four decades and wanted an upward departure. Which Raylan understood to mean, throw the book at him. Raylan would listen to parts of the long-winded arguments, all the legal terms, while thinking about a house in Manalapan and a guy named Chip Ganz and the prospect of meeting him face-to-face, maybe tomorrow, if Dawn was right and Chip hung with the Huggers on weekends. Raylan had been thinking of that more and more, Chip trying to make money off runaways.

Finally he heard the judge say, "Pursuant to the Sentencing Reform Act of 1984, it is the judgment of the court and the sentence of the law that the defendant, Rudi Braga, is hereby committed to the custody of the Bureau of Prisons to be imprisoned for a term of three hundred and sixty months to life as to the indictment."

Raylan heard groans behind him, words in Spanish.

The judge stared out at the audience from the bench, pounded his gavel one time only, and there were no more sounds. He said, "The defendant is remanded to the custody of the United States marshal," and it was over. Everyone rose.

Once they had Rudi in the holding cell, Raylan went back into the courtroom to talk to the clerk.

Milt Dancey was by the railing of the outside hallway smoking a cigarette. He saw Raylan coming toward him with the *United States Sentencing Commission Guidelines Manual* under his arm.

"You're on Warrants," Milt said, "investigating a *kid*napping? How come I haven't heard anything about it?"

Raylan started telling about Harry Arno and the collector Harry was supposed to meet at a restaurant a week ago today, Raylan wanting to give Milt a short version. But he kept talking—what did you leave out?—and Milt kept smoking and by the time he'd finished another cigarette Raylan had told him the whole story.

"What do you think? Have I got probable cause?"

"To get a warrant?"

"Yeah, go in the house."

"What's your probable cause based on?"

"I just told you."

"You don't even know a crime's been committed."

"I'm pretty sure Harry's in there."

"You hear what you're saying? A guy is snatched and kept in the kidnapper's *home*? How do you come up with an idea like that?"

"I'm psychic," Raylan said.

"Oh, well, why didn't you say so?"

Raylan sat at a desk in the court support squad room to call Joyce at home.

"Did she show up?"

"After I sat there for almost a half hour. The reverend goes, 'Oh, have you been waiting long?' She looks like Marianne Faithfull with dark hair."

"I told you she has that hippie look. How'd you get along?"

"I showed her up to Harry's apartment and gave her the key. That was it."

"I thought you wanted a reading."

"The reverend was tired. She said she had to rest and meditate. If I want to come by in the morning she'll see me."

"She's just gonna sit there?"

"I don't know, I've never meditated."

"Well, what do you think of her?"

"In what respect," Joyce said, "her looks, her manner? Do I get the feeling she's sincere, a nice girl? Or do I think she has you believing whatever she tells you?"

"I'll talk to you tomorrow," Raylan said.

Melinda surprised him, walking up only a few minutes after the waiter had served Raylan his beer and conch fritters, on the sidewalk outside the Santa Marta. She said, "Well, hey," coming to him with a big smile. She wore a blue tank top and a little purse that hung from her shoulder on a chain. Raylan had the *Guidelines Manual* open on the table. Sitting down, Melinda looked at it and said, "What's that?" making a face. "Like you're doing your homework."

"Looking up things," Raylan said. "I was afraid you might be in Hialeah, dancing."

"I'm going later." She smiled again. "You were waiting for me?"

People strolling past in their trendy outfits would observe the young girl sitting with the older guy in the only suit and tie on South Beach. Raylan would raise his gaze beneath the hat brim and they'd look away. He said to Melinda, "I've been thinking about you. You okay?"

It seemed to surprise her. "Sure, everything's fine. Except I haven't seen Do-do all week."

"Who's Do-do?"

"Bobby. Everybody calls him Bobby Deo? I call him Bobby Do-do."

"He mind?"

"I don't say it to his face. I did once and he tried to slap me around. I told him, he ever touched me again I'd leave. I don't need that."

"I guess not," Raylan said. He took off his hat and laid it on the table and saw Melinda smile.

"You have nice hair. I thought you might be bald—why you wore the hat. Oh—I phoned Bobby today, where he's working? Some colored guy answered and said he'd left and wasn't ever coming back."

Raylan closed the *Guidelines Manual.*

"Maybe to get rid of you."

"He did. He goes, 'I'm busy,' and hangs up on me. Very impolite."

"Bobby was there yesterday."

"Oh, you saw him? Good. Was he working?"

"Taking a rest."

"He must've finished; that's why he left."

"I don't think so."

"Well, if he was working he'd still be there." She looked up, as though Bobby might be coming along the street. "I should've asked what time he left. *I* sure haven't seen him."

Raylan said, "You really want to?"

Melinda gave him a look with half-closed eyes, putting it on. "You trying to move in?"

"I'm older'n Bobby," Raylan said. "And he's too old for you. Where's home?"

"Perry, Georgia. You know where it is?"

"I've been through there."

"Everybody who comes down Seventy-five has. You work at a motel cleaning rooms, making beds, or you get out of town. Here, I can waitress if I want and have something to do at night."

"Bobby's a bad guy," Raylan said.

She seemed about to speak, maybe to defend him, and changed her mind to think about it first, looking out at the street.

"You can do better."

She looked at Raylan now and nodded. "You're probably right. I mean about him being a bad guy."

Raylan said, "Can I ask you something? What is it about him you like?"

"Not much, when I think about it."

"But you're attracted to him?"

"Well, sure, he's hot. Look at him, his hair. . . . You should see him dance."

"I've got another question. What're you doing tomorrow, around noon?"

"What do you mean?"

"You ever been to a Huggers Gathering?"

It got her to smile again.

"I've been to a couple, yeah, and I went to a Deadhead party at the Miami Arena. I mean in the parking lot, I didn't go to the concert. I don't like the Dead, that grandpa rock. I like Pearl Jam, Spin Doctors . . . It's funny, I think of Huggers and Deadheads as almost the same—they're not *all*, but you see everybody smoking doobs and getting dosed on acid. I've done that and I've done nitrous oxide, everybody going around talking like Donald Duck. Those Hugger girls are a trip, they look at you funny if you shave your armpits. I do mine once a week, and my nails. Yeah, they're fun, Hugger parties, except they're always trying to hug you and I like my space. Where's this one?"

"West Palm."

"Sure, I'll go, I've never been there. But I certainly don't see you hanging out with Huggers."

"That's why I need you," Raylan said, "help me find a guy I'm looking for without showing myself and spook him."

"What'd he do?"

"I'll tell you tomorrow, on the way," Raylan said. "There was something else I wanted to ask you. Did the colored guy say Bobby had finished his work, so he packed up and left?"

"Uh-unh, just that he wasn't coming back."

"Does he have clothes up in the room?"

"A lot. He has like ten pair of shoes, these real nice silk shirts he wears when we go dancing—"

"You sure he hasn't been back."

"I'm positive."

Raylan picked up his beer. "You want to have some supper?"

"I don't mind. Sure."

"Then I'm going to see a lady who tells fortunes."

Melinda squinted at him, smiling a little. "Huggers and fortune-tellers; you're into some weird shit, aren't you?"

"It's different," Raylan said.

He imagined Dawn looking at him through the peephole before opening the door. She had on the same blouse and white skirt, no shoes though and seemed vulnerable, waiting with that expectant look in her eyes, hopeful. Raylan came in carrying the *Guidelines Manual* and she closed the door, not saying a word.

"Did you meditate?"

"Some."

"Have anything to eat?"

"I'm not hungry."

He watched her go to the dining table by the kitchenette, it didn't seem with any purpose. She picked up a deck of tarot cards and laid them down again, idly fanning out the deck on the bright varnished surface. Raylan wondered if she was being a poor soul for his benefit.

He said, "Bobby's gone."

It brought her around.

"Gone where?"

"That's the question. Gone on down the road or gone from this earth plane?"

"How do you know?"

"Louis told a person I know Bobby left and wasn't coming back. I was wondering, you suppose you could check with somebody in the spirit world, find out if he crossed over?"

Dawn kept staring at him. "You're serious."

"Or you could call the house and ask Louis."

She said, "You think Bobby's dead?" Sounding awed at the idea.

"The kind of person he is, the kind of people he associates with, I'm surprised he's still with us—if he is. Bobby left your house with a bad attitude. Louis says he's gone, and I'd like to know what happened to him."

"But why do I have to call?"

"I'm asking you to," Raylan said, "and if you help me it could keep you out of prison." He saw her expression change. "Or reduce your time."

"But I haven't *done* anything."

Raylan walked over and dropped the *Guidelines Manual* on the table. He said, "Look up what you get for kidnapping, page forty-six," and crossed to Harry's desk, the phone sitting there, a white one.

"I told you," Dawn said, "my God, all I did was ask Harry a few questions."

"You were aiding," Raylan said, "taking part. That puts you in it." Raylan picked up the phone.

She said, "If I do this . . ."

"I'll show you my gratitude," Raylan said. He dialed the number and held the phone toward her. He could hear ringing and after a few moments a voice saying "Ganz's residence."

Dawn came over, took the phone from him and started right in. "Louis?" She said, "I want to ask you something," turning away as she spoke, but still close enough to Raylan that he heard Louis's voice again, Louis saying, "What's wrong, baby?"

She had her back to Raylan now, walking away, going to a front window to stand looking out, Raylan seeing her nighttime reflection in the glass. He heard her say, "Bobby's gone, isn't he?" and watched her listening for a moment before she said, "Because I *know*. How do I know anything?" The psychic, using her stuff on Louis, slipping into her role. Raylan had to admire the way she did it, so easily. He heard her say, "Where is he then?" and watched her listening to Louis, staring at her own reflection in the glass. Now she said, "You're lying to me, I know you are." Listened and said, " 'Cause he's *dead,* that's why." Listened and said, "I can see him. Louis, I know he's dead." She listened another few moments, then lowered the phone coming over to the desk and Raylan heard Louis's voice again saying, "Dawn?" Saying, "Baby, you still there?" before she put the phone down and stood with her hand on it.

Raylan said, "What's wrong, baby?"

It got him a mean look, Dawn turning nasty on him, saying, "You want to ask me if he's really dead, and if I tell you yes you'll say, 'Oh, is that right? How do you know?' 'Cause you think you're smarter than I am, you think I make things up. But you know what? You don't know shit. If you don't believe he's dead, go find out for yourself. I'm not helping you anymore."

Chip was in the bathroom during the call but had heard the phone ring; he came in the study asking who it was. Louis told him Dawn, and Chip frowned and asked what was wrong, Louis having a strange look on his face.

"She knows Bobby's dead."

"Who told her?"

"Nobody told her, she just *knows.* It's the kind of thing she knows, man."

"What did you say?"

"I told her she was crazy, but she *knows,* she say she could see him."

"We got to pay her," Chip said. "Jesus."

"She hung up on me. I'm trying to tell her no, the man left, but she can see him."

"In the swimming pool?"

"She didn't say, but she *knows*. You know what I'm saying?"

"You see what she's doing?" Chip said. "We got to pay her. Tomorrow, I'll get some money."

"We leaving tomorrow."

"Before we go," Chip said. "I'll score, don't worry. And I'll sell some of my mother's clothes, make a couple hundred bucks that way. Those Hugger chicks love to dress up and dance around on the grass. They all smell the same, that scent they wear, that patchouli?"

"She say Bobby's dead, I felt the hair stand up on my neck."

"I'll go pick out some things," Chip said and left the study.

Louis sat down on the sofa. He found a good-looking roach in the ashtray, lit it and sucked hard and held it in his lungs till he had to breathe.

He told himself, Okay now, be cool. What did he have to do outside of take Harry his supper? Louis put Harry on the TV screen, Harry among the trash with his bathing cap.

He told himself it was good he hadn't put Chip in the pool just yet and have Dawn see him in there with Bobby and freak thinking he was taking everybody out and she was next, nobody left to tell nothing.

He told himself, Let the man go to the Hugger thing in the park and do whatever he does, sell his mama's dresses. Don't tell him where Dawn was. Put him on Mr. Walker's boat when it came later on and when they got out in the ocean and couldn't see land, push the man over the side.

What else?

Be cool. That's all you have to do, Louis told himself. Be cool till the time comes to leave, then get your ass out, fast.

twenty-seven

They sat at the dining table in Harry's living room, Joyce looking at the deck of tarot cards in Dawn's hands, noticing the slender fingers, the nails bitten down.

Dawn said, "I should tell you before we begin, I do know who you are."

Joyce raised her gaze to Dawn's face, the long, straight hair, the demure Marianne Faithfull look.

"I know you're a close friend of both Raylan and Harry Arno."

Joyce said, "Do you know where Harry is?"

She watched Dawn look up to say, "No, I don't," and shrug her hair away from her face.

Joyce said, "What *do* you know?" and said right away, "I'm sorry, I didn't mean that."

Whether she did or not didn't seem to bother Reverend Dawn, the little-girl psychic in a man's starched white shirt this morning, and jeans. Joyce wished now she had worn jeans instead of the daisy-pattern sundress.

"If you'll shuffle these, please, and cut them into three stacks . . ." Dawn handed her the tarot deck. "The first time Raylan came I saw you and his former wife. I didn't see Harry in the picture, but I do now."

Joyce finished shuffling and cut the deck twice.

"You see Harry in the picture as what?"

"Your lover at one time. You still feel an affection for him."

"Raylan told you that?"

"Anything I know about you," Dawn said, "I told *him.*" She looked down at the table and turned over the top three cards on the stacks. "The Ace of Rods, reversed, the Ace of Swords, and the Judgment card. You're planting seeds, thinking of starting a new life. It's not without stress, 'cause you don't know what will grow out of this situation and become your karma."

Joyce sat back in her chair. "I have no idea what you're talking about. Do you have to use the cards?"

Dawn said, "Let's see," and turned over three

more cards. "The Knight of Pentacles, the Seven of Pentacles, and"—raising her eyebrows—"the Knight of Swords. Okay, you have to understand I'm reading from vibrations, too. When I access your higher self I'm no longer reading the cards. If you want me to simplify this, not tell you what the cards mean . . . It looks like you have a choice to make, the Knight of Pentacles or the Knight of Swords. Do you know what I'm talking about?"

"Go on," Joyce said.

"The Judgment card is the focus; you'll have to live with the decision you make, so be careful. The Knight of Swords is fearless, ready to fight. In a lot of ways he's very aggressive. Jumps on his horse and takes off without always knowing where he's going. The Knight of Pentacles is more stable, good at business, financial matters. He's a Taurus."

Joyce said, "You're making this up."

"I am, in a way," Dawn said, looking up, tossing her hair. "I interpret what I see and what I feel, but it's your call. The cards so far aren't positive or negative. In other words, you're on the fence. Like, Oh, my, what am I gonna do? But you're the one who put yourself there. I don't give advice other than to say you should follow your true feelings."

"I'm not sure," Joyce said, "what my true feelings are."

"You're introspective," Dawn said. "Take a look. You're also somewhat spiritual by nature."

"What does that mean?"

"You think a lot. But sometimes what you see as a logical conclusion goes against what you feel, the spirit moving you. The one who's represented by the Knight of Swords killed a man. . . ."

"He told you that," Joyce said.

Dawn shook her head, still looking at the cards. "I touched his hand, the one that held the gun, and I knew. Now I see you're having trouble with that. How can you feel close to a man who's killed someone? And might do it again."

"He had to have told you that," Joyce said.

Dawn looked up now. She said, "Let's get something straight. Raylan hasn't told me one thing about you, nothing. If you don't believe it, there's no reason to continue."

"I'm sorry," Joyce said. "Go on."

"Do you have a question?"

"Who's represented by that other knight?"

"The Knight of Pentacles," Dawn said. "Tell me who you think."

"Harry?"

"Does anyone else come to mind?"

"No."

"So you've answered your own question. Give me your hand," Dawn said, and swept the cards aside to make room.

Joyce placed her hands flat on the table and watched Dawn's hands cover them.

"Do you have another question?"

"I'm not sure about my true feelings."

"What was the first thing you said to me when we started?"

"I don't remember."

"I said I knew you were a close friend of Raylan and Harry's and you said . . . ?"

"I asked about Harry."

"You said, 'Do you know where Harry is?' He was your first concern."

"I'm worried about him. I don't even know if he's alive."

"He is," Dawn said.

"How do you know?"

"Take my word, he's okay."

"Do you know where he is?"

"I'm not able to see what's around him," Dawn said, "because Harry can't see."

"What do you mean?"

"It's like when I try to get into your head-space and see things through your eyes? It's blurry. You wear glasses?"

"Contacts."

"I see a lot of men watching you, but they're out of focus, like I'm looking at them through your glasses and they don't help me at all. You're moving, your hair's flying . . ."

Joyce watched Dawn frown and then close her eyes.

She said, "You were a dancer," sounding surprised.

"When I was younger."

"The men are all looking at you. . . ."

Joyce waited.

"You danced naked?"

"Topless."

Dawn said, "Oh." She said after a moment, "Is there any money in that?"

"Depending on what you're willing to do," Joyce said.

"I suppose," Dawn said, nodding. "Anyway, you're concerned about Harry 'cause you're a loving, caring person; you don't want anything to happen to him, and nothing bad will. You feel guilty now that you weren't as nice to him as you could've been. I mean just before. You miss him. . . . Well, actually what you miss is taking care of him."

"You're telling me," Joyce said, "those are my true feelings?"

"You create your own reality. You tell me."

"Harry can be awfully difficult."

"Maybe so, but he doesn't ever surprise you, you know he's always there. He represents like stability," Dawn said, "and at your age that isn't a bad thing to have a lot of."

"I thought I was doing pretty well," Joyce said, "for my age."

"I wasn't saying you're old," Dawn said, "I meant at this time in your life you're looking for security, karmically speaking. See, what I'm pulling from you is a low energy level. You might feel you're full of spunk, but what it is, it's anxiety; you're worn out wondering where your life is going. What you'd really like to do is take it easy."

Joyce watched the psychic who looked like Marianne Faithfull sit back shaking her head now, in sympathy.

Saying, "Boy, who wouldn't."

*   *   *

Raylan was waiting in the lobby. He walked up to Joyce as she came off the elevator.

"How'd it go?"

"I need to kick back," Joyce said, "karmically speaking. Sort of let it happen."

"Let what happen?"

"My life."

"Isn't that all anybody has to do?"

She said, "Why don't you go play with your gun."

twenty-eight

When a girl in bib overalls told Raylan she loved him and handed a printed sheet through the window, he read:

HUGGING

Hugging is healthy: It helps the body's immunity system, it keeps you healthier, it cures depression, it reduces stress, it induces sleep, it's invigorating. . . .

Got that far and filed the sheet with the *Miami Herald* and a pair of binoculars, on the seat next to him. If anyone wanted to know what he was doing, sitting in a Jaguar in the parking circle at the north end of Dreher Park, he was taking it easy. Letting it happen, so to speak. When a squad car stopped by, Raylan showed his star and told the sheriff's deputy he was working surveillance and to kindly get his green-and-white out of there. When a bearded guy with snake tattoos on his arms shoved a smudge stick at Raylan and said, "Have a smudge," offering what looked like a joint as big as a loaf of bread, Raylan said no thanks, catching the odor of smoldering sweet grass and sage, new-age incense. The bearded guy said, "Go on, tight ass, take a whiff, it'll do you good."

Raylan turned his head, hat brim low on his eyes, to the bearded countenance in the window and said, "Do you want to have to eat that thing?"

The guy with the snake tattoos left. Raylan watched him cross the grassy park toward picnic tables in a stand of ficus, big ones, where most of the Huggers were gathered, maybe a couple dozen, most of them young. Raylan could hear their voices now and then and drumbeats that would bang away for a minute or so and stop. He saw a couple of girls in their underwear, their panties, trying on dresses and dancing to the drumbeats. The Huggers were to his left, off past the public rest rooms and a phone booth, the old glass-box kind. Straight ahead, a walk skirted a dense woods of banyan and palmettos.

Raylan had sent Melinda down that path to locate the dope tree, where the heads gathered, and look

for Warren Ganz, a middle-aged guy who went by the
name of Cal. In the car coming here Melinda said,
"You're using me in a dope bust?" not wanting any
part of it. Raylan told her Cal was suspected of having committed extortion and the sexual exploitation
of minors, and Melinda was ready to go. The plan—if
Cal was there—Melinda would tell him she'd run
away from home, didn't have a place to stay and
needed money more than anything. Raylan told her
how Cal operated, how he'd talk sweet to her, find
out where she was from, who her parents were, then
phone them and ask for a big finder's fee. "Or," Raylan said, "you're a nasty kid, you work it so it's your
idea to call your folks; he asks for the money and you
split it. You get him to that phone booth by the rest
rooms and I'll take it from there." Melinda walked
down the path barefoot in shorts, the little purse
hanging from her shoulder, and was back inside of
twenty minutes.

"He's there, but I wasn't able to get near him. He's
selling dresses."

"Buy one," Raylan said.

"I'm not supposed to have any money. You forget?" She said, "You should hear some of their weekend names they use. Fat Cat and Cherokee, Reser-
voir Dog; two girls there are Bambi and Ling-Ling.
They go, 'Love you,' or 'Gimme a hug,' and then try
and put their arms around you. I'm in the woods
there taking a leak? This big, hairy pervert comes up,
wants to hug me. He goes, 'Welcome home, sister.
Love you.' I'm telling you . . ."

"Is there much dope?"

"Not out in the open, but it's there. This goomer stops by, he goes, 'Want to get zooked?' and shows me a Visine bottle. I told them my name's Peanut." She stared at Raylan and said, "You're . . . let's see. How about, you're the Cat in the Hat." She left the car again to look for Cal, give it another shot.

It was almost four now; she'd been gone over an hour.

Raylan picked up his binoculars and put them on the groups by the tables, over in the trees, to see Huggers in grungy clothes and tie-dyed outfits, drop-out campers having fun: drinking beer, sniffing the guy with the snake tattoos' smudge stick, banging on drums, sucking on balloons a guy was filling with ni-trous oxide from a tank, Huggers giving new arrivals peace signs and hugs. Dawn had described a sign, WELCOME HOME, and there it was, fixed to a tree. Ray-lan edged his binoculars past other groups, normal-looking picnickers, families.

He watched a girl come out of the rest room build-ing and lowered the glasses, a fat girl coming over to the car now, saying, "I need a hug, bad. Will you give me a hug?" She squeezed her head and shoulders through the window and got Raylan around the neck, pressing his face to her breast before he could pro-tect himself. She said, "Love you," and walked away as he took his hat off and replaced it over his eyes.

Not long after that he saw Melinda coming up the path along the banyan thicket with a skinny guy in jeans and white tennis shoes, a red, white, and green rugby shirt, sunglasses, the guy fairly young, his hair blond in the sunlight—until Raylan put the glasses on him and he became an older guy with gray hair. Finally, the one and only Chip Ganz, the guy slouching along next to Melinda, middle-aged hip, talking, smoking a joint pinched between his thumb and finger. Raylan watched him offer the joint to Melinda as they came past the parking circle. Bringing the stub to her mouth and taking a drag, she looked right at the car. Now they were heading toward the phone booth by the rest rooms, Chip digging into his pocket for change and then counting what he had in his hand. Now Melinda had her little purse open and was feeling inside.

Raylan got out of the car and walked over to them, standing by the phone booth now. He saw Chip look at him and start to look away—at the grass, the trees, at whatever was there that seemed to hold some fascination for him—Raylan was sure Chip knew who he was.

"You need change?"

Chip came around showing surprise now. "Oh . . . yeah, if you could help us out."

Raylan put his right hand in his pants pocket, his left hand in the other pocket and stood this way looking at Chip, not saying anything for several moments. He watched Chip studying his change again to be occupied.

"You see Harry lately?"

Chip raised his eyebrows looking up. "Harry?"

"The one you owe the sixteen five."

Chip put on a tired smile now, shaking his head. "He sent you to collect?"

"That was another guy," Raylan said, "your gardener."

"Oh. Yeah, the one my mother hired."

"While you're down in the Keys."

"That's right, but I did see the guy. I explained it to him."

"What?"

"That I'd pay Harry in the next sixty days or so."

Chip maintaining an innocent look: blank, but somewhat bewildered.

Raylan said, "You came all the way up here to get hugged?"

Chip grinned. "Well, among other things. I like the atmosphere, it takes me back, man, to that time, the peace movement, we were gonna change the world. You must've been around then."

"I was in a coal mine," Raylan said. "You know who I am, don't you?"

"A friend of Harry's. You must be the one stopped by and spoke to my caretaker, Louis? He called and told me."

"While you were in the Keys."

"Yeah."

"Were you going home from here?"

Chip shook his head. "No reason to."

"Is Louis there?"

"I think he has Saturday off."

Raylan said, "Who's there, just Harry?"

He watched Chip frown now, giving it all he had.

"You think Harry's at my *house*?"

Frowning and then shaking his head.

Raylan said, "Where're you parked?"

Chip hesitated. "On Summit. In one of those strip malls. Why?"

Raylan said, "Give me your car keys."

"Why? What for?"

Raylan said, "You want to see my I.D.?"

"I just don't understand why you want my keys."

Raylan held out his hand.

Chip shrugged. He dug the keys out of his jeans and held them up, a finger in the key ring. "Okay, now what?"

"Take off the one for the car."

Chip sighed now, going along, worked the key from the ring and handed it to Raylan. He said, "You know, this would appear to be a car-jacking, except you don't seem the type that goes around boosting cars." His expression turned deadpan, a stand-up comic now as he said, "Hey, but what do I know?" Then seemed to laugh without wanting to, ruining the effect.

Raylan thought Chip was doing the best he could, trying hard to seem innocent, good-humored, but the man was becoming giddy. Raylan doubted he'd be able to keep it together for long.

Handing the car key to Melinda, telling her, "It's a tan Mercedes that needs bodywork," came close to finishing Chip off.

He said, "Peanut?"

The poor guy, betrayed by this nice-looking young girl. She said to Chip, "It's Melinda, just so you'll know who set you up."

"Summit's that way," Raylan said, pointing south.

Melinda nodded. "I'll see you later," and walked off across the grassy park.

Chip watched her with an expression Raylan thought of as forlorn, lost, no one to help him. But then said to Raylan, still with hope at this point, though not much, "How do I get my car back?"

"I don't know," Raylan said. "You don't have Bobby to pick it up, do you?"

That seemed to finish Chip off, at least for the time being. He looked at Raylan with nothing to offer.

Raylan put his hand on Chip's shoulder.

"Come on, I'll take you home."

twenty-nine

Yesterday when Harry said he heard something that sounded like shots, coming from outside, Louis said, "Yeah, is that right?"

This morning when Louis went in the room and saw Harry pulling his bathing cap over his face, Louis said, "You don't need that no more. The one you had to worry about's gone."

Harry said, "The guy that shot King?"

"I fired him," Louis said.

"He left?"

"Gone. You never see him again."

"We still going to Freeport?"

"We going today, so clean yourself up."

"We gonna fly?"

"You see me taking you through Customs and Immigration? The man ask the purpose of your visit? We going by private yacht."

"What time?"

"Be cool, Harry, I let you know."

This afternoon Louis brought Harry his snack and Harry asked if they were going now.

"Pretty soon," Louis said. "Tell you what I'll do, I'll take the plywood down off the window; you can look out, see the boat when it comes."

"I could hear the ocean out there," Harry said. "I like to just sit and look at the ocean sometimes."

Porky little guy looking up at him.

"Me too," Louis said.

"You know I don't have any clothes," Harry said. "I'm gonna look like a bum over there."

The little guy worrying about his appearance.

"You be fine," Louis said. "You don't even need shoes. We gonna walk out in the ocean—walk in the water like Ramsey Lewis, no relation to me. Get in a rubber raft to take us to the yacht. My man was gonna pick us up in the Innercoastal, but he say he look at his charts and don't like the way it becomes so narrow by here. He like it where if the Coast Guard's coming you can see the motherfuckers before they down on you."

Louis remembered Harry the first few days asking

was anybody there and then yelling, saying he wasn't gonna say nothing if they didn't talk to him, so fuck you. Acting tough way past his prime. Now Harry was submissive, as Chip had said he'd become, but without it taking weeks. Louis felt, in a way, he had made a friend of Harry, had saved his life, kept Bobby from killing him; so there wasn't anything wrong with letting Harry give him half his money. Like it wasn't a crime kind of gig no more.

This waiting was a bitch, sitting around thinking. Having time to think, work out what he'd do, was good. It was while thinking about walking out in the ocean with Harry, and having Chip along too, Chip whining, bitching, Louis decided the best thing would be to put Chip in the swimming pool soon as he got home. Not wait to drop him in the ocean. Do it and don't think no more about it. Having too much time to think wasn't good. Then you began to think of different ways your plan could get fucked up and you'd change your mind.

As soon as they were driving out of the park Raylan had begun to break Chip down with consequences.

"Here's how it is. For kidnapping, abduction, or unlawful restraint, you're looking at fifty-one to sixty-three months in a federal prison, a real one, not some army base with tennis courts. Now if you demanded payment—and I don't see you'd have a reason to hold him if you didn't—you're looking at ninety-seven to a hundred and twenty-one months. If Harry's injured, sustained any kind of bodily injury, you're looking at more time over and above the basic offense level. If a dangerous weapon was used you go up two levels. If Harry is released, allowed to walk out or turned over to law enforcement authorities within thirty days, you'll save yourself a couple of years. I'm gonna assume you did not abduct Harry for any reason that would come under sexual exploitation. Am I right?"

Poor Chip. "How can I answer that?"

"With a simple yes or no."

"If I say either one I'm admitting Harry was kidnapped."

"All right, let me ask you," Raylan said, "is Harry in your house at the present time?"

Chip didn't answer.

"I'll give you an easier one. Is Louis?"

He said, "I don't know."

"If he isn't," Raylan said, "I bet I know where he is, with Dawn."

"What're you talking about?"

"You didn't know he's been pokin' her? I thought maybe you'd handed her down, like an old pair of shoes." Raylan glanced at the poor guy sitting there, helpless but agitated. "That Dawn," Raylan said, "she's something. She can touch you and tell what you had for breakfast. I guess she's been touching Louis enough to know what's going on. She's sitting on the fence now waiting to see how it turns out. I told her, I said, 'Honey, you're liable to get your tail in a crack sitting there and go down with the boys.' You and Louis. We don't worry about Bobby no more, do we?"

No answer. Chip over there with his own thoughts.

"Since nobody's home," Raylan said, "you gonna invite me in your house?"

Chip said, "Why would I do that?"

"You don't have to. You can tell me to go to hell or go get a warrant, one." Raylan glanced at him again. "I haven't threatened you in any way, have I?"

"You just finished saying I could go to prison for a hundred and twenty-one months."

The high number sticking in his mind.

"It wasn't a threat," Raylan said, "it's how the sentencing guidelines read for the crime you're committing. It's in black and white, partner, the letter of the law. So, are you giving me permission to enter your house?"

Raylan let Chip take his time. He felt the man was all the way into himself now, looking around in his head and not seeing any hope left.

Chip said, "I guess so."

"The traffic's not too bad on Saturday," Raylan said, heading down 95 to Lantana to take the bridge over to Manalapan, "but we could still use another north-south freeway. What do you think?"

Louis switched the video picture from the front drive, waiting for Chip's car to come nosing in, to Harry upstairs shuffling in his chains from the window he could see out of now and had opened, to his cot, turning but not sitting down, then shuffling back to the window, anxious.

Louis was becoming anxious himself. If Chip wasn't home by the time the boat got here they'd have to wait for him, Louis not wanting any loose ends to trip him up. But it would be close to dark in half an hour and Mr. Walker wouldn't be able to spot the white house with the red roof from out in the ocean. Louis had told him he'd put the backyard floodlights on just in case. Look for them like two miles north of the Boynton Inlet and collect fifty thousand. He'd said, "Nothing to it, my man; Mr. Walker, the salty sailorman."

Nothing to it, shit. It was getting close. Too close. Mr. Walker could even be early.

That got Louis out of the sofa, leaving Harry on the screen. In the sunroom he switched on the flood-lights, went outside and looked up at them mounted on the roof, weak spots of light in the dusk. He walked out past the scummy swimming pool, across the yard and into the palm trees and sea grape, fol-lowing the path to where the property sloped down full of scrub and driftwood to the beach. He saw the ocean wasn't doing much, a lazy kind of surf coming in green, easy for a rubber raft to make it all the way here and they wouldn't get too wet. Louis had on his new black silk jacket, but thought now maybe he should put it in the hanging bag with the rest of his things. He'd filled a carry-on bag with snacks, Fritos and salted peanuts—not that dry-roasted shit, real peanuts. Peanut brittle for Harry, the man loved his peanut brittle. What else?

The shotgun, in the chest in the study; no sense leaving it in the house. He had buried the Browning he'd used on Bobby, had the other one in his hanging bag, and Bobby's piece, the Sig Sauer, in with the snacks to give to Mr. Walker. The sky was already dark out on the ocean, misting up out there under big heavy clouds, a few boats. . . . What looked like charter fishing boats coming in, but another one he couldn't tell if it was or not. Maybe Mr. Walker.

Louis hurried back to the house, ran upstairs to get his hanging bag—decided to leave his new jacket on —and stuck his head in the hostage room.

"Five minutes, Harry."

The man came around from the window looking more anxious than before. He said, "I got to go to the bathroom."

"Well, hurry up, man. Gonna take my things down and come back for you."

Louis ducked out, leaving the door open.

He got the stubby shotgun from the study, went in the kitchen for the snack bag and believed that was it. Outside, he crossed the yard again, made his way through the palms and sea grape down to the beach this time—deserted either way he looked—to set his things down in the sand, the shotgun on top the hanging bag.

The boat that might be Mr. Walker's didn't seem any closer. Louis watched it thinking, It still could be him. He turned around to see the floodlights up on the house looking a little brighter now.

Time to get Harry.

Raylan turned in past the PRIVATE DRIVE, KEEP OUT sign and eased the Jaguar through the shrubs. He thought about checking the garage for Bobby's car, but would do it later. Right now his mind was set on entering the house. He told Chip to get out and then told him to wait and came around the car looking at the vegetation.

"Your mom needs a gardener didn't learn his trade in prison."

Chip said, "And I guess I need a lawyer."

Raylan hesitated. "We going in or not?"

"If that's what you want to do."

Raylan hesitated again. He said, "Wait," and went back to the Jaguar, opened the trunk and took out an extra pair of handcuffs he slipped into a side pocket of his coat, ducked his head in again and came out with his Remington 12-gauge.

Chip, watching him, said, "What's that for?"

"Whoever wants it," Raylan said.

"I told you no one's home."

"I know you did. Would you open the door, please?"

Raylan followed Chip to the front stoop and watched him unlock the door, push it open and step aside.

"After you," Raylan said, motioning with the shotgun.

Chip said, "I have no reason to go in."

Sounding like a different person on his home ground, as if his hope had been restored.

Raylan said, "You think Louis'll save you?"

Chip didn't answer. What Raylan saw him do was come to a decision, like it was now or never for him. He seemed to square his shoulders as he looked at Raylan. And stepped inside. Raylan followed.

He was in the house.

Some window light showed in the front rooms bare of furniture. From the foyer the hallway became gradually darker to where a square of light lay on the floor, coming from a doorway down at the end.

"That way," Raylan said and kept two steps behind Chip moving along bare walls in no hurry, cautious in a house that was supposed to be empty. They approached the doorway now that showed light inside, a soft lamp glow. Raylan kept his eyes on the doorway, past Chip's left shoulder, almost there when Chip moved, yelled out, "Louis!" and flattened against the wall. Raylan kept going, went through the doorway to the study and put his shotgun on Harry in chains, Harry full length on the TV screen, turning from an open window.

Louis paused in the sea grape to look out at the ocean again. The boat seemed closer now, but not much. If it was Mr. Walker he was easing his way in, careful of reefs maybe, or sandbars. Louis turned and hurried across the yard, glancing at the pool hiding Bobby, went in the doors off the patio and through the sunroom to the study. Who was standing there waiting but the Chipper.

"Hey, you made it."

Louis grinning at Chip till he saw Chip wasn't looking at him but at the TV. Like hypnotized. Louis turned to look. What he saw was Harry sitting on his cot and the *man*—seeing him from behind, the man bent over fooling with the chains—but it was the man, the cowboy, no doubt of it, wearing his hat, the suit. . . .

"You crazy?" Louis said. "You let him in the house?"

Chip turned to him all eyes. "We got to get out."

"Leave Harry?" Louis said. "Leave the cowboy knowing all about us? Man, you *are* crazy."

It seemed to wake him up some. Chip went to the chest saying, "The shotgun."

"It's out on the beach," Louis said. "Shit, everything's out on the beach," and ran from the study through the sunroom. He heard Chip.

Chip yelling, "Where you going!"

Asshole. Louis wanting to stop and say, where you think? But not having the time. He knew where Chip was going for sure, in the pool. Him and the cowboy both.

Louis was across the yard and into the sea grape when he thought of the window in the hostage room, uncovered now, but didn't turn around to look. Man, he had to *move*. Get the shotgun and the Browning—shit, dig it out of the hanging bag—and get back in time to do the cowboy in the room still bent over. Or coming down the stairs, see the man's face. Say to him, Surprise, motherfucker. *Boom.*

Harry said to Raylan, standing at the window now, "You could open these with a screwdriver, for Christ sake. You don't need the key."

"What'd he tell you exactly?"

"He said be ready in five minutes, and that was about ten minutes ago. He had to take his stuff down first."

"He didn't have anything with him," Raylan said,

watching the date palms and clumps of sea grape at the edge of the property, the trees hiding the strip of beach.

"He said he'd be back for me."

"I think that's what he did," Raylan said.

"Then why didn't he come upstairs?"

It took Raylan maybe two seconds to decide what it meant and say, "He knows I'm here," and start for the door, in a hurry to catch Louis outside.

Harry had time to say, "Wait a minute, will you?" He yelled at him, "Get me out of here!" too late.

Raylan was gone.

Harry's gaze, coming away from the door, stopped on Raylan's shotgun, lying on the other cot.

Louis stood in the path through the sea grape studying the house, taking in that upstairs window now free of plywood. Nobody up there watching that he could tell. He pumped the stubby shotgun to put one in the chamber. The Browning was stuck in his waist beneath his new black silk jacket. He needed to hurry, catch the man by surprise, but didn't like having to cross the yard out in the open, exposed. So what he did was sprint across hunched over, like anybody looking out a window then wouldn't see him. He came past the swimming pool, got to the patio and stopped, seeing one of the French doors come open.

The cowboy stepped out, nothing in his hands, and stood looking right at him. He said, "You don't want to get shot, do you? Put down the gun. Drop it on that chair."

Louis was where he'd stood when he did Bobby
only turned around, facing the house instead of the
swimming pool, a lounge chair next to him. He said,
"What'd I do?"

"You have two years coming for that illegal
weapon," Raylan said. "I won't discuss the kidnapping with you at this time. Put the gun down and
come over here, your hands behind your head."

"You telling me all that," Louis said, "you don't
even have a gun pointing at me."

"If I pull it," Raylan said, "I'll use it. You understand? You make a threatening move I'll shoot you
through the heart."

Louis held the sawed-off pointed down and against
his leg. He said, "Man, all I got to do is raise this
thing."

"I have to advise you, though, to put it down."

Louis said, "We like in the movies, huh? The two
hombres facing each other out in the street."

"That's the only place it ever happened," Raylan
said. "In the movies. You ever shot a man?"

Louis liked the way this was going, knowing he had
the advantage, holding a shotgun he'd hardly have to
aim. He said, "Lemme see. Yeah, I did, just the other
day."

That stopped the man. But he believed it, asking,
"How close were you?"

"About like this far, me and you. Was Bobby, the
Puerto Rican gunfighter. You know Bobby."

The man's suitcoat was open and he had his
thumbs in his belt now in his U.S. marshal pose.
Louis watched the man's right hand.

He said, "You killed Bobby with that gun?"

"No, man, we drew on each other with pistolas, did the deed like you suppose to." With his left hand Louis opened his coat enough to show the Browning. "Used one like this on him."

Raylan said, "Now you want to try with the shotgun?"

"I don't see no other way. Do you?"

The man raised his hat and set it on his head again, on his eyes, and it gave him a look—not just the hat but the man's whole manner standing there—that made Louis hesitate and wonder did he have the advantage here or not. The man saying, "I'll tell you once more to put down the gun."

See? Like he thought *he* had the advantage.

The man saying, "You don't put it down by the time I count to three I'll shoot to kill. One . . ."

Louis thinking, *Hey, shit, wait.*

"Two."

And saw the man's hand come out of his coat with a pistol. *Cheating,* the man drawing on the count of two. Louis saw the muzzle hole looking at him the same way Bobby's had, swung his gun up from his leg now, quick, and right then heard a shotgun blast that wasn't from his, that got him to look up to see Harry with a gun barrel sticking out the window, the gun going off again with the smoke and noise it made and Louis felt the load hit him high in the chest to punch the breath out of him and slam him off his feet. He wanted to say come on, man, wait now, looking at sky, that's all, the sky turned darker from what it was a minute ago, and thinking, The man never said *three.*

Thinking, Was Harry. But how could it be? It was too quick, how it happened. He wanted to start over and do it right this time, no cheating. He was looking at sky, then looking at the man's face in the hat looking down at him . . .

Raylan touched Louis's throat and closed his eyes with the same two fingers.

Chip looked like he was approaching the edge of a cliff, coming within a few feet of Louis and turning away. Raylan sent him to get Harry.

"Nine days up there in fucking chains," Harry said, coming across the patio, eager, his eyes full of life. "I nailed him, didn't I? Like a split second before he was gonna shoot." Harry turned to Raylan. "I saved your life, you know it? You realize that? You come to rescue me and I end up saving your ass."

Raylan said, "Is that what you think?"

t h i r t y

It was Sunday morning now, half past ten. Dawn asked Raylan if he'd like a cup of coffee; he said he wouldn't mind and followed her to the kitchen. It seemed bare, hardly ever used. She stood at the range, her back to him, in jeans and a white shirt, her hair combed. Raylan, by the Formica table, had his hat on. He said to her, "You saw Harry?"

"Last night, but only for a few minutes. I told you he was okay."

"For a man who spent a week chained up," Raylan said, "blindfolded, eating TV dinners."

"He was nice to me," Dawn said, sounding hopeful, coming to the table now with the electric coffeepot. "I told him I was sorry, but there was really nothing I could do. He said he understood that. You want toast?"

"I've had breakfast."

"He said if I needed a lawyer he'd get me one."

"Harry did?"

"He's not mad at me. He kept telling Joyce how he's shot and killed three bad guys in his life, making the point, more than you have. Joyce was all over him. She even fixed him a drink, saying 'cause he deserved it. I left."

Raylan watched her pour coffee into ceramic mugs. Sugar and powdered milk were on the table. He pulled a chair out and sat down. "I understand they're going away."

"Yeah, to Vegas," Dawn said. "I love Vegas, I wouldn't even mind living there. Maybe when this business is settled. . . . What about Chip?"

"His first appearance hearing's tomorrow afternoon. He'll be charged and a bond set."

She said, "I suppose I'll have to appear sometime."

Raylan watched her lean over the table, her shirt open in front, to put three spoons of sugar in her coffee and stir it. He said, "The sheriff's people will talk to you, then it's up to them." He had to ask her, "What do you see happening to you?"

"It's not real clear yet."

Raylan said, "I think you see things the same way I

do except you have that Grand Trine in your natal chart, so you believe you have a gift. I've never understood people wanting to know their future. I'd rather let it happen and be surprised."

Dawn put the spoon down. She moved around behind him and placed her hands on his shoulders. She said, "You'd like to go to bed with me." She said, "That's how psychic I am. You can deny it, it's still true."

"I admit it's crossed my mind," Raylan said.

"See? Come on then, let's go."

"Wanting to is one thing," Raylan said, "doing it wouldn't be appropriate."

"Ap*pro*priate—gimme a break. If you want to and I want to . . ."

"I'm not gonna arrest you."

There was a pause.

"You're not?"

Raylan felt her hands slip from his shoulders. She was sitting down now at the table, hunching her chair in close, all the while looking at him.

"How come?"

"It's not my case. I was never *on* a case, I was looking for Harry. I'll be asked what I know, but mainly it'll be Harry's word, and you said he was nice to you."

"Yeah, but what'll you tell them about me?"

"Only what you told me, you were threatened, they made you do it." Raylan paused. "You said the other day, when we were talking about that woman's murder and how you conned the detectives—"

"I did *not.* I saw the murder weapon, that book-end."

"You took a chance, guessed there were two book-ends and reasoned it out from there. I called you on it and you said, 'What's wrong with wanting to do better?' Wanting to get ahead in the world, be some-body. See, I think the way you go about it," Raylan said, "you give yourself enough problems without my adding to them."

"You're not gonna testify against me?"

Sounding like she wanted to be sure about it.

Raylan shook his head. "Why put you in prison? This place is bad enough."

"Then why can't we go to bed?"

He said, "I'm getting out of here before I do some-thing foolish."

She said, "What's wrong with being foolish some-times?"

It was a good question.

A SNEAK PREVIEW OF

RAYLAN

BY

ELMORE
LEONARD

Featuring U.S. Marshal Raylan Givens

Available in hardcover from

wm

WILLIAM MORROW
An Imprint of HarperCollins*Publishers*

BUZZ HICKS, the senior detective in the room, said, "Now we're getting to it, aren't we? You're lookin for Reno's little girl, aren't you? Jackie Nevada."

Raylan said, "Isn't Reno her stepdad?"

"That's right," Hicks said. "The name on her birth certificate's Rachel Nevada, but Reno started callin her Jackie when she was a kid."

One of the detectives down the table said, "Her mom was called Jackie. She got knocked up by some loser passin through and took up with Reno. She has the child and acts like a mother till she got tired of home life and hit the road. Was Reno named her Rachel, after his own mother, but started callin her Jackie before too long. Had a soft spot for the broad walked out on him."

Hicks said, "Lloyd, how'd you come up with all that?"

"Talkin to her," Lloyd said, "while we had her in custody."

"So now," Hicks said, "she's raised by Reno, this suspected colored guy passin as Latino and runnin a sports book."

"They musta got along," Raylan said.

"Well, they lived in the same house," Hicks said, "till she went to Butler. Listen to this, and paid her way through college playin poker at night. The only girl livin in a house with seven guys, all students. You know what they called her? 'Mother.' She had a poker table, cards and racks of chips. You wanted to play you had to bring your own chair or borrow one. We went over there and talked to 'em. They said you oughta see her shuffle cards."

"I understand," Raylan said, "she won twenty grand betting Duke over her school."

"That's right, but Reno says he covered her for ten, in case Butler managed to pull off a win. We asked Jackie—" Hicks turning to look down the table. "Lloyd, what'd she tell us?"

"That game," Lloyd said, "Reno put up *nada*. He was too busy losin on the spread. Jackie said the students laid down twenty and that's what she picked up."

"You look into it?" Raylan said.

Hicks said, "What are we, the gaming commission? It was Duke minus seven, the spread *BetUS Sportsbook* was offerin online, and Reno took a bath."

"How'd Jackie take gettin busted?"

"Didn't make a fuss. I guess thinkin about the hole she was in, broke. This A student who plays poker you might say for a living. I asked the woman runs poker games we busted. Elaine? I said, 'You musta known those guys'd eat her alive.' Elaine said, 'She lost her cool. But you could tell the girl's a player.' We set Jackie aside while we're arm-wrestlin these high-priced lawyers and she walks out."

"Didn't show up in court," Raylan said.

"Took off on us," Hicks said. "Reno swears he hasn't heard from her. What do you think this girl's doin now?"

Raylan said, "Well, I hear she's sticking up banks to get back on her feet. You got tape on her?"

"Jackie and two other girls," Hicks said. "We have 'em in different banks in Lexington. Now take a look at what she's doing." Hicks glanced down the table. One of the detectives—it was Lloyd—slid the stack of surveillance prints to him and Hicks passed them on to

Raylan, telling him, "We showed Reno. He said his little girl don't rob banks. These are some girls lost their way. He said, 'But they're mellow, riding some kind of high.' He said, 'My little girl don't do drugs either. She keeps her mind on poker.' "

Raylan went through the tapes, seeing the girls with shopping bags at separate tellers.

Hicks said, "Watch 'em come away, the two looking back at the one still at a window. They're stoned. Had to get fixed to rob the bank."

"I've heard of ones have to get ripped before they go in," Raylan said. "These girls look like they just cashed their paychecks."

"What do they get paid in," Hicks said, "yen? Have to bring store bags to carry it?"

"I guess what I mean," Raylan said, "we don't see that many women stickin up banks. I think it's maybe five or six out of a hundred. Here you've got three at once. Which one you think's Jackie?"

"The one wearing the baseball cap," Hicks said, "down on her eyes. Some of the other tapes you'll come to, you see her lookin up." He stood to watch Raylan go through the prints.

Lloyd said, "Buzz, you recall we had two girls doin banks at the same time?"

"Not around here," Hicks said.

"Was down toward the state line," Lloyd said, "seven, eight years ago. They'd hit a bank in some dinky town off sixty-four and cross over to Louisville. A guy with the girls was teachin 'em how to rob banks."

Hicks said, "How you remember that?"

"It stuck in my mind," Lloyd said. "I remember a confidential informant fingered them, but were released for lack of evidence."

Raylan said, "You remember what happened to the snitch?"

Lloyd was squinting, trying to recall before nodding his head. "A guy blew off his right arm with a shotgun."

Raylan said, "Delroy Lewis?"

"*That's* the guy was questioned," Lloyd said, "about the bank jobs."

"You mind," Hicks said, "if we settle on this job here?" and said to Raylan, "That one, where she's lookin up. All of us but Lloyd said that's Jackie Nevada or her twin."

"It could be," Raylan said. "I stopped by Butler and got a look at her picture. I can't see the girl in the yearbook playing to a surveillance camera."

"We like her motive," Hicks said. "She needs dough."

Raylan was shaking his head. "These two comin out, mugging right at the camera."

"Doped up and think it's a hoot. It's your people in Lexington," Hicks said, "sent us all the bank photos. They picked out Jackie and asked for our confirmation."

"The three almost look alike," Raylan said. "Young, the same size. Three girls having fun."

Hicks said, "Robbin banks."

"Your fugitive," Raylan said, "I can see why you want her to be Jackie. I hope you're right and I'm dead wrong. But I can't see three girls wanting to rob banks. I *can* see some guy putting 'em up to it. Gives the girl's some toot and drops 'em off. I don't know for sure, but we'll find out, won't we?"

"We respect your opinion," Buzz Hicks said, "but hope you're wrong this time. We been followin you since you called out that Zip in Miami, Tommy Bucks? You gave him twenty-four hours to get out of town. He drew on you and you put him down."

"And got demoted to Harlan County, Kentucky."

"But then shot it out with that transplant nurse."

"You're havin fun with me, aren't you?"

"Well," Hicks said, "you're doin a job the way we like to see it done."

LIZ BURGOYNE CAME in the sun parlor from the patio to see Jackie Nevada waiting, getting up from the sofa, and it made Liz think of Raylan, the time she walked in and he asked her about Cuba stealing kidneys. Liz crossed the room in jeans and cowboy boots offering her hand, saying:

"Jackie Nevada. Harry's told me about his poker-playing buddy. He makes you sound like a little girl, but you're quite something else, aren't you?" Liz smiling now. "Harry mentioned you're wanted by the police?"

"It's a misdemeanor thing," Jackie said. "I didn't show up for a hearing."

"Picked up in a raid," Liz said. "Harry told me about it. He said you like manhattans, is that right?"

Jackie said, "If that's what we're having."

They were both on the sofa now, the nearly empty pitcher on the cocktail table, both smoking cigarettes.

"You ever cheat?" Liz said.

"Why do only women ask that? You mean at poker."

"Or on a guy."

"Poker, I've never had to."

"You're that good?"

"You have to work with another player. Didn't you see *Rounders*? They cheat playing with a bunch of cops. I've never cheated on a boyfriend either. Right now I don't have one, but I live with seven guys. You know what they think is funny? Farting."

"Why do guys love to fart?"

"They're expressing themselves."

"You hop in the sack with any of them?"

"Nope. There's some fooling around, girls come for a party and we get high, but I don't recall anything really inappropriate. You might hear a girl tell some guy to quit grabbin her ass. We have great parties."

Liz said, "You like to go down on guys?"

"Not *guys*, no. But I have polished the occasional knob."

"Wow," Liz said. "You're not bashful, are you?"

"You know what I'm talking about or wouldn't've asked."

"You have to meet some of my friends from olden times, they'd love you."

"I'm not a lay," Jackie said. "I've only gone to bed with three guys in four years, ones I thought I was serious about."

"What happened to them?"

"They graduated."

Liz poured the rest of the manhattans.

"You like to do it standing up?"

"I never have," Jackie said. "In movies they look like they're ringing the bell, but I think it would be uncomfortable."

Liz said, "I bet I know the movie you're thinking of. The girl walks in the bar—"

"That's the one."

"She can't get any attention and yells out, 'Who's a girl gotta suck around here to get a drink?' "

"She gets into the cute guy's pants, in the booth."

"Then you see them in back doing it standing up."

"You ever do it with a black guy?"

"No, and I'm not racist," Jackie said. "Or maybe I

am and didn't know it. I've never had any chills and thrills yet when I meet black guys at parties. I know you have."

"Our driver at the time," Liz said, "Harry thought was from West Africa, so Cuba always had to put on an accent, one he picked up from cabdrivers." She said, "I can't imagine Harry trying anything with you."

"Why?" Jackie said.

"He's too old. He might ask you to strip, promise he'll just look."

"Would that upset you?"

"Not in the least, if he can pull it off."

"He sure goes to the bathroom a lot."

"His tired kidneys," Liz said. "And here's your boy-friend now."

Harry came in from the hallway telling Jackie, "I got three guys so far want to play you: my friends the breeders, Ike and Mike, and a World Series of Poker pro they dug up called Dude Moody."

Jackie was nodding.

"He's been at the final table. I think he won a couple of bracelets. They call him Moody Blues or just Blues."

"I said to Ike and Mike, 'For Christ sake, what do you guys need help for?' And there's a guy in town I asked to stop by. You met him, Liz, Raylan Givens? The marshal lookin for that driver we had. He called, I asked him to come by for a drink and say hello."

Jackie said, "Harry, don't tell him I play poker, okay?"

Jackie watched Raylan take off his hat shaking hands with Harry and they stood talking for a few minutes. Now they were coming over to the sofa, Raylan saying, "Don't get up, ladies, you look comfortable."

"We *have* had a couple," Liz said. "Raylan, it's so

good to see you. It seems to me that you and I sat here having martinis one time. Harry, where were you?"

"Tendin business. I believe I was helpin a foal come into the world. She's still lookin like a possible."

Jackie saw Raylan stare at her for a moment and turn to Liz again, Liz saying, "This time my guest said she might try a manhattan. They seemed to've worked just fine." Jackie wondering how she'd be introduced. These people got in conversations and forgot she was there.

Not Raylan.

Harry said, "Liz makes it sound like she's never had a manhattan."

Jackie watched Raylan smile, being polite, watched his eyes come back to her. She said through her buzz, "Hi, I'm Jackie."

Raylan came over to shake hands telling her not to get up, but she did and stood with her feet planted.

"Harry's latest partner," Liz said.

Raylan gave her hand a nice squeeze and said, "Is that right?"

Jackie told herself she'd get out of this or she wouldn't, and said, "Harry's my banker, he stakes me to poker games, but doesn't pay too much attention." Smiling then to show she was being funny. "He has no idea how we're doing."

No one laughed. Liz said, "If you've been playing no limit for the past week you're winning, or Harry would've left you off somewhere."

Harry said, "You make me sound heartless."

"I'll bet," Liz said, "she's up at least a hundred grand."

Raylan said, "You play poker as an occupation?"

She said, "I'm not sure. I'm looking at it."

"You were in a game," Raylan said, "in Indianapolis recently that was raided, weren't you?"

Jackie said, "You know how much I lost?"

Harry said, "You never want to be in a game when the cops bust in. They take all the cash and chips as evidence. What happens to the dough after that?" Harry said to Raylan. "Maybe you can tell me."

"Isn't part of my job," Raylan said.

"I'm always careful," Harry said, "pickin games for Jackie. What I do is call the chief of police, tell him who I am, and say I want to play some poker without gettin in the way of a raid. I ask him if there's a police fundraiser I could help out."

Liz asked Raylan if he had time for a drink. He said, glancing at his watch, he'd better get back. "We're tryin to locate a guy wants to shoot me on sight."

Liz said, "I'd think you'd have them lining up."

"Well, some are dead," Raylan said, and looked at Jackie. "I'd like to hear more about what you're doin. I haven't played a lot of poker but've always had a good time. Are you stayin here by any chance?"

"Till we hit the poker trail again," Harry said. "Jackie's takin on some guys tomorrow in a big cash game."

Raylan touched his coat pocket and said, "Excuse me," taking out his cell phone and turning away.

Jackie watched him, telling herself it was a case they were putting him on and he had to leave right now, forget about her walking out of jail, and heard him say, "Come on, you're kiddin." He turned his back to them now and stepped away to listen. *Come on, you're kiddin,* his voice raised but not much, was all she heard. She watched him fold his cell and come back to stand with her as he told Liz and Harry, "I'm sorry, but that was my job callin."

"About the guy who wants to shoot you?" Liz said.

"Something else," Raylan said. Then paused, like he

was getting around to what he wanted to say. "You don't mind, I'd like to have a word with Ms. Nevada."

Liz said, "I hope you're not going to cuff our guest. Are you?"

"I'm not arrestin her," Raylan said. "There's something I'd like to talk to her about."

Jackie gave Liz a shrug and walked out to the hallway with Raylan.

"Where we going if you're not turning me in?"

"I want to talk to you," Raylan said. "The first time I came here I said, 'This's a sun parlor? I'd like to see what they call the living room.' Liz told me it's been a sun parlor for eighty-five years."

Jackie stopped. "If you're not arresting me, where we going?"

"Forget about Indy," Raylan said. "I'll appear at your hearing and tell the court you owed a shylock and was hopin to pay him out of the twenty grand you blew." Raylan, turned enough to see the Burgoynes watching, said, "Come on," and they continued walking down the hall, Raylan telling Jackie, "I stopped at Butler and saw your picture in the yearbook. I said to myself, Whatever it was, you didn't do it."

"I have no idea," Jackie said, "what's going on."

"I want to take you out," Raylan said, "if you're not playin tonight. You are, I'll come and watch."

She said, "Like a date?" Thought for a moment and said, "You know those two girls who were murdered? I'd love to see where it happened."

"There's nothin there now but police tape. He paused a moment and said. "Hey, you want to come with me? I'll show you a scene hard to believe."

New York Times **bestselling author Elmore Leonard brings back U.S. Marshal Raylan Givens, hero of the hit FX series "Justified"**

With the closing of the Harlan County coalmines, marijuana has become a big cash crop. A hundred pounds can gross three hundred thousand dollars, but that's chump change compared to the quarter million a human body can bring in—especially when it's sold piece-by-piece.

When dope-dealing brothers Dickie and Coover Crowe decide to branch out into the body business, they enter the crosshairs of laconic, Stetson-wearing, fast-drawing U.S. Marshal Raylan Givens.

Dark and droll, *Raylan* is pure Elmore Leonard—a page-turner filled with the sparkling dialogue and sly suspense that are hallmarks of this modern master.

**On Sale January 31, 2012.
Available wherever books are sold.**

Friend and follow Elmore Leonard on Facebook and Twitter!

**Hardcover
ISBN 978-0-06-211946-9
$26.99 ($34.99 Can.)**

WILLIAM MORROW
An Imprint of HarperCollinsPublishers

SPEND MORE TIME WITH
RAYLAN GIVENS
THIS WINTER

JUSTIFIED FX

NEW SEASON COMING 2012

Stay Connected at facebook.com/justifiedFX

#justifiedfx

THE COMPLETE SECOND SEASON

THE COMPLETE SECOND SEASON

SEASON 2
COMING TO
BLU-RAY &
DVD EARLY
2012

SONY PICTURES TELEVISION   SONY PICTURES HOME ENTERTAINMENT

© 2011 Sony Pictures Television Inc. and Bluebush Productions, LLC. All Rights Reserved.

THE UNDISPUTED MASTER
OF THE CRIME NOVEL

DJIBOUTI
A Novel

978-0-06-173521-9 (trade paperback)

Elmore Leonard brings his trademark wit and inimitable style to this twisting, gripping—and sometimes playful—tale of modern-day piracy.

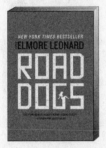

ROAD DOGS
A Novel

978-0-06-198570-6 (trade paperback)

The further adventures of Jack Foley, out of prison but right back into trouble.

PRONTO

978-0-06-212033-5 (trade paperback)

A brilliant combination of suspense and black humor featuring Raylan Givens, the inspiration behind the FX series *Justified*.

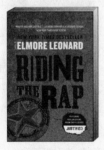

RIDING THE RAP

978-0-06-212247-6 (trade paperback)

Raylan Givens returns to bust open a kidnapping ring in the sequel to *Pronto*.

FIRE IN THE HOLE
Stories

978-0-06-212034-2 (trade paperback)

This short fiction collection features a few beloved Elmore Leonard characters, including Raylan Givens in the title story that was the basis for the pilot of the hit FX series *Justified*.

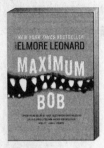

MAXIMUM BOB

978-0-06-200940-1 (trade paperback)

Florida Judge "Maximum" Bob Gibbs has thrown the
book at so many felons, it's beginning to look
as if one of them is throwing it back at him.

TISHOMINGO BLUES

978-0-06-200939-5 (trade paperback)

The Dixie Mafia is aiming to shoot high-diver Dennis
Lenahan from the top of his 80-foot ladder.

RUM PUNCH
A Novel

978-0-06-211982-7 (trade paperback)

Cops try to use Jackie Burke to get at the gunrunner she's
been bringing cash into the country for, but she hatches a
plan to keep the money for herself.

FREAKY DEAKY
A Novel

978-0-06-212035-9 (trade paperback)

It's only after he transfers out of the bomb squad that
Chris Mankowski begins playing with dynamite.

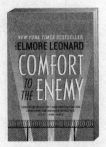

COMFORT TO THE ENEMY AND OTHER CARL WEBSTER STORIES

978-0-06-173515-8 (trade paperback)

First time in print in the U.S.
A collection of 3 stories about the legendary lawman
Carl Webster.

GET SHORTY
A Novel

978-0-06-212025-0 (trade paperback)

A Miami shylock, Chili Palmer, goes to Hollywood
and becomes a movie producer. Why not?

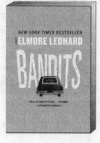

BANDITS

978-0-06-212032-8 (trade paperback)

An unlikely trio targeting millions of dollars is
sure to make out like bandits—if they survive.

KILLSHOT
A Novel

978-0-06-212159-2 (trade paperback)

After witnessing a scam, Carmen and her husband
must outrun the thugs bent on eliminating any
living evidence.

MR. PARADISE
A Novel

978-0-06-211905-6 (trade paperback)

Elmore Leonard presents a whole new cast of
characters—the kind that only he can create—in
this Detroit homicide book.

GLITZ
A Novel

978-0-06-212158-5 (trade paperback)

A classic Elmore Leonard novel, spinning from the lazy
beaches of Puerto Rico to the mean streets of Miami to
the non-stop jangle of Atlantic City's one-armed bandits.

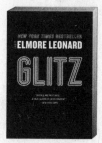

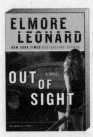

OUT OF SIGHT
A Novel

978-0-06-174031-2 (trade paperback)

Minutes after pulling into a prison parking lot, Deputy U.S. Marshal Karen Sisco meets legendary bank robber Jack Foley and the fun begins.

THE COMPLETE WESTERN STORIES OF ELMORE LEONARD

978-0-06-124292-2 (trade paperback)

This collection is a must-have for every fan of Elmore Leonard.

SWAG
A Novel

978-0-06-174136-4 (trade paperback)

Used car salesman Frank Ryan sells Ernest Stickley, Jr. on his "10 Rules for Success and Happiness in Armed Robbery".

LABRAVA
A Novel

978-0-06-176769-2 (trade paperback)

Ex-Secret Service agent Joe LaBrava gets mixed up in a scam involving a former movie actress and bad guys.

BE COOL
A Novel

978-0-06-077706-7 (trade paperback)

Chili Palmer searches for his next big hit as murder blurs the line between reality and the big screen.

SPLIT IMAGES
A Novel

978-0-06-212251-3 (trade paperback)

When homicide cop Bryan Hurd takes a vacation, he lands in Palm Beach and finds murder in the Sunshine State.

Visit www.AuthorTracker.com
for exclusive information on your favorite HarperCollins authors.
Available wherever books are sold, or call 1-800-331-3761 to order.